Hannah looked straight at Rex. "Tell me why you walked out on me that night."

"I had to," he said.

She sighed, then looked away. "What about children?"

God, she was covering six years of ground here, while he was thinking of one step at a time. He thought of his own miserable childhood, how he had vowed he would never visit that kind of pain on himself. "Kids were never part of my plan."

Something shuttered in her eyes. She was closing him out as he watched. He reached out. She gently pushed his hands away and closed her eyes as tears slid out from under her lids.

He didn't know what to say.

Dear Reader,

This is a month full of greats: great authors, great miniseries…great books. Start off with award-winning Marie Ferrarella's *Racing Against Time,* the first in a new miniseries called CAVANAUGH JUSTICE. This family fights for what's right—and their reward is lasting love.

The miniseries excitement continues with the second of Carla Cassidy's CHEROKEE CORNERS trilogy. *Dead Certain* brings the hero and heroine together to solve a terrible crime, but it keeps them together with love. Candace Irvin's latest features *A Dangerous Engagement,* and it's also the first SISTERS IN ARMS title, introducing a group of military women bonded through friendship and destined to find men worthy of their hearts.

Of course, you won't want to miss our stand-alone books, either. Marilyn Tracy's *A Warrior's Vow* is built around a suspenseful search for a missing child, and it's there, in the rugged Southwest, that her hero and heroine find each other. Cindy Dees has an irresistible Special Forces officer for a hero in *Line of Fire*—and he takes aim right at the heroine's heart. Finally, welcome new author Loreth Anne White, who came to us via our eHarlequin.com Web site. *Melting the Ice* is her first book—and we're all eagerly awaiting her next.

Enjoy—and come back next month for more exciting romantic reading, only from Silhouette Intimate Moments.

Leslie J. Wainger
Executive Editor

Please address questions and book requests to:
Silhouette Reader Service
U.S.: 3010 Walden Ave., P.O. Box 1325, Buffalo, NY 14269
Canadian: P.O. Box 609, Fort Erie, Ont. L2A 5X3

Melting
the Ice
LORETH ANNE WHITE

INTIMATE MOMENTS™
Published by Silhouette Books
America's Publisher of Contemporary Romance

 **SILHOUETTE BOOKS**

ISBN 0-373-27324-X

MELTING THE ICE

Copyright © 2003 by Loreth Beswetherick

LORETH ANNE WHITE

As a child in Africa, when asked what she wanted to be when she grew up, Loreth said a spy…or a psychologist, or maybe marine biologist, archaeologist or lawyer. Instead she fell in love, traveled the world and had a baby. When she looked up again she was back in Africa, writing and editing news and features for a large chain of community newspapers. But those childhood dreams never died. It took another decade, another baby and a move across continents before the lightbulb finally went on. She didn't *have* to grow up. She could be *them all*— the spy, the psychologist and all the rest—through her characters. She sat down to pen her first novel…and fell in love.

She currently lives with her husband, two daughters and their cats in a ski resort in the rugged Coast Mountains of British Columbia, where there is no shortage of inspiration for larger-than-life characters and adventure.

To Pavlo for believing in me, JoJo for her support
and Susan Litman for making it all happen.

Chapter 1

"They found a body."

Hannah looked up from her computer. Al's face was ashen.

"They think it's Amy. Up in Grizzly Bowl." The forty-five-year-old publisher of the *White River Gazette* dug his hands into his hair, held his head, as if trying to keep reality from seeping in.

Hannah pushed her chair back. She said nothing but moved quickly across the newsroom toward Al. He was shaking, the dial tone still buzzing from the telephone receiver that lay on his desk. She took it, gently replaced it in the cradle and sat next to him.

"Was that the police?" she asked softly.

He nodded. "They're waiting for the coroner to come in from Vancouver by chopper."

"God, I'm so sorry, Al."

He wiped his upper lip with the back of his hand. "Hell, Hannah, I guess I always knew the news would come sometime, but—'' he looked away from her, out the floor-to-ceiling windows toward the wild sun-kissed peaks that rose in an amphitheater around British Columbia's White River Valley ''—it still comes as a gut slammer.''

It was last October, almost a year ago, that Amy had vanished, seemingly into thin air. A winter had come and gone. Upwards of two million skiers had carved tracks into Grizzly Bowl on Powder Mountain, where a woman's cries had been heard by hikers last fall. And once the snows had begun to melt, thousands of sightseers had been ferried via gondola to hike the Grizzly Traverse and look back out over Grizzly Bowl, the glacier and the spectacular Coast Mountain scene below.

How could they have missed her?

Hannah reached forward and took Al's rough, sun-browned hand in her own. ''How'd they find her?''

He cleared his throat. ''Wildlife activity. It alerted mountain staff this morning.''

Hannah knew search-and-rescue personnel had told Powder Mountain employees to keep a watch out for any abnormal wildlife activity as snows receded. It was standard procedure in these parts. But nothing had turned up in the spring. Nothing throughout the summer.

And, as long as there'd been no body, no proof that Amy had died, there'd always been hope. Al had hung on to that. All the while he had hoped. And he'd kept paying the rent on Amy's apartment. ''Just in case,'' he'd said.

He turned to her, eyes, the same azure as Amy's, shimmering with emotion. ''Sven was the one who found her.''

Hannah's chest felt tight. Sven Jansen was the mountain guide Amy used to go out with. Things cut so close in a small community like this. As a foreign correspondent Hannah had covered wars and natural disasters, yet there was nothing to compare; this touched her in ways those stories seldom had. When tragedy hit a town as small as White River, it touched everyone. It became personal.

Al dragged both his weather-beaten hands through his thatch of white hair. "God, Hannah, I was supposed to be watching over her."

"This is beyond your control, Al, we all know that."

Several phones were ringing. The news of the discovery was out, and media hounds would be baying for information. Amy's parents were well connected in Canada's political circles, and the *White River Gazette,* as Amy's workplace, was part of this story no matter what.

Hannah placed a hand on Al's shoulder. "Why don't you go home. I'll handle this for now. We can regroup when you're ready."

He looked up, angst deepening the age lines that mapped his craggy face, his effort to compose himself visible. "Thanks. I think I will. I need to call my sister." He reached out and took Hannah's hand. It was an unusual gesture for Al, a man as independent and robust as the Coast Mountain terrain. She had a sense it was more than her hand he was reaching for. He was reaching for answers.

"I don't know what I would've done without your help this past year, Hannah."

"It's okay, Al. I owe you. You've always been there for me."

The phones shrilled, relentless. Al stared at the flashing red message lights. Reality calling. It wasn't going to go away. "This is one of the biggest news stories to hit this valley. I guess the *Gazette* should have someone up there on Grizzly."

"I know. I'll see to it." She patted his hand. "Go home, Al."

He stood, paused.

She knew what he was thinking. That Amy's death wasn't an accident. She couldn't believe it, either. Especially after the suspicious break-in at Amy's apartment at the same time Amy went missing. "I'll be there. Don't worry. We'll get to the bottom of this. I promise."

He nodded.

Hannah watched as Amy's uncle left the office, his usually powerful posture crumpled.

The gondola doors swung slowly shut. Hannah was cocooned in the little cabin as it swung from its moorings and lifted into the air, swaying slightly from side to side.

It was a twenty-five-minute ride to the top and then a short hike up to the traverse.

She always found the gondola soothing, with its quiet mechanical hum. It was meditative, lifting her above the world, separating her. It helped her think. And she needed to think. She needed to compose herself for what she might find on Grizzly Glacier. She wondered what clues Amy's body might yield after sleeping for so long under the ice.

The late-August sun was balmy, and bits of light white fluff, the seeds of the fireweed, waltzed on warm currents of air around the gondola. Summer snow—that's what Danny called it. Hannah smiled, thinking of her boy. She was glad she had relented and let him go and stay with her mom for the last two weeks of his summer holidays.

She had never let him go to his gran's smallholding on Vancouver Island for so long but Daniel had conspired with his granny to twist Hannah's arm. Hannah had hoped to join them there for the Labor Day weekend, but with this latest development, she didn't think she would be able to make it. She was pretty much working full-time at the *Gazette* now, balancing her schedule around Danny's needs.

She had slipped into this routine after Amy disappeared last year. She had wanted to help Al out. It wasn't a bad job, and with Danny going into first grade next month, she would have even more time.

The gondola lurched as it passed another lift tower. Hannah could see a black bear and its cub down on the ski run. White River Valley was a sparkling jewel far below, a community built around a string of glacier-fed lakes. From up high the lakes were shimmering beads, with hues from chalky green to crystal-clear sapphire. The town got its name from the river that cascaded down through the gorge separating Powder Mountain from neighboring Moonstone Mountain. The river was milky with glacial silt and the waters gushed frothing and creamy white into frigid Alabaster Lake below.

So beautiful, thought Hannah, yet so harsh. They always made her think of Danny's father. Beautiful but hard. Cold. Secretive. Rex Logan was like these peaks around her, carved from stone and scarred by time. There was an underlying sense of wildness and danger about him. She should have recognized from the start that he would hurt her.

She hated herself for having fallen for him, for naively believing that he was the one she would spend the rest of her life with.

Never again would she let passion overrule her common sense. Never again would she be so deceived, so lacking in guile.

Never.

She would always stay in control.

Hannah left the gondola station and made her way along the rocky trail that led up to the traverse above

Grizzly Bowl, which cradled the glacier and looked like a giant's scoop out of the mountain. A marmot ducked and scuttled for cover as she approached.

She could see police tape up on the trail above the glacier. It screamed crime scene, except Amy's death was supposed to have been an accident. The bright-yellow ribbon fluttered in the Alpine breeze against a backdrop of painfully bright blue sky and glacial snow. Behind it a crowd of curious tourists and media gathered on the hiking trail. They were all looking down, watching a group of search-and-rescue personnel and police officers on the glacier below.

Hannah could hear the dull *thuck-thuck-thuck* of a helicopter somewhere, closing in. From her vantage point below, she aimed her camera lens up at the crowd, focused, clicked.

She was used to having her own Canadian News Agency cameraman on a job, but this was not Africa and her CNA days were over. Balancing a career that could see her in Angola one month and Sierra Leone the next was no life for a child. She had experienced what that kind of lifestyle had done to her father, to her family.

As Hannah clicked, the yellow tape was sucked from its moorings into a brutal whirling frenzy. The chopper was coming in for a landing just off the trail, churning up everything in its path. A red hat went flying. People held their hair, ducked their heads. Gray glacial silt boiled up in a cloud around them.

Hannah kept shooting.

She jogged up the steep trail as the blur of the two lethal rotor blades slowed and came into focus. She recognized the coroner and members of a television crew as they alighted from the mechanical beast. A man in a suit followed. He stood out amongst the windbreakers and fleece. This story was pulling them all in, even the suits. Hannah guessed he was with one of the big U.S. outfits.

She joined the crowd, out of breath. There were other newspaper photographers capturing the scene. She tried to peer down into the glacial bowl but couldn't really make out what was happening below. The TV crew started filming.

"Hannah, over here." The Swiss-German accent and granular rasp was unmistakable.

"Hey, Gunter." She moved over to join the plastic surgeon. He was deeply tanned with a head of thick salt-and-pepper hair and clear hazel eyes. Hannah couldn't help thinking he carried his years exceptionally well. But then, Dr. Gunter Schmidt was devoted to the pursuit of youth. It was that same promise of eternal youth that attracted the rich and famous to his White River Spa.

"I was on a walk up here on the mountain." Gunter could not pronounce words with a *w*. He said them as if they started with a *v*. But despite his pronunciation oddities and Germanic syntax, his English was good.

"And then I see all this commotion. They say it is Amy." He was also out of breath. "That is right? They have found her?"

"It looks that way, Gunter."

"Ach, poor Al. He must be taking it hard, ja?"

"He is. He's struggling." Hannah looked away from the scene below, her eyes following the trail she knew so well. From here, it climbed a little farther then leveled out along the ridge toward the ski area boundary. Then it rounded the ridge and led to a series of small, rustic cabins designed for overnight use. A hiker could spend a week doing the full loop. Back-country skiers used the cabins in winter. "I just can't figure what Amy was doing up here."

"She was perhaps hiking," the doctor offered, following her gaze.

"No, Gunter. I don't buy it. Her clothes were wrong. The weather, the timing, the break-in. Nothing fits."

The doctor frowned.

Hannah lifted her camera and peered through her lens at the scene below on the glacier. She could make out the form of Sven Jansen. She clicked the shutter as the team started to slowly make their way with a body bag back up the glacier toward the chopper.

Rex Logan's heart missed a beat.

Anyone watching him in his air-conditioned Toronto office would not have noticed a thing. He never showed his emotion. That came from his British Special Air Services training. That, combined with his medical specialty, was one of the reasons the Bellona Channel found him so valuable.

But the picture on page three of the *Toronto Star* had upped his pulse rate.

He leaned forward to press the button on his phone. "Hold all my calls, Margaret."

He loosened his tie and flattened the page out onto his desk. It was Hannah McGuire.

In grainy black-and-white.

He scanned the headlines. A body had been found on Powder Mountain in White River. Hannah had been captured by a news photographer among a crowd on the mountain. She was holding a camera in one hand, looking toward a body bag. Her long hair was blowing across her face. She was trying to hold it back with her other hand.

Rex ran his forefinger slowly over her grainy image. He knew the feel of that hair. Her knew her smell. He knew the sensation of her golden skin. Her image haunted his dreams at night.

He absently fingered the small Ethiopian silver ring on his finger as the hot memories welled up and assaulted him in his cool office. He could almost smell the crushed frangipani blooms, hear the sound of night insects, taste the salt on her skin, see her eyes. Those eyes, leonine, with the color and fire of fine whiskey.

Rex closed his eyes and slowly sucked in air. The memories of Marumba often came like that. They would wash over him before he could send the unbidden images scuttling back into the recesses of his tired brain.

He knew Hannah was in White River. He knew that much from the Canadian News Agency office. Once, just once, when he had a whiskey too many, he'd called the CNA headquarters. It was a lapse of reason. She was the only one who did that to him, skewed his judgment. He'd wanted to know where he could find her. They'd put him through to a photographer who used to work with Hannah on her Africa assignments. He told Rex that Hannah had quit and moved to White River.

Why the hell she had dropped her career as one of the best damn foreign correspondents this country had known was beyond him. She was at the peak of her profession. And now, here she was, in a photo on his desk that had caught her looking out over a body on a mountain in White River.

White River, where the International Toxicology Conference was due to start in one week.

His contacts in Cairo had indicated that several rogue nations were planning to send agents to that conference. The list of participants was already starting to read like a who's who in the world of biological warfare. Red flags were going up all over the place. Something was going down. And the Bellona Channel board members wanted him there. Only trouble was, Rex didn't want to go.

He didn't want to run into Hannah McGuire.

Rex pulled open his desk drawer and fished out a magnifying glass. He hungered to see her more clearly.

Useless. It just made things bigger, blurrier, grainier. He put the magnifying glass back into his drawer and rubbed the heels of his hands into his eye sockets before reading the story.

There was no reference to Hannah. The article noted that the body was presumed to be that of Amy Barnes, a young reporter who'd gone missing last fall.

He looked at the photograph again. Then something new caught his eye and, for a second time, his heart beat faster.

It couldn't be.

In his preoccupation with Hannah he hadn't noticed the man standing near her. It had been six years since he'd last seen him. If it wasn't him, the likeness was incredible.

Rex needed to know more.

This was more than coincidence. Two people on Powder Mountain, both linked to a tumultuous period in his life six years ago. Hannah and this man. The last time he had laid eyes on either of them was in Marumba.

He leaned forward and pushed the phone intercom button to ring his secretary. "Margaret, did you tape the news last night?" She usually recorded the CNA news. It aired at six o'clock, before she returned from work. She liked to watch it when she got home.

"I always tape the CNA, Rex." Margaret's voice came back through the intercom. "It comes on again later at night, but way past my bedtime. Even an old-timer like me needs beauty rest."

"You're beautiful to me, Margaret. I need that tape." There would be something on the CNA news, he was sure. The missing girl's parents were high profile, and the search for Amy Barnes had been one of the biggest search-and-rescue missions mounted in recent years.

* * *

Rex took his pizza slice out of the microwave and cracked open an ice-cold cola. He had to do something about his eating habits. Always on the run. He settled in front of his television set, inserted Margaret's tape, took a bite of pizza and pushed the play button.

It had been a long time since he'd watched Hannah on TV. The last he'd seen of her work was her acclaimed CNA documentary on conflict diamonds in Africa. That was what she'd been working on when she had first caught his eye and held his libido hostage in Penaka, the capital of Marumba.

Rex leaned forward as the camera cut to a TV reporter on Powder Mountain. The reporter was saying there would be an autopsy. Then, as the camera moved to pan the faces in the crowd, it caught the gold of her hair and lingered on the profile of a woman made for television. Hannah McGuire's lambent image sprang to life, invading his living room.

She stole his attention from the rest of the news report.

Rex slowly swallowed his mouthful of food, fixated with her image. She was in khaki hiking shorts and a green jacket. She was lightly bronzed from a summer of sun, the way she had been in Marumba, her limbs long and strong.

And then she was gone.

Rex quickly rewound the clip, took a swig of his cold drink and focused on the other faces in the crowd.

There was no doubt. It was him in the suit, standing near her on that mountain. Mitchell. The CIA agent Rex blamed for botching the Marumba laboratory raid.

If it hadn't been for Mitchell's preemptive strike on the secret biological weapons research lab in Marumba six years ago, they would have in custody the man the world had dubbed the Plague Doctor.

Mitchell had called in the Marumba government troops too early. And he had made too much noise about it. Dr. Ivan Rostov, the Plague Doctor, had been forewarned. He had slithered back into the murk of the underworld, taking his lethal secrets with him.

The question now, thought Rex as he remembered the pizza cooling on his plate, is why U.S. Central Intelligence was interested in the death of this young Canadian reporter. And why Agent Mitchell in particular? His specialty was biological warfare intelligence. Perhaps he was in White River early for the toxicology conference. The CIA always kept tabs on get-togethers like these. Yet, the conference wasn't due to be held for at least another week.

There was no way Rex could avoid going to White River now. And if he knew the Bellona Channel board of directors, they would want him on a plane yesterday.

He reached for his secure phone and punched in the number of the Bellona Channel board chair, Dr. William J. Killian.

"Killian, it's Rex Logan."

"Rex, how the hell are you? I heard you were back in Toronto."

Rex did not waste time on platitudes. "We have a situation developing, Killian. We need to get the board members together for direction. I have some interesting data from my Cairo trip, and there are some developments in White River. Could be related. Looks like a hot spot."

"Give me one or two hours Rex. I should have everyone assembled for a secure telecon within that time."

"Standing by."

Killian, a reclusive eighty-year-old billionaire and founder of Bio Can Pharmaceutical, knew firsthand the blight of biological weapons. In his youth he had worked for a United Nations special commission to disarm rogue states of their offensive bioweapons programs.

The billionaire was widely regarded as a visionary. He believed biology in the wrong hands could ultimately spell the end of the human race. Killian felt governments around the world had not fully grasped the implications of the biological threat. In his mind not enough time and resources were being thrown at the problem.

He set out to do something about it.

He formed the Bellona Channel. It was a civilian organization and civilian funded, but the Bellona Channel operatives assembled by Killian were all gleaned from the elite ranks of some of the world's crack government organizations including the Navy SEALS, the CIA, Britain's Special Air Services and MI-6, Israel's Mossad and the FBI.

Killian had hand picked Rex from the SAS in Britain and brought him to Canada to head up the indigenous-medicine arm of Bio Can Pharmaceutical. The position served as a cover for his covert work with Bellona.

Rex grabbed the phone at the first ring.

"Rex, we have the full board present, go ahead."

"Evening, gentlemen."

The greetings were hearty and intimate, coming in from around the world. For some it was an ungodly early hour. Rex was proud to work for this team. The Bellona board was comprised of some of the brightest minds of this age. They shared Killian's vision and were bound by loyalty and a common code of ethics.

Once the social niceties were over, Rex outlined the scenario. It was his mention of CIA agent Ken Mitchell's presence in White River that really piqued the board's interest.

"The way things unfolded with that lab raid in Marumba, I wouldn't be surprised to find Ken Mitchell was double dipping,'' noted Killian.

''A double agent?'' The question came from the Australian director.

''It's feasible. The question now is, what is he doing in White River? We need to find out and we need you on the job, Rex. You're the one with the background on this case.'' There were murmurs of agreement at Killian's assessment.

Rex felt a sick little slide in his stomach. There went his hope of sending a replacement to White River. Hannah's lambent image swam back into his brain. He squeezed it out and channeled his attention back to the teleconference.

''Right. I'll make arrangements. Any word on the Plague Doc?'' Since the botched lab raid, the hunt for Dr. Ivan Rostov, one of the biggest international manhunts in history, had turned up nothing. Not even a lead. The Bellona Channel was just one of the many intelligence agencies after him.

''Nothing so far, Rex. It's been six years now. For all we know, he could be dead.'' Killian cleared his throat. ''But he did escape that lab fire with his latest work, the work on ethnic bullets. And that's what has us worried. Even if Rostov was taken out, his work could still be completed by another rogue scientist and sold to the highest bidder.''

Rex grunted in acknowledgment. *Ethnic bullets* was the term the Bellona Channel had given to the Plague Doctor's efforts to genetically modify a range of lethal viruses including smallpox, Marburg, Ebola and bubonic plague. The Plague Doctor had started designing these bugs in his Marumba lab so that they would target only people with a specific genetic makeup, creating scourges that could potentially kill only people with blue eyes, for example, or only people of a particular race. The Human Genome Project had made this possible.

The potential was horrendous.

"We need you in White River immediately, Logan."

The waters of Howe Sound sparkled in his rearview mirror as the road twisted and climbed up into the thin air of the Coast Mountains.

Margaret had seen to it that Rex had a rental vehicle waiting at the Vancouver airport. He'd asked her to make sure he got something with off-road capability. He was heading into rough country.

The narrow, treacherous road snaked up through forest and raw canyon. The view of the tortured Tantalus range in the distance was breathtaking. Rex felt his spirit wanting to soar as he gained elevation, but as he neared White River, he saw dark clouds up ahead.

They were massing over the distant snow-capped peaks, threatening to unleash their heavy burden.

The road sign ahead indicated the White River turnoff. Rex took the next exit and began the steep climb up through the valley toward White River and Powder Mountain. There were road-block booms at intervals along the road. They were raised up now, but Rex knew that when the winter weather turned foul and the roads deadly, the black and yellow booms would be lowered.

He felt a slight chill on his skin as he gained elevation. The bruised-ochre sky added to his sense of unease as he closed in on the ski town. Thunder rumbled faintly in the hills.

Well, he would just have to do his job and try to stay out of Hannah McGuire's way for the next week or so.

With a stroke of luck, he might not see her at all.

"Take a seat, Hannah." Fred LeFevre, Royal Canadian Mounted Police Staff Sergeant, motioned to a gray plastic chair. "Mind if I eat my lunch?"

"No. Go ahead. Thanks for seeing me." She despised

the way the RCMP staff sergeant allowed his eyes to range over her unabashedly. He was doing it now.

She sat. "Did you manage to get one of the guys to look into Amy's case again?"

He unwrapped his cheeseburger as he spoke. "I did, as a favor to you. But there's nothing there. You should let it rest."

Hannah leaned forward. "But, Fred, you have to agree, the timing of the break-in was curious. Al and I went through all her things. The place was ransacked, but nothing is missing. Her CDs are there, her mountain bike, her video equipment, her climbing gear—"

"Hannah, Hannah." Fred held up his stubby-fingered hands. "The robbery was one in a series last year. There's no point in rehashing this now that we've found her."

Anger prickled. "I'm not rehashing. It's just that this whole business feels wrong. *Especially* now that we have found her. Amy wasn't dressed for the weather. She had no gear. She left no note. It just raises more questions."

She didn't think Fred had even heard her. "We think the reason nothing was taken from her apartment was because the perpetrators were interrupted." He lifted his cheeseburger with both hands and bit into it. Sauce slopped out the sides and splotched onto the waxed wrapper on his desk. The thick smell of fried onions permeated the air in the small office.

Hannah shook her head. "I just can't believe it was unrelated to her disappearance. Neither can Al. It was like someone was looking for something."

"Look, it's out of my hands now. The coroner has ruled her death accidental." He spurted ketchup onto his fries. "It's hard. I know. But you have to let it go. We may never find out exactly what happened. Unless there is evidence of a crime, I'm obliged to close the book at my end." He chewed as he spoke, squeezing his words around the fast-food mash in his mouth.

"Al still has the lease to her apartment. Maybe you could take one more look?"

Fred took another chomp out of his cheeseburger and followed it with a fistful of fries. He chewed a little before opening his mouth to talk again. "Like I said, there's no evidence that the B and E is connected to her accident. I just don't have the resources to—"

"So you're not going to try and find the people who did this?"

"There were no prints. Nothing to go on."

She rubbed her hands over her face, scrubbing at the frustration. This was a dead end. He was no help.

Fred stopped chewing. "Hannah…I'm sorry."

She stood. "It's okay. Thanks for your time."

"Look, if you come up with something concrete, anything that will justify opening up the case again, I will."

"Thanks, Fred. Enjoy your lunch." She turned and walked out, feeling his eyes on her behind.

There *had* to be something. She just needed to find it. She'd promised Al she would help get to the bottom of this. Perhaps she might still find some clue in Amy's apartment. Maybe she and Al had missed something a year ago.

Outside the RCMP detachment, the sky was darkening with the threat of a storm. The light in the village was a dim and unearthly amber under the bruised clouds, and there was a distant grumble of thunder up in the peaks. Branches nodded in grim deference to the mounting wind.

Hannah stood on the stairs and zipped up her jacket, irked at how the weather always affected her moods. The brooding clouds seemed to hold ominous portent. The sudden chill seeped up and into her spine. She felt as if things were closing in on her as she stepped out into the wind.

Chapter 2

The concierge at Rex's hotel was right, the Black Diamond Grill had one of the best patios in White River. It was located near the gondola station at the base of Powder Mountain, and the view of the grassy ski slopes was unobstructed.

The patio was buzzing with the Friday-afternoon lunch crowd. People were lapping up the sunshine after last night's fierce storm.

Rex was shown to a small table under a red umbrella at the rear of the patio. He counted himself lucky to find a spot. Luckier than he had been in his hunt for CIA Agent Mitchell this morning.

There was no Ken Mitchell registered at any of the hotels in White River. But that was not surprising. Mitchell would hardly use his real name. Still, Rex wanted to rule out the obvious.

A waitress with auburn braids approached his table.

"I'll have the special. And I'll try the White River ale."

She took his menu, and Rex settled back to survey the ski town scene. The village was packed with tourists. He could hear British and Australian and American accents. The couple at the table next to him were conversing in Spanish, and next to them was a boisterous party of Japanese teens. Their animation was infectious.

His beer arrived. He spilled the cool amber liquid into his mouth, letting it pool around his tongue before swallowing. The local brew was good.

He stretched his legs out under the table.

And then he saw her.

How could anyone miss her?

Sunlight glinted gold off her hair. The waitress was showing her and two older men to a table at the far end of the patio.

Rex didn't move despite the quickening of his pulse. He maintained his posture of relaxation. He did not want to draw attention to himself.

One of the men pulled out a chair for her. She sat with fluid grace, her back partially to him. He could just catch her aristocratic profile, her high cheekbones, the shape of her lush mouth. Rex closed his eyes and inhaled deeply, calming the edgy rush of adrenaline coursing through his veins. He felt as if he'd been winded. A punch to the solar plexus. Nothing could have prepared him for this. So many times he'd dreamed of her, conjured her up from the caverns of his mind. But this hit him straight in the gut. The sight of her in living, breathing, pulsing flesh was a physical assault on his system.

Time slowed. The patio buzz faded.

"You all right, sir?" His waitress was putting his club sandwich in front of him.

He opened his eyes. "Thanks. Just drinking in the summer weather while it lasts." He was back in control. Cool. Composed. At least, outwardly. He had an ideal vantage

point from the back of the patio under the umbrella. He
donned his dark shades. She wasn't likely to see him here.

He took another swig of beer, his eyes fixed on the
woman who was once his lover. The woman he still ached
for. Her hair was longer than he remembered. More feminine. The thick waves skimmed below her shoulders. It
fell softly across her profile as she leaned forward to touch
the arm of one of the men. It was a gentle, consoling
gesture. He felt his stomach slip. That was Hannah
McGuire. A mix of intelligence and compassion, guts and
lithe grace. He was a voyeur, studying her jealously from
the shadows. But he couldn't tear his eyes away. Not for
a minute. She was wearing white linen pants, a white tank
top, her arms bare and sun browned. Fresh off the pages
of a fashion magazine. He drank the sight in.

Every pore in his body screamed to go to her. Touch
her. Hold her. Tell her he was sorry. He should've known
it would be close to impossible to avoid her here. White
River was a small town. Perhaps deep down, at some
primal subconscious level, he'd even wanted to run into
her. Perhaps that's why he'd accepted this mission instead
of trying to insist on Scott as a replacement. His body
had brought him where his mind refused to go. Hannah
McGuire was like a drug to his system. And the sight of
her now, after all these years, made him feel like an al-
coholic must feel after taking that first forbidden sip.

Forbidden. Hannah was off-limits. He forced his attention to the company she was with.

The man was talking to her, shaking his head, as if in
disbelief. Rex didn't recognize him.

But the other, there was something about the other man
that butted sharply up against the deep recesses of his
memory. He was familiar. Very. But Rex couldn't place
him.

The man sat ramrod straight, broad shoulders pulled

back. Tanned, fit, strong. His dark hair was flecked with silver, but from this distance it was difficult to pinpoint his age. Rex mentally filed the facts, trying to come up with a match.

All three of them looked up as a fourth man approached their table.

Again his pulse quickened. Agent Ken Mitchell.

Rex bit into his sandwich and slowly chewed as he watched. Now, this was getting really interesting.

Gunter, Al and Hannah all looked up as the tall man approached their table.

"Hello again, Hannah." It was the Washington reporter she'd met on the mountain, the one in the suit.

"Mark, hi. Please join us, take a seat," Hannah motioned to an empty chair.

"Thank you." He was wearing dark glasses, a crisp white shirt. Formal for this resort town. He'd brought his big-city sensibilities with him.

Hannah made the introductions. "Mark Bamfield, this is Al Brashear, publisher of the *Gazette,* and this is Dr. Gunter Schmidt from the White River Spa." She turned to Al. "Mark works as a freelance writer. He came to the *Gazette* office this morning to talk about Amy."

Mark Bamfield shook hands. "Actually, I'm here for the upcoming forensic toxicology conference. I'm generally a medical and science writer, based out of the States." He pulled up the chair, sat down and lifted his sunglasses. "But since I'm here, I've been asked to pick up the Amy Barnes story." He turned to Al. "This must be difficult. I'm sorry."

Al nodded. "I understand the news value. I'm still a media man."

"I was hoping I'd get a chance to meet you, Al. I want to do an in-depth color piece on your niece. With your consent, of course. Something that captures the spirit of who she was. I was wondering if I could take a look at some of the articles she'd been working on, get a sense of her life, her work.''

Al looked weary. ''Of course. Feel free to call me at the office. We can set something up.''

''I appreciate that. Thank you.''

Gunter stepped in, changing the topic, breaking the subtle tension that had settled around his friend. ''Tell me, Mark, the toxicology conference, is there anything in particular, any specific speakers you are interested in?''

Mark turned to Gunter. ''I plan to attend most of the sessions, see what grabs me. Will you be there?''

''Ja, but of course. It's not every day one of these things comes to your doorstep. You are covering this for a newspaper?''

''Magazine. *Spectra*.''

Hannah knew of it. High profile. ''Nice gig.''

''Not bad. Now that you mention it, you had a pretty good one yourself.''

''What do you mean?''

''I realized, after I met you yesterday, you're Mac McGuire's daughter.''

Hannah tensed. She felt instantly cornered, always did when anything about her past sneaked into the present she'd so carefully carved out for herself and Danny.

''Yes. Mac was my dad.'' She forked a piece of lettuce from her Caesar salad but couldn't find the impetus to bring it to her mouth.

''You were following in his footsteps for a while there, McGuire. One of the best. They were even calling you Mac, Jr.''

''You been checking up on me?''

Mark laughed. ''Mac's a legend in media circles. So

why'd you quit? What brought you here?'' *To this media backwater.* The words hung unsaid.

She forced a smile. "I needed a change. And I like the skiing."

Mark raised his brows, studying her. She had an uneasy feeling about him. Like he could see into her, like he knew something. She forced the lettuce into her mouth.

Al was watching her, too. She'd never spoken to him about Mac. But she figured he knew she was the daughter of the famous Canadian international correspondent. She loved Al for the fact that he never pried, that he sensed her need to put the past away. That he just let her be while the scabs of her wound grew strong.

She saw Gunter Schmidt studying her, too, as if the fact she was Mac's daughter suddenly meant she had to be judged by new standards. But the plastic surgeon made no comment. He pushed his empty plate to one side. "Well, that was good." Gunter dabbed the corners of his mouth neatly with his napkin. "But my patients, they are waiting." He called for the check.

Rex watched as the man with gray-flecked hair called for the bill.

So, Hannah knew Ken Mitchell. No matter how he looked at it, he was not going to be able to avoid her. She was working her way into his investigation. He'd need to ask her about Mitchell. And the other man, the one tugging at his memory.

He watched them stand, say their goodbyes. Hannah shook Mitchell's hand. She looked unhappy. It tore at him.

Do you remember me, Hannah McGuire? Do you hate me? What is making you sad, my lovely? God he wanted to ask her those questions. He'd have to shelve those for another life. Right now he needed to ask her about Mitchell. But how to approach her after all these years? For the first time in his adult life, Rex Logan felt lost. Helpless. He hadn't planned for this. The cold, calculating, fearless agent was not only lost, he was afraid. But with the anxiety that sloshed in his belly was a sharp little zing. A spike of adrenaline. Unwanted, but there. It hummed through him at the thought of coming face-to-face with Hannah McGuire, hearing the smokiness of her voice, seeing those tiny forest-green flecks in her gold leonine eyes.

But not now. Not yet. He wasn't ready. Right now he'd tail Mitchell. He watched them make for the exit, giving them time.

Mark Bamfield held out his hand. "Good to meet you, Al, Gunter. Thanks for inviting me to join you."

He turned to Hannah and took her hand in his. "Nice to see you again, Hannah. Maybe dinner sometime?"

She just nodded and watched him go. He'd left her unsettled, off-kilter.

"You okay, Hannah?"

"Yeah, Gunter. Just tired. Thanks for lunch."

"Anytime. You look after Al now, ja?"

"Ja, Ja." Al jokingly waved his friend off, mimicking his raspy German accent. "You go back to your filthy-rich patients. I can take care of myself."

Hannah affectionately took Al by the arm as they made their way down the pedestrian walkway back to the office. Sometimes she felt he was the father she never really had. "So you can look after yourself, huh?"

"Damn right. Just need a little time." *To find out what really happened to Amy.* The words went unsaid. Hannah knew Al wouldn't heal until he had the answer.

The sun was warm on their backs as they strolled through the summer crowds. Much warmer than an hour ago when Hannah had needed the extra comfort of her sweater. She realized suddenly it was missing.

"Oh, Al, my sweater. I must have left it at the restaurant. You go on ahead. I'll see you back at the office."

"No, no. I'll come with you. Too nice out. Any excuse to extend my break is welcome." He fell in step with her as she headed quickly back to the Black Diamond.

Al waited at the restaurant entrance as Hannah stepped up onto the patio and made her way back to the table. They had been gone only minutes. Her sweater was still draped over the back of the chair.

She gathered it up, turned to head out.

Then froze.

He stood in shadow at the far end of the patio.

He was looking directly at her.

The world around her faded away. Hannah reached absently for the back of a chair as her vision narrowed. She needed to steady herself. Her chest was like a vise. She couldn't breathe.

He didn't move.

She told herself it couldn't be. It was someone who looked like him. But she knew. In her gut. She knew the lines of him, the stance, like she knew her own son. Her mind reeled. Irrational panic licked through her blood and gripped at her throat. For so long he had lurked in the shadows of her mind. Now he stood, in flesh and blood, in the shade of the patio.

Here, in White River.

The shock of it was too much. She wasn't ready to deal with seeing him.

She turned, walked woodenly toward Al, clutching her sweater.

"Hannah, what's the matter? You look like you've seen a ghost." He grabbed her elbow in support.

"I...I think I am coming down with something. I just

need to get out of here. I…I'll see you back at the office.''
She pulled away from Al and started to weave quickly
through the groups of tourists thronging the walkways.

She headed for the park with its network of trails that
ran along the White River.

She broke into a run when she reached the gravel path,
ignoring the sharp little stones that slipped into her sandals. Usually running eased her pain. Now the air rasped
in her lungs.

She stopped only when she reached the little waterfall.

She sat down on her rock, close to the water's edge.
Daniel called it Mommy's Rock. The little one beside it
was Danny's Rock. They would often come to the park
and picnic here beside the river. They would watch the
whitewater churn over the boulders and throw a fine mist
into the air. Danny liked the way the droplets would catch
the sun and spin the light into a myriad of rainbows.

Hannah turned her face toward the raging water. She
let the sound wash over her and the fine mist kiss her
cheeks.

The knot in her gut slowly loosened, unraveled and
bubbled up through her chest, threatening to spill out in
a warm release of tears. She tilted her head back, scrunch-
ing her eyes, angry with herself.

Fool.

Fight or flight. She'd had the classic response to a
threat. And she'd flown. She'd run like hunted prey. The
way she'd been running emotionally for the last six years.
She knew she would have to face him one day. She just
didn't think it would be now. Like this. Here, in her
mountain sanctuary.

And she was scared. She'd built something here for
Danny and herself. A home. She couldn't let his presence
in White River rock those foundations. She couldn't let

him hurt Danny. Thank God her boy was away. She
needed to figure out how to deal with this.

Hannah took a deep breath, drinking in the damp, cool
air, filling her lungs to the bottom in a bid to steady herself, calm the heart jackhammering in her chest, marshal
her thoughts.

But her heart leaped straight back into her mouth at the
sudden firm pressure of a large hand on her shoulder.

She spun round and stared up, straight into eyes, pale
blue as the sky behind him.

Danny's eyes.

She opened her mouth but no words came. He seemed
bigger, his face harder. There was no laughter in those
ice eyes. Yet there was still that sensual mouth, that powerful masculine aura. He took her breath away.

"Hannah, we need to talk."

He still had a trace of British accent, refined in sound
even as it was rough and seductive in tone. It melted her
core in an instant.

"Rex—" His name came from her lips in a breathy
whisper. "Please…please don't touch me." She couldn't
bear it. His hand on her. The sensation. The heaviness.
The warmth, the crashing kaleidoscope of bottled memories that came spinning, splashing out through her brain.

He let go of her shoulder and she caught the glint of a
silver ring. Her breath choked in her throat.

He was still wearing her ring. The little Ethiopian silver
ring she had bought for him at a market in Marumba. It
had been a lark. They'd been deliriously happy. She'd
been in love, or so she had thought. She had joked that
as long as Rex wore that ring, he belonged to her.

And he was still wearing it. On the little finger of his
left hand.

Hannah was suddenly overwhelmed with six years
worth of conflicting emotions. They surged up in waves

and crashed over her. Her need for him. Her hate. Her bitterness. Her anger. Her desperate need to understand.

She started to shake inside. All those things she had thought to say to him if she ever ran into him again were obliterated, deleted, at the sight of those darkly fringed eyes of blue ice. And the ring.

She looked up from the ring into those wolf eyes. They bit back into her with Arctic intensity, searching, probing. She felt naked under his scrutiny. He held her captive with his gaze as he slowly came round to sit on Danny's rock.

"What are you doing here, Rex?"

"I came for the toxicology conference."

Not for her. His words cut deeper than they should have.

"You…you didn't know I was here?"

He leaned forward, as if to touch her, held back. "I knew, Hannah."

What else did he know? She felt a talon of fear claw at her heart. What had he really come for? "You were hoping you wouldn't run in to me?"

"I was going to look you up. We need to talk."

There was so much to say. She had so many questions. *Why did you leave me like that?* She wanted to scream it at him. Damn her pride. She wanted to hit that hard, muscular chest with her fists. She wanted to shake him. Hurt him. Run her fingers through that gloss of ebony hair. Feel the give of those sculpted lips under the tips of her fingers. God, she just wanted him to hold her.

She tried to stand. The world seemed to have shifted on its axis, leaving her unbalanced. She fought the buckling sensation in her knees. She needed to stand over him. Feel the height. Find some strength. "I don't think there's anything to say, Rex. You made that clear in your note." She needed to buy time. To think.

She took a step back, turned to leave.

"Wait, Hannah!" He was off the rock, gripping her wrist. She could feel her pulse beating against the strength of his fingers.

She looked up into his eyes. "I did, Rex. Six years ago I waited. I've waited long enough."

He stiffened, eyes narrowing like those of a Siberian husky. A small muscle pulsed in his jaw. But he said nothing, just loosened the grip on her wrist, let it fall.

It was the ultimate rejection. He was doing it to her all over again. Hot wetness spilled up into her eyes. She turned so that he wouldn't see. And she started up the riverbank, half hoping he'd call out to her and explain.

He didn't.

She held her spine stiff. Ignoring the bite of stones in her sandals, she walked smoothly, proudly, away. But inside she cried. Like the child who had cried for the love of her father. Like the woman who had vowed never to need a man to make her whole.

Rex watched her go. A proud and beautiful woman, her long hair swinging gently across her back. A woman once his. His body screamed to call out to her. To tell her the truth. To explain that he'd had to leave. That he could never be with her. That he'd made the biggest mistake of his life. And nothing…nothing in this world had cost him more than that one act. He'd left her, alone in that tent, sleeping under an African sky. And with her, he'd left his heart.

Chapter 3

"'**N**ight, Danny. Love you."

"Love you more."

"You know that's not possible. Bye, sweetie. Be good." Hannah put down the phone, picked up her mug of cocoa and walked barefoot out onto the deck.

At least Danny was enjoying himself. She stood at the railing, looking out over Alabaster Lake, cradling her cocoa. She missed him more than she could have imagined. She missed his constant chattering, his incessant questions. His funny little quips. His mess of toys all over the living room floor.

She sipped from her mug. Dusk was settling on the valley but the snow-capped peaks still basked in the sun's attention. They were bathed with soft peach Alpenglow. So beautiful. So distant. She couldn't remember when she last felt so alone. She watched as a canoe cut across the glass of the lake, two people paddling in harmony, perfect balance. Their unity lent power to their strokes, purpose to their direction. But she was alone. She'd been left to paddle her own canoe. And she had. Her stroke was not as strong, but she'd found a balance of sorts. She'd been content, if not happy.

Until now. Until today.

Rex had brought a storm into the valley, whipping up waves and rocking her fragile boat. She had to find a way to steady it. She couldn't see that way right now.

Damn him. He hadn't even tried to explain. She wouldn't humiliate herself by asking.

The sun slipped off the peaks and the chill deepened instantly. She set her mug on the railing and reached for her fleece, pulling it tight around her, blocking out the searching fingers of cold.

She had to figure out what to do. This past year Danny had started asking more and more about his father. She was not going to lie to him. She'd told him his dad had left before he was born.

But last month, when Danny asked if his dad even knew that he had been born, she'd been stumped. She'd panicked, changed the subject—and been eaten by guilt since. She hadn't been ready to deal with it then and she sure as hell wasn't ready now.

Danny had a right to know the truth. If she didn't tell him soon that Rex Logan was his father, he would find out himself one day. And at what cost? Yet Hannah was so damn afraid that even if she brought it all out into the open now, Danny would end up feeling the same kind of rejection she had as a child.

She wasn't ready to shatter her boy's life.

She had to find a way to sound Rex out. Would he reject Danny outright? Would he be bound by a sense of duty and poke his nose into his son's life and screw with his head every time his guilt got too big?

Like Mac had?

God knows, Mac had tried to be a father to her, a husband to her mother. But he'd been programmed to roam wild, to chase adventure around the world. Hannah had no doubt Mac had loved her mother once. And he'd tried to do his duty once Hannah was born. But all he did was tear his own soul in two and destroy his family in the process. Sheila McGuire had never really truly been free until Mac lost his life on assignment in the Congo.

God, she was a fool to have fallen into the same trap. She'd fallen for Rex in spite of the fact she'd vowed never to be like her mother. Now she couldn't see her way free.

And she didn't have much time. Danny would be home Friday.

The phone rang inside her condo, making her jump. She padded inside, pulling the slider closed against the cold behind her.

She picked up the receiver, half-afraid it was Rex.

"Hannah, it's Al. Are you okay? You didn't make it back to the office this afternoon."

"Yeah. I'm fine. Thanks. I was just feeling queasy. Must've been something I had for lunch."

He paused. "There was a man at the Black Diamond. He followed you."

She was quiet. So Al had seen Rex. Had he seen her boy in the man?

"Hannah?"

"Yeah, I'm here."

"Look, if you ever want to talk, if you ever—"

"Al, I'm okay. Really. I wasn't feeling well. That's all."

"All right." He cleared his throat. "I was just worried about you…and I wanted to tell you the coroner's report came through this afternoon."

She'd been so wrapped up in her own angst she'd forgotten they'd been expecting it, hoping it would tell them something others may have missed.

"What did it say?"

"Well, Amy had a badly broken left leg." Hannah could hear the strain in his voice. "It probably happened in the fall. Judging from where she was found, they figure she tried to drag herself along that rock band that forms a lateral moraine halfway down Grizzly Bowl. But from there it's vertical blue ice, nowhere to go. She died of exposure."

"But why didn't they find her? They combed that area?"

"The pathologist figures that her body heat melted her into the glacier. Then the rain that fell the first two nights froze and sealed her under a sheet of ice."

So that's why the dogs couldn't find her, why there was no telltale hump in the snow that came after the rain. Amy had slept in a tomb of frozen glass all winter while a million skiers had played over her.

"It's final, Hannah. I've given up the lease on her apartment. I have to get her stuff packed and out by the end of next week."

Hannah knew how Al had struggled the last time he had gone into Amy's home, touched her things. "Would you like me to help?"

"I can't ask you that."

"Of course you can. I want to help."

"I really shouldn't let you do this—"

"Al, at least let me get started. I'll get her things into boxes. If you want, you can take it from there."

"Hannah...I can't thank you enough."

"No worries. Really. I can start going through the apartment this weekend. I still have a key."

Hannah hung up and began to pace in front of her living room windows. They yawned up from floor to ceil-

ing and looked out over the water. On the opposite shores
of the lake, lights were beginning to twinkle in White
River village. The town was nestled between the feet of
Powder and Moonstone Mountains which were themselves cleft apart by the icy river that gushed between
them.

Chairlifts reached out from the village and stretched up
the flanks of Powder. Moonstone, however, fell outside
the ski area boundary and was untouched by lift lines.
The only development on Moonstone was on a large
swath of land at the base, to the south of the village. It
was home to the exclusive White River Spa.

The sky was clear tonight. Calm. A world away from
how Hannah felt inside. A moon was rising, the light of
it already glinting off mica in the rocks on the peak of
Moonstone.

It was up in those mountains that Amy had slept in her
ice tomb.

Hannah stopped pacing to stare up at the peaks. An
accident. It was all there in the official report. But it still
didn't explain why Amy had gone up there in the first
place, why she had left the roped-off trail and fallen to
her death, why her apartment was ransacked. There was
no way Hannah would be able to sleep tonight. As ex-
hausted as she felt, she was strung tight as a wire.

She may as well go and take a look at the apartment
now. She could start sorting Amy's things. And maybe,
just maybe, she'd find some answers.

The moon threw a trail of glimmering gold sovereigns
onto black water as Hannah drove the deserted road
around the lake and headed toward the lights of the village. She parked her Subaru in the underground and
climbed the stairs to the pedestrian-only stroll.

Groups of people clustered around doorways that led

down to nightclubs pulsating with primal beats below street level. Some were smoking. Couples strode by, arm in arm, laughing. Restaurants were still busy.

It was quieter down the cobbled path that led to Amy's apartment on the edge of town. There weren't as many decorative streetlamps in this less-touristy area.

Hannah felt in her fleece pocket for the key and looked up at the second-story window.

She stopped in her tracks.

She could have sworn she saw light flicker briefly in the window. She waited to see if it would come again. Nothing.

Just jumpy, she told herself. Been a weird day.

She sucked in the cool night air, calming her jittery nerves, and entered the apartment building. She climbed the stairs up to number 204, the place Amy had called home since she'd moved to White River.

The hall light was out.

Damn. Bulb must have blown. Hannah fumbled in the dark trying to get the key into the lock. She swung the door open and stepped blindly into the black apartment, groping for the light switch.

It was instantaneous.

White pain spliced through her shoulder as her arm was wrenched behind her back.

Panic punched her in the stomach. A scream surged through her body and erupted into her throat. It got no further. It was suffocated by leather.

A glove.

She fought to gasp in air. She could see nothing through the blur of blackness.

The door slammed shut behind her, cutting her off from the outside world.

She flailed behind her with her free hand and tore at a

handful of hair. An expletive. Male. More pain as he increased the pressure on her arm.

"Shut the hell up or you get hurt." He spat the words into the dark. Harsh, hoarse. Her lungs screamed for gulps of air. But each time she struggled to move, the pain tore at her shoulder.

Stay calm, Hannah. Stay calm. She forced herself to hold still.

The iron grip eased slightly, as if her attacker was testing. She could feel hot breath at her ear.

He swore and immediately let go of her mouth.

"Hannah?"

A thin beam from a flashlight cut through the dark. Slowly he turned her head and body round to face him, still pinning her arm behind her back. She blinked blindly against the sudden brightness as he looked down into her face.

"Sweet Jesus." He let the light fall so she could see him. It caught the hard ice of his eyes.

She felt faint.

"Rex?" Her voice came out hoarse, barely audible.

"What the hell do you think you're doing, McGuire? You could have gotten yourself hurt." He kept his voice a low whisper. His mouth was so close she felt his breath on her lips.

She wrenched free and lunged for the light switch. Light flooded the small apartment.

She whirled round to confront him. "Damn you, Rex Logan! What in hell are *you* doing in Amy Barnes's apartment?"

"Lord, woman." He pushed past her, drew the blinds in a deft movement. "Keep your voice down."

Uneasiness prickled up the nape of her neck. He looked lethal, dressed in black from head to foot. Dark stubble shadowed his jaw. His hair was black gloss, and he'd let it grow. It gave him a wild look. The only light thing about him was the glacial ice in his stare. A devil with Arctic eyes. The contrast was startling, unnerving. Almost inhuman.

"You shouldn't be here, Hannah." His words were low, threatening.

"*You're* the one with no right to be here." Anger started to boil up, displacing her fear. She could feel the heat of color spilling back into her cheeks. "Give me one good reason not to call the cops and have your sorry ass kicked behind bars, Rex Logan." She realized she was shaking.

"You do that and you won't find out what really happened to Amy Barnes."

She was stunned into silence.

He took a step closer. "Talk to me, Hannah. Tell me why you're in a dead woman's apartment at night." He was unnerving her with his steady blue gaze. She was determined to hold it, not to look away and give him the upper hand.

"What makes you think I believe *anything* happened to Amy?"

"I know you, Hannah. You don't let things lie. Never did. That's why you were good. One of the best. That's why you're here, tonight, isn't it? You're looking for something."

She pushed the hair back from her face in an effort to clear her head. Rex stepped even closer. The air crackled between them. She edged backward, toward the phone. Blood drummed in her ears.

"What has any of this got to do with you, Rex?"

"I'm looking for answers. Like you. I don't believe Amy's death was an accident."

Hannah took another step back toward the phone and reached behind her for the receiver.

He was on her in an instant, had her pinned up against the wall, her heart jackhammering against her rib cage. He reached and took the receiver from her hand. Placed it firmly back in the cradle. "No cops."

She was afraid now. This man was no stranger to attack. He moved like a black jungle cat and had the same power. Hannah swallowed, her throat tight. She tried to speak. "What do you want from me, Rex?"

He held her, up against the wall, a brutally intimate embrace. He leaned in, placing his mouth between her fall of hair and her ear. "More than you'll ever know, McGuire." The hot whisper, painfully seductive, snaked through her. A serpent of unwanted desire.

He reached up, slowly took a handful of her hair, gently twisted it through gloved fingers and let it fall back onto her shoulder. It was an achingly intimate gesture. She began to tremble inside. Emotion pricked hot behind her eyes. Damn him. Damn this man from her past. He was pulling the threads of her life apart.

"Come." He took her wrist, led her to a chair. She was powerless.

"Sit."

He faced her, seated on the coffee table, his knees almost touching hers. "You gate crashed my party, Hannah. You play by my rules now. That means no police."

"I…I don't understand. Who *are* you, Rex? What's going on?"

"I found something. Something that makes me think Amy Barnes got herself into trouble. It may have gotten her killed."

Confusion spiraled through her brain. "You don't mean murder?"

"I think she was sticking her nose where it wasn't wanted."

"What…what did you find?"

Again he sidestepped her question. "But if you take this to the cops, you'll get nowhere. No answers. The police are not going to help you. Trust me on this."

Trust? She'd trusted Rex Logan once before. She thought she'd known this man. She looked at him now; he was a stranger. A dangerous one. And the cops were his Achilles' heel. Why?

"And if I *do* go the cops, what happens to you? You going to try and stop me?"

"You'll tie me up in bureaucratic red tape, that's what. Then it'll be too late."

"For what?"

He dragged his hands through his hair and blew out a stream of frustration. "Christ, Hannah, why'd you have to walk into this?"

"What, exactly, have I walked in to, Dr. Logan? Who the hell are you?"

He stared at her, assessing.

"Look, either you tell me what the hell is going on or I go to the RCMP detachment right now."

He stood up, paced, turned to face her. "I can't tell you. It's classified."

She pushed herself to her feet. "What do you mean you can't tell me? What do you mean 'classified'?"

He stepped forward, taking her hands in his. "Hannah, work with me on this. Trust me."

"Work with you? *Trust you?* You won't tell me what the hell is going on. You won't tell me who you are, why you're sneaking around like a thief and you expect me to *work* with you?"

"You shouldn't have come here."

"Screw you, Logan. I had every right to come here." She pushed past him and stalked from the apartment, slammed the door behind her.

Hannah stepped out onto the pedestrian walkway into

the clean night air still shaking with adrenaline. She'd done it again. Fled. Damn him. She looked back up at the second floor. Amy's apartment was once again in darkness.

Rex lifted the blind slightly with the back of his hand and looked down into the street to watch her go. He saw her stop, turn and look back up at the window. Instinctively he shifted farther back into the dark shadows. Her hair shimmered pale gold in the lamplight, like an angel's.

Blast.

Hannah was not working her way into his investigation, she had crashed slap-bang into the middle of it. So much for trying to stay out of her way while he was in White River.

And after finding what he had in Amy's apartment, Hannah could be at risk if she insisted on digging. If his suspicions were correct, Hannah's curiosity may already have landed her in hot water. Very hot water.

Oh, the bittersweet irony.

He'd walked out of her life six years ago to keep her safe.

Now he could not walk from her. This time he would have to stay close to keep her from harm.

She was sticking her nose into the business of people who played for keeps. She had no idea what she was up against. She would need his help. She would need his protection. And he needed to make sure she didn't blow his cover by going to the cops.

He watched her turn and stride down the dimly lit street. He watched the sway of her hips.

It was that same purposeful stride that had caught his attention in Marumba. The same sway that had sparked fire in his groin.

Yes, she needed his protection, but who would protect him from her?

He'd made a mistake falling for her once. He wasn't doing much better the second time around. The woman was a drug. He'd already let himself slip.

This must be his retribution.

Then his pulse quickened.

Rex saw a hooded figure step out from under the cover of the dark portico across the walkway. Whoever it was began following Hannah toward the festive heart of White River village.

Chapter 4

The early-morning air was crisp, the clear sky pale and colorless, yet to be kissed by the sun. Within the hour it would burst over the mountain in a crashing symphony of gold chasing the chill into valley shadows until evening.

Hannah knew it would be a glorious August Saturday. It made the bizarre and sinister events of last night all the more incongruous. Was it really possible Amy had been murdered? What did Rex Logan have to do with it? What did he find in Amy's apartment that they'd all missed? What was he really doing in White River?

She couldn't go and talk to Staff Sgt. Fred LeFevre. Not yet. He'd laugh her out of the office. She needed to learn more from Rex.

But right now, this time was hers. She crouched down to tighten the laces of her runners. She would do hills today. She needed a good workout to clear the scuzz from her sleep-deprived brain and ease the kinks from her body.

Hannah broke into a slow run, rhythmically sucking the cool air down into her lungs and blowing it out into crisp clouds of vapor. She followed the trail from her condo down around the lakeshore to the point where White River flowed under the Callaghan Road bridge.

She jogged under the bridge, picking up one of the gravel trails that snaked through the park and up into the Moonstone foothills.

Her breathing was hard, deep and rhythmic now. She felt strong, in control. She found her pace as the sun peeked over the ridge and spilled suddenly into the valley, its warmth immediately noticeable on her back.

She had the trails to herself this morning. She could feel her body working, smooth, like an engine, warmth pulsing with each heartbeat through her limbs. The cold air was rough against the back of her throat. It felt good.

She slowed slightly, her body switching gears as the trail climbed into the trees. Her feet were cushioned as gravel gave way to spongy pine needles and fallen leaves. As she entered the woods, the trees strangled the morning sunshine off into cool dank shadows.

All Hannah could hear now was the sound of her own hard, steady breathing and White River, swollen and raging in the distance.

A crash in the undergrowth stopped her dead.

The noise was just ahead. Brush cracking.

Her brain identified the sound as her body screamed to flee.

But she held her ground. Hannah had been in these mountains long enough to learn not to run from a bear.

She started, one foot behind the other, backing down the trail, very slowly, just as the large ursine beast crashed through the undergrowth ahead.

It lumbered onto the trail. Hannah caught her breath. It was massive, well on its way of achieving its hibernation weight. She was used to seeing bears in White River but the primal awe at the sight of such a beast never left her.

The bear caught wind of Hannah and surged up onto its hind legs, opening and closing its mouth and swaying its head.

It was trying to get a better scent. Hannah kept backing away slowly.

Stay calm, give it space. She ran through a mental bear encounter checklist as she backed off.

She was so tightly wound she almost screamed when two little cubs scampered out of the trees in front of her, across the trail and into the brush on the other side. The big sow dropped to all fours, chomped her mouth and huffed at Hannah in warning before lumbering into the brush after her cubs.

She could feel the blood thudding through the arteries at her neck with each rapid pound of her heart. Filled with exhilaration and the adrenaline of fear, Hannah laughed out loud in release.

She waited until she could no longer hear the undergrowth crushing under the clumsy weight of the bruins before she again broke into a run.

But she was uneasy now. She couldn't regain her stride. She kept glancing over her shoulder and hearing sounds in the trees, in the shadows.

She thought she could hear the thud of feet in the soft ground behind her. She felt like the hunted must feel, her senses heightened, nerves strung like a bow.

She heard the thud of feet again. And she felt a presence.

She stopped, swiped her damp brow with the back of her hand. Listening. Silence. Nothing.

Then a sharp crack in the brush.

Hannah uncoiled into a sprint, cut onto a trail that led to the suspension bridge, a lifeline over White River that would lead her to the village, people. Fear burned with cold air in her chest as she sprinted through the trees. Sweat dripped into her eyes, blurring her vision. She ran onto the bridge. Slats of wood bounced under her weight throwing her momentarily off balance. Water raged below. She stumbled, grabbed the cable railing, and made her way across to the wooden ramp that led off the bridge. She hit solid land, sprinted over a mound and turned sharply to her right. And ran straight into him.

He reeled back under the force of the collision, grabbing her shoulders in an effort to steady them both.

"Hannah. What is it?"

She pulled away from him and bent over, hands on her knees, trying to catch her breath, the nausea of exertion rising in her stomach. "Rex…you…startled…me." Her words came out in rasping gasps.

"Talk to me. What spooked you?"

Still bent over, panting, she looked up at him. He was also in workout gear. His dark hair hung tousled and damp over his brow. Was *he* chasing her?

"Nothing…bear and her cubs. I lost my head."

He raised a brow. He didn't believe her.

"Someone was following you." He said it so matter-of-factly. As if he already knew. He scanned the trees on the far side of the river. "How long do you think he's been watching you?"

"What?" She stood upright, hand pressed tight into the pain of the stitch at her waist. "What do you mean 'how long'? Why would someone be 'watching' me?"

"Keep it down."

She glanced back into the woods, following his gaze. He was making her really uneasy.

He put a hand on each shoulder. "You're not safe, Hannah, not until I get to the bottom of this." He looked into her eyes. She felt suddenly self-conscious. She caught the wild strand escaping from her ponytail and brushed it behind her ear.

"Listen to me, you need protection."

She attempted a laugh. It came out hollow. "And who's going to protect me? You? The guy who breaks into apartments?"

"Damn right I am."

She pulled away from him. "Don't be ridiculous."

"Hannah, someone followed you when you left Amy's apartment last night."

She closed her eyes and drew in a deep, steadying breath. Her brain could no longer cope. It was in total overload.

"Hannah, we *have* to talk." He looked around, then into her eyes. "But not here. Come, let me buy you breakfast."

Coffee, she needed coffee. She needed space. He was crowding her, invading her life.

"Let's go." He took her arm and started to lead her down the path. She struggled to match his long gait as he ushered her along the trail toward the village. She was losing control, he was sucking her down into a confusing, gray maelstrom. She had to take a step back.

"Wait, Rex."

He stopped.

"I…I'm going home to change first." Besides feeling like something the cat had dragged in, the perspiration on her skin had cooled and set her shivering. "I'm cold."

Rex skimmed his eyes over her, a twinkle brightening the ice for an instant. He grinned. Quick and wolfish. "Yes. I see. I'll come with you."

She wrapped her arms over her chest. "No. I'll go alone and meet up with you later."

"Hannah, you're not getting it. You're in the same kind of trouble Amy was. You have to trust me on this."

There it was again. That word. Trust. She glanced back into the forest. She felt as if she was trapped between the devil and the trees. She was sure someone had been following her. What if Rex was right? Had she been tailed last night?

Hannah sat silent in his four-wheel-drive vehicle as he drove her around the lake.

He had the wheel and all the control. She had none. She had no idea what she had gotten herself into. She was being forced to trust him. Look where that had gotten her before.

They were approaching her condo. "Here. This one."

He pulled into her driveway. "Nice place."

"It's mine." The words escaped her mouth before her head even registered them.

"Still a nice place."

"Thanks." She'd made a decent investment in this property. She'd lived frugally during her foreign correspondent years. Her clothes had been utilitarian, her accommodation and food on the company tab. But she'd earned well and invested well. It had secured her this home. Now her freelance work plus the hours she put in at the *Gazette* supplemented her income. She and Danny were doing fine.

She climbed out of the car. He followed. He was going to come in. Into her home. Thoughts of Danny streamed through her brain. His room. His little bicycle. His toys. The photographs of him all over her condo. She turned to him. "Rex." Her voice was firm. "I don't want you in my house. Can you wait?"

He angled his head, curious. "Why?"

"I just don't."

"I'll just come in and take a quick look around. Make

sure things are safe. Then I'll leave you in peace while you change.''

Panic licked at her stomach. ''No. Please.''

Rex frowned, studying her face. Then he turned away and scanned the surroundings. He looked back at her. ''And if there's someone inside?''

''I'll yell.''

He shook his head, looked up at the sky, blew out a stream of air in frustration. But he wasn't pushing her. She had to hand him that.

''Wait.'' He strode back to the SUV and fished a cell phone out of the glove compartment. He punched in some numbers and handed it to her. ''Here. Press one and I'll be there in a flash. Don't lock your door. I'll keep watch out here.''

Hannah stepped into her home and closed the door quietly behind her. She took her time. Not so much to spite him as to absorb and process the events of the past twenty-four hours.

Rex Logan had walked back into her life and turned it upside down, spilling it all directions like a box of kids' toys. She turned on the shower and let hot water sluice over her limbs, beat at the dull ache in her shoulder. She was going to have to play along with him for a while. She had no other option. Fred LeFevre would laugh her out of his office if she came to him with a conspiracy theory and zero proof to back it up. And what if Rex *was* telling the truth? What if she did tie him up in bureaucratic red tape? Would that mean they'd never find out if someone had taken Amy's life? And why?

Hannah steeled her resolve. She'd march to the beat of his drum for now. God help her. Because once they'd solved the mystery of Amy Barnes, she was going to have to deal with the fact that this stranger in her life was Danny's father.

And she was going to have to try and resolve it all before Friday. Before Danny came home.

She toweled off and rubbed a mild gardenia-scented lotion over her body.

Hannah changed three times before she settled on a lemon-yellow sleeveless dress hemmed about two inches above her knees. It offset her tan and showed her limbs to best advantage. She couldn't remember when she'd last worn a dress. Not this summer, anyway.

She appraised the result in the mirror, then muttered a curse. Why did she even care?

"Well, I'll tell you why you care." She leaned forward and addressed her reflection, wagging her finger at her alter ego. "You want to look cool and groomed and un-fazed by his little charade. That's why." Her very feminine core, deep down, also wanted Rex to see what he'd lost. A part of her wanted him to eat dust.

Satisfied, she grabbed her sunglasses, sweater and purse and headed back to his car.

"You took your sweet time." But the gruffness of his words belied the glint of obvious approval in his eyes.

And it sparked a small glow of warm triumph in her belly.

Rex said nothing as he drove.

She looked like a golden goddess, this woman sitting next to him. The soft floral scent of her freshly showered body stirred painful memories of crushed frangipani blooms.

He lowered the window, letting in the fresh air. He wanted to blow the scent of her from his nostrils.

He'd had altogether too little sleep in his SUV. After he'd seen that hulking figure step out from under the por-tico and walk in her footsteps, he'd followed Hannah home, parked across the street, just out of sight until he could be sure she hadn't been tailed all the way.

When she set off for her run earlier this morning, he'd followed her in his vehicle but lost her when she cut into the forest. He'd dug his gym bag out of the car, changed into his sweats and tried to catch up to her, but she was packing a mean pace and he'd lost her, until she crashed into him near the suspension bridge. He would have to keep closer tabs on her.

Seeing her in the forest this morning, vulnerable, tousled, flushed, breathless, the damp T-shirt molding the soft roundness of her breasts, had near driven him wild.

He not only wanted to protect her, he needed to. It was a primal urge. He wanted to gather his woman in his arms and keep her safe from the evil of the world.

Only she wasn't his woman.

And she could never be.

He gripped the wheel and stepped on the gas, negotiating the bend in the road.

The silence hung thick and charged between them.

Rex led her to an intimate booth in the back corner of Ben's Bistro. A private cocoon in the midst of the lively clatter of plates and cutlery and steady buzz of voices. The sun spilled warm through small windowpanes, throwing square patterns onto the red-and-white checked tablecloth.

"We can talk here."

She took a seat opposite him.

"Try the eggs."

Hannah perused the menu. "I'm not that hungry. I'll have the fruit cup. And a coffee."

"The eggs are good. I had them yesterday. You look like you could do with some protein."

"I'll have the fruit."

She watched him as he placed their order. He was still in his T-shirt and sweatpants, but that did nothing to diminish his dark aura of authority. He cut a powerful figure. She watched the muscles twist under the tanned skin of his forearm as he handed the menus to the server and checked his watch. Her eyes were drawn by the motion, the silver of the watch, the dark hair on his arm, the solid breadth of his wrist. She'd forgotten the beauty of his fingers. Long. Strong. Those hands. They could be so rough yet so achingly gentle. He had run them over her hot skin once. Moved from her ankles up, slowly, along the inside of her thighs—

No. She yanked her mind back into the present. He was watching her. Intently. His eyes deep, unreadable pools. His lids with their thick fringe of lashes low. God, he'd been reading her mind.

Shaken, she lifted her water glass, gulped and silently thanked the waitress for her timing as she arrived with a pot of coffee.

Hannah's hand was unsteady as she poured cream into her coffee, remembering that he took his black. Funny how little details could stick in your mind over the years.

Rex spooned sugar into his cup, still silent.

"Are you going to tell me what's going on?"

He leaned forward, forearms on the table. His words were low, for her ears only. "Keep your voice down. Don't whisper. Mumbling is better. The sound doesn't carry as well. Got it?"

She nodded.

He looked deep into her eyes, searching. "I shouldn't be telling you this. I don't want to involve you."

"Rex, I'm in this whether you like it or not."

"I don't. And what I'm going to tell you has to remain between us. Hannah, I have to trust you. Lives could depend on it."

"You're a fine one to be talking about trust, Logan."

She saw the slight narrowing of his eyes, the shadow that flitted through them. But he let her jibe pass. He wasn't going to be drawn there. "You're a reporter."

"I can keep a secret, Rex. Believe me. I haven't gone to the cops." *Yet.*

He took a sip of his coffee, watching her over the rim. "Well, what did you find in Amy's apartment?"

"Two library books and a document."

"Oh, that *definitely* means she met with foul play."

He wasn't amused. "It's the subject matter. Amy Barnes was reading up-to-date information on biological warfare."

"What?"

"It wasn't just biological weapons she was interested in. She was reading up on genetically engineered BW technology."

"Okay. I'm having real trouble joining the dots here. Help me out."

"We have reason to believe that Amy came across something here in White River that landed her in trouble. Something to do with biological weapons."

"We?"

"Bio Can."

"What's a pharmaceutical company got to do with this?"

"Let's just say Bio Can has a highly specialized division focused on developing antidotes and vaccines for bugs with a potential to be weaponized."

Her head was spinning. "But I thought your field was more indigenous medicine." *At least that's what you told me in Africa.*

"It is. I work in both divisions." He stopped talking as the server arrived with their food. Rex tucked into his egg and bacon platter, savoring a mouthful before continuing.

Hannah stared at her fruit. Biological weapons? What in the hell had Amy been up to? "Maybe she was just researching something, Rex, for a story."

He chewed, nodded. "Maybe. But there was a piece of paper in one of the books. On it is the name and number of a CIA agent, one who specializes in biowarfare intelligence."

"Oh my God."

He sipped his coffee. "How's the fruit?"

The question seemed suddenly so inane. Hannah looked at the plate in front of her, picked up a fork and jabbed at a strawberry. "Fine." She felt ill.

"And I checked Amy's computer last night. The hard drive has been cleaned out."

Hannah stiffened. "That's it. The break-in. That's what they took. Electronic data. No wonder the cops didn't find anything."

"Well, whoever took the data didn't find the library books."

"But who?"

"That's what I'm here to find out. I'm hoping you'll help."

"I don't get it, Rex. Why White River? What's the connection?"

"We don't know. But the forensic toxicology conference is a common denominator here. We suspect something may be going down."

"Like what?"

"A deal. An information exchange, maybe. We haven't got much time."

"But what does a conference like that have to do with biological warfare, anyway?"

Rex pushed his plate aside. "There is a component on

the conference agenda that covers lethal viruses and new research in the field of forensic detection. It's that kind of stuff that draws top scientists from around the world. Ideas are exchanged. Connections made. Deals made. Most of it happens offstage. Bio Can likes to keep on top of these kinds of developments. So do a lot of other agencies.''

Hannah looked out through the little window panes at a group of young people gathered in the sun on the patio across the village square. Amy should be with them, laughing, planning her next snowboarding trip, her next surfing expedition. She had been cheated out of her future.

She turned back to face the man in front of her. ''So you're telling me you're one of the good guys?''

''*Good* is a subjective term.''

''Is that why you don't want the cops involved?''

''This is beyond small-town cops, Hannah. This is the big league. The global league.''

She pushed her uneaten fruit bowl aside. She felt as if all the blood had left her head.

He leaned forward as if to take her hand. Hannah braced for the touch but it never came. He seemed to catch himself, lifting the coffeepot instead. He held it up. ''Refill?''

She shook her head. ''What happens now?''

He poured seconds for himself. ''Now, you tell me about Ken Mitchell.''

''Ken Mitchell?''

''This slices both ways, Hannah.''

''Rex, I don't know any Ken Mitchell.''

''You were lunching with him at the Black Diamond yesterday.''

Hannah felt something slip in her stomach. ''You mean Mark Bamfield, the freelance writer?''

''Try CIA.''

"I see." Her brain was numb.

"So he's calling himself Bamfield. What's his cover?"

She cleared her throat. "He said he was a freelance reporter from Washington, that he was here for the toxicology conference and that he was doing a story on Amy Barnes."

"See the links now?"

She nodded. She didn't like what she was seeing at all.

This time he placed his hand over hers. "And, Hannah, if you go to the police now, if you tie me up with bureaucracy, you could end up getting yourself killed."

She looked down at the large hand covering her own. She could feel its warmth, its roughness. It was the hand with the ring, the token of her love, the symbol of her naïveté. She looked back up into his eyes. She couldn't read them. "That sounds like a threat, Rex."

"No, Hannah. A warning. I don't want you to get hurt. You've crossed the line. There's no going back now. Now you play by new rules."

He was right. She didn't see how she could turn back. Her world hadn't only shifted on its axis; she'd been thrust into a whole new one where she didn't know the players and she didn't know the rules. And she sure as hell didn't know the man sitting in front of her.

She pulled her hand out from under his. "What do you want me to do?"

Something flickered through his eyes. Then it was gone. "Can you get me into the *Gazette* office? I need to take a look at Amy's work computer, see if she left any trail there."

"I can do that."

"Now?"

She looked at her watch. It was early on Saturday. The *Gazette* offices would likely be empty. "Now's good."

He stood up. "Let's go and see what we can find before

it's too late. And then I need a shower and a change of clothes.''

He moved around to Hannah's side of the booth. ''Coming?'' He held out his arm for her to join him. He cut a paradoxical figure. A striking but unshaven British gentleman in sweats. She stood up and took his arm.

He steered her out of the bistro and into bright Saturday sunshine. ''Now,'' he said, ''we must discuss the little matter of keeping you safe. Perhaps you could check into the hotel for a while. Your place is a little isolated on the other side of the lake.''

Chapter 5

She stood her ground in the middle of village square. "I will stay away from the police. I will show you around the *Gazette* office. I'll help you because I want to find out what happened to Amy. But I will *not* move out of my house."

He dropped his voice to a gravelly whisper. "You're making a scene. Keep moving. For Christ's sake act normal." Rex tucked his arm around her waist and led her down the cobbled walkway toward the *Gazette* office. "It would just be for a while, until I can figure out what's going on."

"That's ridiculous."

Yet, after her scare this morning, after what he'd revealed at the bistro, she wasn't so sure. She wasn't sure of anything anymore.

He kept her close with his arm. Solid, fluid strength, guiding her down the path. *But what path?* Where in hell were they headed?

"Rex," she whispered. "I don't want a bodyguard."

"Well, you got one."

She slipped out from under his possessive hold and climbed the concrete stairs ahead of him, pushing open the glass door with the *White River Gazette* logo emblazoned on the front.

She marched in without holding the door open behind her. She had a photograph of Danny on her desk and she wanted to make sure he didn't see it. Not now. She didn't want to have her precious boy play any part in this. She herself couldn't seem to grasp what was happening.

"Hey, Hannah. Didn't expect you in today. It's been like a train station this morning."

She stopped short. "Georgette?"

Hannah hadn't anticipated seeing anyone at the *Gazette* reception desk on this weekend morning, especially not the village gossip. "I didn't think you'd be in, either." She turned to motion to the arrogant man in her wake. "That's Rex." She didn't use his last name. She didn't want Georgette putting two and two together and linking little Daniel Logan McGuire with this man. She had a hunch Al had already made the connection. She sure didn't need the town windbag to do the same. "I need to show him some archived stories on Amy's disappearance. Rex, this is our superefficient office coordinator, Georgette." Hannah started to make for her office down the corridor, anxious to slip that photograph of Danny into her drawer.

"Archives, huh?" Georgette called after her. "That's what Al and that freelance writer were after earlier today."

Hannah stopped dead in her tracks, spun round to face Georgette. "What freelance writer?"

"Mark Bamfield. He met Al here this morning." Georgette chuckled, turning her smile up a few watts for Rex.

"And there I was thinking I'd have a peaceful Saturday doing catch-up."

"Don't worry. We won't disturb you, Georgette." Rex flashed that sharp white smile of his at the office coordinator, and Hannah felt something twist inside her gut.

Georgette tilted her chin and brushed a lock of hair behind her ear. "No problem, Rex. Take as long as you like."

Hannah stalked off to her office, leaving Georgette batting her eyes at Rex. So he had a way with the ladies. Little did they know he was a love-'em-and-leave-'em cad who sneaked off in the dark. The sooner they got to the bottom of this business, and the sooner he got out of her life, the better.

Hannah scooped Danny's picture off her desk and slipped it into her purse.

"What's the big rush?" She heard Rex behind her and jumped. The newsroom seemed to shrink in his presence.

"Uh, I'm worried that Bamfield…Mitchell whoever, has gotten to the files." She spoke quickly as she booted up the computer and seated herself in front of the terminal.

"Well, no amount of rushing now is going to change that." Rex pulled up a chair and squeezed it in beside Hannah's.

He was invading her space again. Her chest felt tight.

"Perhaps you could shift over just a tad, or do you plan on doing this yourself?" he said.

She glared at him and edged her chair over an inch. He pulled his seat in, bringing his arm almost into contact with hers. They sat side by side looking at the computer screen as it crackled to life. She could feel it, the intensity, the energy mushrooming warm between them. It raised the fine hair along her limbs in little goose bumps. She rubbed her arms.

He said nothing. The silence was thick.

She cleared her throat. "Where do you want to start, Rex?" *Where did one start after six years?*

He turned to face her. He was so close. She could feel her heart rate increase, her breathing become more shallow. His glacial gaze held her. She couldn't look away. She watched as the light in them shifted from crystal to dark, the center starburst of indigo radiating out with the heat of his gaze. It knocked her completely off guard. She felt herself being drawn in, being physically pulled, her body leaning imperceptibly toward his.

She swallowed.

He turned and looked back at the screen, clearing his throat. "So, where are Amy's files stored?"

Hannah felt overwhelmingly relieved to have a clear task. A defined road. "This was her terminal," she told Rex. She needed to refocus. "It's basically what I inherited when she went missing. It's a Macintosh system. Most small newspapers use Macs." She was babbling.

Hannah clicked open a file and showed him where Amy's work had been stored. "This is not the morgue. This is…was, her personal working stuff. I didn't delete anything, just filed it here. Amy's notes are in here." She clicked. "Her interviews, contacts and stories." Hannah moved the mouse. She could feel the heat emanating from the body almost touching hers.

"Um, once Amy completed a story she would have filed it here." She clicked on network folder that was shared by all the computers in the office. "This is where Al would have picked it up for editing before dumping it into another folder where production would access it for layout."

His fingers brushed over hers as he gently took the mouse from her hand. Her breath caught in her throat. Those long, gently tapered fingers that had once stroked slowly up the inside of her thigh touched hers. Hannah felt warmth pool, unwanted, delicious in her belly.

Her hands were trembling.

This was ridiculous.

She jerked off her chair, stalked over to the large newsroom windows. There were tufts of white cloud over the granite peaks. She could see the lift lines, chairs winking as metal caught sun, and she could see Grizzly Bowl, where Amy had lost her life.

Hannah turned back to face him. "Take a look and see what you can find in there, Rex. If you have any questions, I'll be in the next office."

His blue gaze bored into her. "Don't go anywhere, Hannah, I might need you." The timbre of his voice was low, rough.

She stared at him, a battle of emotions raging in her brain and in her heart. *And where were you, Rex, all those years ago when I needed you? Where were you when I went into labor with your child? Where were you when he got his first tooth? Where were you, Rex, when he asked if he had a daddy?*

She wanted to shake him. Strike him. She wanted to ask him why he deserted her that night. Why he'd left the warmth of their sleeping bag and stalked off into the African veldt. She wanted the touch of those hands on her skin. Heaven help her. She wanted him. And she hated him.

"Fine. I won't go anywhere."

From where she stood she could see the small muscle pulsing on the right side of his jaw, just near his ear as he watched her. She knew by the look in his dark-rimmed sky-blue eyes that he felt it, too. That unspoken frisson, that undeniable seductive pull. It was that same sensual vortex that had sucked them down together in Marumba.

Silence stretched thick and elastic between them. She could think of no words to break the spell that held them.

The light from behind her played unforgivingly on his features but did nothing to diminish them. God he was striking. More rugged than beautiful. And hard, as hard as this unforgiving terrain, this mountain playground she called home. She watched the white sunlight catch in his eyes.

They made her think of a pool. An ice-cool pool that lay still as glass under summer heat. But when a swimmer plunged with breathless delight into its cold depths, the surface would shatter into refracted, laughing light and dancing crystal.

She suspected swimmers didn't play there often.

His eyes held her prisoner as he slowly pushed his chair back and moved over to her. She was incapable of backing away, like a small mouse mesmerized by the hungry stare of a serpent.

He came closer. Closer.

Breathe, Hannah. She seemed to have lost the ability to do what came so naturally. *Breathe.*

He lifted his hand and hooked a knuckle under her chin, tilting her face up to him.

There were dark fathomless depths lurking in those glacial blue pools now. Swirling undercurrents. They mirrored the dark passion that swam warm inside her.

He softly traced the outline of her lips with the roughened pad of his thumb. She felt the world around her recede, her vision blur.

She allowed her lips to part slightly as he pushed against them, and she let the tip of her tongue test the salt of his finger.

In response the pressure of his finger became a little more urgent, more forceful, parting her lips wider. The sensation of wanting to take his whole finger into her mouth, to suck him into her, was overwhelming as she felt the rivers of warmth in her body threaten to overrun their banks.

Her legs were unsteady.

"You feel it, Hannah." His voice was throaty, rough with want. "You feel it, too, don't you? I can see it in your eyes." He ran his finger forcefully along the edge of her teeth. His other hand found the small of her back and he started to pull her in close to his hard body. She felt her breasts push up against his chest.

She wanted him. All of him, deep inside. She wanted to wrap herself around him, drink him in. Six years had not dulled the edge of her hunger for him. It was sharper. She ached with a raw need she thought she had buried all those years ago.

No. She couldn't go there. Couldn't repeat it. Her drugged brain scrambled to pull at threads of rationality. "No. Rex, please. No!"

He backed away instantly. For what seemed an eternity they just stood, close. Trying to compute the depth of what still existed between them.

Then he reached up and gently brushed a lock of hair from her cheek.

The retreat, the tenderness of the movement as he touched her hair was too much for Hannah. What had been locked inside spilled out in hot silent tears onto her cheeks.

"Damn you." She pushed against his chest. "Damn you, Rex."

She felt his muscles brace solid against her hands as she tried to shove him away.

It had happened in Marumba. She had let passion override reason. It had been a mistake. She was not going to make that mistake again. Especially not now. There was too much at risk. There was Danny.

She turned her back on him to face the timeless peaks. She held her arms tight about herself, trying to hold in the ache, the pain, the need.

"Hannah." He put a hand on her shoulder.

She jerked out from under his touch. "Leave me alone, please, Rex." She swiped the back of her hand across the wetness of her cheeks and turned to face him. "I'll be in the next room."

She forced her knees to bend, she made her legs walk across the newsroom to the door. Her limbs felt like rubber.

Rex stalked down the concrete stairs from the *Gazette* office, following Hannah into the village streets. He battled to hold his raw anger in check. He was used to being in complete control of emotions. It was a requirement of the job. But this woman had power over him. The power to turn off his internal controls. He was furious he'd stepped over the line. He wanted her. He'd wanted to take her right in that office. Sweet Jesus. How could he do that to her? How could he hurt her like this?

"Where are we going?"

He took Hannah by the elbow and steered her down the walkway. The afternoon sun had turned a soft yellow but it did nothing to mellow the naked emotion that seethed between them.

Rex had found that CIA agent Ken Mitchell had indeed accessed the office files. Mitchell now knew what they knew, that Amy had demonstrated an unnatural interest in biological weapons and urban terrorism and that she had a file of information devoted exclusively to the topic, along with Website addresses.

"I said, where are we going?"

"My hotel. I told you I need a shower."

"Well, I don't." She pulled free. "I'm going home. If you need me you can call me there."

"No." He grabbed her arm. "I need you to make a phone call to the Vancouver library, find out about those books—when Amy took them out, what else she may have borrowed. You can do that from my room."

"You expect me to jump at your command? You've got the social grace of a military despot, you know. Didn't your parents teach you anything?"

She was lashing out at him. Good. It was better that way. "You're right, they left my education to the military. Everything I learned about life, I learned in the army."

She seemed to halt at his words, her eyes flared briefly in question. But she said nothing.

"Come." He ushered her up the wide stone stairs of the White River Presidential Hotel.

The doorman snapped to attention as they approached, and held open the door. Rex gave his thanks with a curt nod and escorted Hannah into the cavernous hotel lobby.

She said nothing as he ushered her into the elevator and pressed the button for the sixth floor.

The doors closed them in. Just the two of them, alone, as the elevator started to hum. It threw their predicament into stark relief.

After six years of nothing, no contact, they were now trapped together. But the feelings between them were no different. Only deeper, darker, more convoluted. He had to try to stay clear of that abyss. He had to keep his head and keep her safe. He had to clear this case and get the hell out of here. Leave before they destroyed each other.

But she was sucking him in, even now as she watched the numbers of the floors flash by. He could feel her feminine presence touching him in this confined space. He could feel the energy coming from her, waves of it. Passion and anger and hate and pain. He yearned to reach out and quell it, stroke it away.

He thrust his hands into the pockets of his loose sweat-pants. *Deal with it, Logan. A few more days and you'll be out of her life.*

Hannah just about leaped through the elevator doors as they opened onto the lush carpet of the sixth floor. She started quickly along the corridor to the left. He reached out and caught the fabric of her dress in the small of her back. "No, this way."

He turned and made his way down the corridor to the right. She stormed after him, the carpet swallowing the angry impact of her feet.

Hannah stood in the hotel room. There was one large double bed. Soft white diaphanous curtains were tied back from French doors that opened onto a small balcony.

A bathroom led off to the right. The only sign that anyone occupied the suite was a laptop on the black-lacquered desk under a small window that was graced with the same white bridal curtains.

Rex pulled his T-shirt over his head and tossed it onto the bed. He yanked open the drawer of the bedside table, pulled out a telephone directory and tossed it onto the desk. "There. You'll find the Vancouver Public Library number in there. And here." He tossed a bag onto the chair. "Amy's library material is in that bag."

Hannah could see the scar that sliced across the left side of his chest from underarm to nipple. She saw the dark hair that ran in a slim dense whorl from below his navel into the track pants slung low on his narrow hips. The suggestive swirl of hair lured her eyes down his flat belly. It whispered of what lay beyond. She'd been there. Her hands had once traced that line...her mind swam back.

He was watching her again. She grabbed the phone book and started flicking through the pages, looking for the library number.

Rex marched into the bathroom. The door closed behind him with a click. Hannah could hear the shower. She picked up the phone and punched in the number of the Vancouver library. She glanced at her watch. There should still be someone there this time on a Saturday.

"Vancouver Public Library, how may I help you?"

"Yes, hi, I have a couple of titles here." She rummaged quickly in the bag, pulling them out. "I think they belong to a deceased friend of mine and I was wondering if you could help me out by telling me when they were borrowed."

"Certainly. One moment."

Hannah was put through to another person who asked for the titles. It was the first time she'd seen the books, and as she read the titles out loud, the seriousness of the situation started to seep in. *Biological Agents Used in Assassination,* and *Mapping Human Genes—Implications in Biological Warfare and Genetically Engineered Biological Weapons.*

What on earth was Amy up to?

"Okay, I've pulled up the file here." The voice was perky. "Yes, those were signed out by Grady Fisher on the fifteenth of September last year. They're almost a year overdue but we can certainly waive any charges under these circumstances."

"Who did you say signed the books out?"

"Grady Fisher."

Hannah didn't know any Grady Fisher. "Ah…do you have an address registered on file for Mr. Fisher?"

"Sorry. I thought you said the borrower was deceased, a friend of yours."

Hannah's mind raced through the possibilities. "Well,

her books must have been signed out in someone else's name. Is it possible to get this Grady Fisher's address?"

"Sorry. Library policy. We can't give out that sort of information."

Hannah hung up.

Grady Fisher. Perhaps one of Amy's friends knew who he was. Perhaps if they could find Grady, he might have some answers.

She stood up from the desk and walked over to the French doors. She pulled them open with both hands, and the scents of the mountain immediately blew into the room in a rush of fragrant air. It smelled of straw and honey and earth.

Hannah stepped out onto the small balcony. Six floors down lay the sparkling pool. There was nothing between the back of the hotel property and the ski slopes. In winter, skiers and boarders carved their way right down to the hotel doors, or they crunched along the pathway to the village as steam rose from the heated pool.

Hannah drank in the late-afternoon air. She could see why the hotel was a favorite of honeymooning couples and why the White River marriage commissioner did such a brisk trade. People came from all over the world to tie the knot in these mountains, hoping their love would be as enduring as the snow-capped granite peaks that inspired them.

But she had run to White River as an escape. She had run from love. Well, at least for her it had been love.

Hannah watched as a couple, the man with a baby in a carrier on his back, picked their way slowly down the hiking trail toward the hotel. She had always known she would have children. She had dreamed that she could make it all possible, kids, her successful career, a proper family…a storybook family.

Well, that was for storybooks. She did have a child. It

was not the way she had planned things, but she had a wonderful, beautiful son and she was going to make the best of what she did have. She had been doing fine, until now.

Danny, she needed to phone Danny. She needed to make contact with him, to hear his little voice, to ground herself.

Hannah stepped back into the hotel room and eyed the phone. No, not here. She didn't want Rex to be able to hear.

He was still in the shower; she could hear the splash of the water.

Now was her chance.

She gathered up her purse and sweater and walked quickly across the soft carpet to the door. She put her hand on the knob, pausing to listen for the shower.

It stopped. She'd better hurry. She pulled open the door and made a dash for the elevator.

Rex stepped out of the shower in a fog of steam, feeling vaguely human again. He wrapped a towel around his waist and rubbed a circle clear in the misted mirror. He slathered shaving cream over his jaw, pulled a trail through the creamy froth with his razor, rinsed the blade and took it to his face again.

As the steam once again started blurring the edges of the clearing he'd rubbed on the glass, Rex's mind drifted back in time, back to that day he'd first seen her in Marumba, that small pocket of troubled country nestled between Sierra Leone and Liberia, near the Ivory Coast.

She'd been in that bar, celebrating with a raucous crowd of foreign journalists and photographers. She'd just broken a story about illegal diamonds being smuggled from Sierra Leone through Marumba.

He'd been downing beer, internally seething over the botched lab raid and his wasted time.

Rex had been just hours away from doing a deal with the Plague Doctor himself. It had taken him months of undercover work to infiltrate the Marumba research lab that posed as pharmaceutical plant. He'd won the confidence of the Plague Doctor who'd then given Rex a tour of his facility. Once in the lab, Rex saw the extent of his evil. Most of his experiments with biological agents like the plague, hemorrhagic fevers, anthrax, e-coli or HIV had been carried out on dogs and baboons.

He knew for certain then that the Plague Doctor had been responsible for an Ebola outbreak in Kenya that had killed hundreds. He could also be linked to an outbreak of hoof and mouth disease in animals in Britain.

The doctor personified evil, and he sold his secrets to the highest bidder, to the country or army with the deepest pockets. He was a scientific mercenary in the biological weapons war and he had no conscience.

Rex had almost had the proof he needed, almost had access to the Plague Doctor's new genetic research on ethnic bullets. A few more hours and the Bellona Channel would have had evidence in hand, knowledge it could use in the fight against the proliferation of biological weapons worldwide. Knowledge Bio Can Pharmaceutical could in turn use to create antidotes.

The CIA had also been watching the lab, aware of the Bellona Channel's work. It wasn't unusual for the two organizations to cooperate. But then Mitchell had blown the whistle too early and the troops had moved in.

The result was a fire, a raging white-hot blaze, an ecological nightmare. Everything in the lab was burned. But there were no biological agents found in the fire-safe refrigeration unit in what was the Biosafety Level 4 sector and most of the staff had escaped—including the Plague Doctor.

Rex dragged the razor over his skin, cursing the CIA agent under his breath. He swore again as he nicked his skin with his blade.

It was as if Mitchell had deliberately tried to thwart the Bellona Channel and facilitate the escape of Dr. Ivan Rostov.

It was in that bar, after the disastrous raid, that he'd first seen Hannah. She'd been leaving for Ralundi the next day. Rex also packed his bags that night. But he didn't ship out to Canada as planned. When the pink copper sky over the Marumba mountain range promised dawn, he'd left for Ralundi, a small town on the Marumba coast, telling himself he needed a break.

That decision six years ago to leave for Ralundi had cost him his heart.

Rex splashed cold water over his face and ran his hand over his jaw, testing the result of his shave. He wondered if Hannah had had any luck with the Vancouver library.

He opened the bathroom door and was greeted by cool early-evening air billowing the gauzy curtains out from the French door. He didn't see her. He didn't need to, he could sense she wasn't in the room.

He stalked over to the open French doors and pushed aside the pregnant drapes. "Hannah?"

There was no one on the balcony.

He whirled round and stormed back into the room. "Hannah!"

She had gone.

He swore as he opened the door into the hallway. Nothing but silence along the empty corridor.

He muttered an expletive and yelled down the row of room doors. "Hannah!"

Where in hell was she? Didn't she get it? She wasn't safe. This was no time to play games.

Rex started down the hallway toward the elevator before remembering the towel around his waist. He cursed again and turned back to find some clothes.

She didn't have her car with her; she'd be on foot. Knowing her stubborn streak, Rex figured she'd probably decided to walk all the way home. That meant she would have to go back through the park.

He didn't like this one bit.

He pulled on a white T-shirt and black jeans. Then, as an afterthought, he lifted the mattress, pulled out his .38 and shoved it into the back of his pants.

Chapter 6

A mounting sense of anxiety squeezed in around her heart as she ran down the wide stone stairs of the five-star White River Presidential Hotel.

She almost tripped, catching her balance at the bottom. She stopped momentarily to take stock. She felt as if she was suffocating. She needed to break free from Rex. His presence here in White River was sucking her down into a vortex of emotions she couldn't bear to confront. She had to get home. She had to speak to her little boy, hear his voice.

She didn't have her car. She could catch a bus home. No, the walk would burn off some of her frustration. It was getting cool but there would be enough light for a while yet.

Hannah shrugged into her sweater, clutched her purse under her arm and strode purposefully down the brick-paved walkway.

The eclectic White River boutiques still had their wares

displayed out on the stroll. Summer tourists picked among the displays for treasures to take to their loved ones back home. Others were enjoying sundowners on the patios. Music spilled out into the mountain twilight from restaurants, coffee shops and little bistros. She could smell garlic, wood smoke and barbecue.

But she felt oddly detached as she hurried through the crowds, untouched by the holiday atmosphere. Biological weapons. Murder. It was all too bizarre, too impossible to contemplate against this serene backdrop.

She turned down the path that led to the suspension bridge over White River. She wanted to speak to Danny, go to sleep and wake up realizing this was all just a bad, bad dream.

The walkway cobbles gave way to gravel as the path narrowed and started its descent down through the heavy conifers toward the river. The scent of pine resin was thick in the evening air.

It was darker and cooler as she got closer to the river. She could hear it, rushing swollen from melting glacial ice, ice that hadn't melted in years, the ice of Amy's tomb. It was this unusual melt, she thought, that had brought her body to light and Rex into her life. It had set a series of dominoes tumbling.

Hannah stepped onto the wooden slats of the narrow swinging bridge, conscious of the white froth churning below her feet. She could see the water through the gaps in the wood. She gripped the cold, damp metal of the steel cable that served both as a railing and support for the structure.

The bridge crossed this point in the river because it was most narrow here. The very narrowness of this rocky little gorge, however, drove the body of glacial water in a broiling surge through to the calmer pools and eddies below.

She was halfway across the water, heading for the Moonstone side of the river, when she felt the bridge beneath her jerk. She steadied herself as it began to rock and bounce. Someone else had joined her in crossing. Probably some kids jouncing the bridge. Danny liked to do that.

Gripping the railing, Hannah turned to look over her shoulder. A man, advancing, was making exaggerated movements that caused the bridge to buck and sway under her feet.

The set of his shoulders, the way he filled the space between the railings, reminded her of a football player in line for the tackle. The hood of his voluminous gray sweatshirt was pulled low over his brow.

Everything about his posture was threatening.

Hannah froze and clung to the railing as her brain computed facts. His pants were baggy, wide, cut snowboarder-style. His clothes gave him no form, just bulk.

She was stuck in that space before perceived danger is recognized as real and adrenaline kicks the body into action, that space where time warps into slow motion.

As he moved closer she saw the red-and-white bandanna wrapped over his mouth and nose. He wore reflective sunglasses. He was faceless. His hands were covered with pale latex gloves. Fear fell like a cold stone in her stomach.

Hannah dropped her purse and took a step back, her heart stampeding in her chest. He'd cut off access to the village. Her only escape now was to run into the dark woods on the Moonstone bank.

She turned, ran, staggering like a drunkard as the bridge lurched under her.

He was toying with her. He wasn't rushing. He wanted to see her paralyzed with fear.

Perhaps that's all he wanted, to get a kick out of frightening the life out of some woman. She would outrun him. She reached the end of the bridge where the slats dipped in a little gangplank down onto the dank trail.

She uncoiled into a sprint the minute her feet hit solid ground but was jolted up short as her sweater snagged on the dry fingers of a dying Douglas fir.

She wriggled free just as he hit her with his full weight, the force smacking her into the ground.

The air in her lungs exploded from her rib cage as he sandwiched her to hard earth. She was stunned, winded, and sharp pain sparked and crackled along her ribs.

Hannah groped in the dirt, grasped a cold rock. She could do no more than hold on to it, she was pinned flat into the soil and pine needles by his weight.

What did he want? Is this what happened to Amy?

Pinprick sparks of light started crowding into the periphery of her vision. She blinked them back with tears of pain.

Focus, Hannah, focus. She fought the blackness circling her mind. She could taste soil in her mouth, grit against teeth.

Focus.

She allowed her body to go limp, waiting to see what he wanted from her.

He grabbed a handful of hair, yanked her head sharply round. She used that moment, twisting violently under him, to swing the rock up to his skull.

She felt stone meet skin as it cracked into his cheekbone, shattering the mirrored lens of his glasses.

He grunted, swung back grabbing his cheek, momentarily off balance. She seized the instant, pushed up on her arms, pulled out from under him.

Hannah scrambled up, started to flee, but he reached forward and caught her ankle. She tried to writhe out of his grasp as she fell, but the sideways movement crashed her down onto the rocks that hung over the river.

She felt, more than saw, the angry water waiting below.

Something dribbled into her eye. Warm. Blood. She could taste the metallic tang of her own blood in her mouth.

All that held her back from the frigid froth below was her assailant's painful hold on her ankle.

She twisted her head, looked up at the faceless form that held her life in his hand. Blood oozed thick and black from the gash in his face, soaking into the bandanna over his mouth. She could see the yellow of her own dress refracted into a million shards in the broken mirror of his lens.

He looked down at the water below, then at her.

"Please." She didn't recognize the hoarse croak as having been uttered by her own swollen lips. "Please. Don't. I have a son. Please."

He lifted the hand holding her leg and he let it go.

Gravity did the rest.

Hannah flailed out, grabbing blindly at rocks and roots as she tumbled down into the roiling maw below the bridge.

Pain exploded through her skull as her head glanced off a rock and the glacial cold swallowed her body.

Everything went instantly black.

It didn't go right. This would cost them. Perhaps he could still make it look like an accident. He got up, hurried to retrieve her sweater from the snag, dusted it off and laid it neatly on the rocks over the gorge. His bandanna was sticky with blood from the gash on his face. He cussed as he made his way back along the bridge and gathered up her purse.

He glanced up, made sure he was still alone and opened

it. She had a wallet with ID. Good, they'd know it was hers. They would think she had slipped and fallen.

Then he saw the framed photograph. Her son. Dark hair, unusual pale blue eyes. He stuffed the small frame into the back pocket of his baggy pants before retracing his steps over the bridge and dropping her purse onto the rocks alongside her sweater.

He would have to make his way downriver now, to see if he could find her body. He had to be sure she was good and dead.

But before he could move, a blow across the back of his shoulders shot the wind out of him. He instinctively ducked and rolled, forward and low, flowing with the force before spinning around grabbing his assailant's ankles and bringing him down to join him in the dirt.

He'd been hit by a piece of log. He grabbed for the log and swung it up into his assailant's face before scrambling to his feet and hightailing it into the forest.

"Did you see a woman, tall, in a yellow dress, honey-blond hair?"

Rex could see the young doorman wasn't sure how to answer. "My wife." Rex laughed as he fished a twenty out of his wallet and tucked it into the doorman's vest. "Women. You know how it is. She wanted Chinese, I wanted Italian. So she storms out in a huff."

The lad relaxed. "Yeah, typical." He nodded in conspiratorial agreement. "Women."

"Did you see which way she went, buddy?"

"Yeah." He grinned. "Hard not to notice her. She went that way." He pointed down the stroll that led past the shops to the park and the river.

"Didn't happen to see if anyone was following her, did you?"

A wariness flickered back through the doorman's puppy brown eyes. "Pardon me, sir?"

"Never mind. Thanks, mate."

Rex bounded down the stairs. As he suspected, Hannah must be making for home, on foot.

The sky was still pale violet with streaks of pink cloud, but in the trees near the river, it was almost dark.

Rex trotted over the suspension bridge, keeping his center of balance low, absorbing the bounce and sway of the slats in his knees.

He caught sight of the small pale bundle on the rocks on the opposite bank when he was halfway across the river. His pulse doubled its pace. Panic was something he didn't allow. He couldn't use it to his advantage. He pushed it down.

He dropped off the gangplank onto the trail and climbed down onto the rocks before he saw the sorry bundle for what it was. Hannah's sweater, her purse.

His breath caught in his throat. He dropped down onto his haunches and gently touched her possessions. He saw marks in the dirt above the rocks. It looked as if she could have slipped and fallen.

He could see nothing in the churning foam below.

Rex picked up her sweater and saw dirt, bits of twig and traces of blood. He lifted the soft fabric to his cheek. He closed his eyes and took a deep breath, inhaling her scent. When he opened them, he was in control. Years of British Special Air Services training had slammed into gear.

He'd have to hurry, make best use of the fading light. His eyes followed the marks and scuffs where pine needles had been scraped back to reveal fresh tracks in the damp earth. Rex recognized signs of a struggle. There was blood on a piece of log on the trail. He dropped to the ground and picked up a sticky clump of needles and sniffed. More blood. It looked as if one set of tracks led up the trail into the trees.

He looked up, squinting into dark woods. He channeled the anger that had begun to boil acrid in his gut down to where he could use it as a controlled, combustible fuel that could drive him endlessly, calm and rational, like an oiled and lethal hunter.

He knew bush fighting, and he was no stranger to taking life. Rex set off, crouched low, into the trees along the top of the riverbank. If Hannah had fallen, or been pushed, into the water, she would have washed downstream. He ducked under a low, heavy hemlock bough. That was if she was lucky. If not, she could be trapped underwater against the rocks, under pressure from currents.

The bank dipped closer down to meet the water as White River started to widen and relax into pools and deep back eddies. The roaring sound of the whitewater quieted into a peaceful chatter and chuckle as small rocks knocked together in the shallow currents.

In the dimming light, Rex could see him. Just ahead. A man, with blood down the side of his face. He was bent over her, a limp heap in pale yellow. She lay on the loamy soil of the bank, water lapping at her ankles.

Rex crouched, balanced on one knee, pulled the .38 slowly out from the back of his jeans, eyes fixed on his target. Any sound he made was lost against the low burble of the river.

"Step back or I shoot." His voice carried clear. A visible jolt shocked through the man. He scrambled to his feet, started to run for cover.

"Halt or I'll shoot!"

The man ducked under a branch and bounded up a narrow trail. Rex fired. The crack rang through the woods. But he was gone. No use following him now. Hannah was the priority. Rex dared to hope he would find her alive.

He scrambled down the bank.

It took a split second to absorb the scene, but what met his eyes made no sense. She was barely conscious. It looked as if she had been dragged up through the mud from the water.

She'd thrown up, was gasping softly for breath. It looked as if the man he'd tried to maim with his bullet had been trying to revive her. His blood was smeared on Hannah's face.

Rex dropped to his knees and checked her air passages before touching his lips to hers and breathing warmth and life into her lungs. She coughed, wretched and fell back limp in his arms.

At least she was breathing. He checked her pulse. Weak. He couldn't see much in this light. He had to get her someplace warm. The gash above her eye looked superficial, but her skin was bloodless and felt cold as death.

The river hadn't claimed her, but if he didn't hurry, hypothermia would.

He had to risk moving her.

"The angels were smiling on you, darling." He whispered into her tangle of hair, knowing she wouldn't hear. She was sleeping soundly now, her breathing regular. He'd kept up the two-hourly checks throughout the night. There was no overt sign of concussion, and her temperature was back up into an acceptable range. Rex had managed to keep her out of the more advanced stages of hypothermia that would've required hospitalization.

He lay now, undressed against her naked body. Skin on skin. Sharing his physical warmth. He'd done this throughout the night, keeping her core temperature up. Now, pale gray fingers of dawn searched through gauzy white curtains and touched her face. She looked so fragile. It took his breath away. He stroked her hair and kissed the bandage he had applied to the cut above her eye.

"You put up quite a fight, my angel, but you're going to have some bumps and bruises for your effort." He ran a finger lightly over her cheekbone. She stirred.

He pulled back.

He didn't want to wake her. She needed sleep.

Holding her naked and vulnerable body through the night, Rex had not slept himself. He'd listened to her breathe, his pulse quickening every time there was a slight change in rhythm.

Holding her like that was like nothing he'd experienced before. It had sown something in him. A tiny seed that had sprouted, grown and blossomed with warmth through him. He felt as if he had a sublime purpose. To keep her safe from harm. To be here for her.

The sensation that surged and swelled through his chest was so absolutely foreign it frightened him, awed him.

She moaned slightly and moved. His heart skipped. The motion of her breast, the weight soft and warm against his arm was arousing. It sent hot blood to his groin. But what he was feeling was not about sex. The stirring in his loins was an automatic physical response to a sexual stimulus. It was the sweet ache in his chest that overwhelmed him, swallowed him. "You're getting soft in the head, Rex," he muttered to himself, throwing aside the covers.

He sat on the edge of the bed, facing the gray dawn, and told himself that what he was feeling was a normal response to the stress of almost losing someone. It was just that he hadn't quite felt anything like it before. He'd never cared enough about losing anyone.

A shower would set him straight. He couldn't afford to lose his edge. That was one of the reasons the Bellona

Channel had recruited him—for his steel edge. He was a loner. Didn't need people, relationships. Sex yes, relationships no. You couldn't reconcile that sort of thing with the work he did.

Rex scrubbed his hands through his hair. Hannah had derailed him once in Marumba. He'd been blindsided. He couldn't let it happen again. Look where it had gotten his friend Scott. Scott had tried to balance a wife and kid with his Bellona work. He got the threat the same time Rex did. Now Scott's family was dead.

Rex had saved Hannah from a similar fate six years ago, but only by leaving her the minute he got the note.

He should walk away now. But now he couldn't. This time her life could depend on his staying. Christ, coming to White River had brought him full circle to finish everything that had been started in Marumba.

He picked up the phone, dialed room service. He ordered, hung up and rubbed the hair on his chest. He was running out of time. The toxicology conference was key in all this. It was the common link. Delegates would start arriving in a few days. He had to get moving.

Someone was holding her hand, calling her name. Nothing.

Blackness.

Voices.

Cold, so very cold.

Voices, she could hear voices again, far away. Head hurt.

Blackness.

Hannah drifted in and out of thick gray sleep.

She could hear voices now. They faded as she slipped back. Then she could hear them again. Dark. Far away.

No, they were near. She could hear two men, hushed tones.

She didn't know where she was. Couldn't see. She was naked, warm. She was in a bed.

Dark. No, not dark. Her eyes were shut, stuck shut. She struggled to open them. Her lids were gummed together. They were heavy, thick as she strained to open them. Then winced as bright white light lanced into her brain.

"Thanks, you can leave it here."

Rex, she could hear Rex. She struggled to open her eyes again. "Rex." She mouthed the word but heard no sound. Her tongue was too big for her mouth. The sides of her throat were stuck together. She felt as if she was groping her way out of a deep black hole.

"Rex, is that you?" She heard the words now, a raspy sound. They were her words.

"Hannah." He was by her side, his hand shielding her eyes, gentle. "Take it easy, take it slow."

She tried to sit up and gasped at the pain in her ribs.

"Hey, take it easy, I haven't ruled out broken bones yet."

She could see him now, a dark blur bent over her. She tried to bring her surroundings into focus. Fighting the pain, she pulled herself into a semisitting position. The bedcover slipped, exposing her naked breasts.

His hand came forward, pulled the cover up.

"Where am I?"

Memories, images, they were filtering slowly back into her brain. The back of her head was a steady pulsing pain.

"You're one lucky lady, Hannah McGuire." He was holding her hand, sitting beside her bed. No, his bed. This was not her bed.

The hotel room swam into focus. It was not the same room. Bigger. Another door. She squinted up at him, careful not to move her ribs. "Where am I? This is not your hotel room."

"Nothing wrong with your head, I see." He lifted her

hand and brushed it lightly against his lips. "I got them to change my room for a double." He smiled, a slash of white across his jaw. "I thought you might like some privacy since you're going to be here awhile."

"My head." She gingerly touched what felt like a baseball of a bump on the back of her skull.

"You took a bad knock. Not sure if he did that to you or if it happened when you went into the water. I can't tell you how lucky you are. I've seen people survive worse whitewater and I've seen lives lost in a lot less. It's the luck of the draw. You drew lucky."

It crashed back into her brain. The man on the bridge. The fear. The water churning below. Falling.

"Rex." She reached out and grabbed his arm. "He tried to kill me."

"Easy, easy." He was stroking her hand. "Do you remember who tried to kill you?"

She pulled her hand free of his and held the bed covers over her chest as she tried to sit upright. "My clothes. I need my clothes. I need to phone Dan— Uh, I need to make an urgent phone call."

"Okay. One thing at a time. We'll get you some clothes and I want you to try and get some food into you." He got up and headed over to the tray left by room service. Steam curled up in a wisp from a deep-blue china pot as he poured tea. "Who do you need to phone?"

Her head was thick. She leaned back into the pillow. "I…I think I want to phone my mother. What day is it?" Danny, she must phone Danny. He might have tried to reach her at home. He would be worried.

Rex placed a cup of tea in her hands. She was so thirsty. She took a sip. Her lips felt dry, cracked. The tea was warm, sweet. So good. She took a gulp. It hurt as it went down.

"It's Monday. You lost a day."

"Work, I'm supposed to be at work."

"I called them already." Rex grinned. "I told them you had a rough weekend and that you'd check in later. Georgette thinks you have a hangover. Here, have some toast."

Hannah was surprised to realize she was ravenous. That must be a good sign. Tea, toast and marmalade—so British. She watched him as she crunched into the toast. His hair was damp. He must have undressed her. She found the thought unsettling. She felt vulnerable. She needed clothes and she needed to make that phone call.

He seemed to be reading her mind. "You can wear something of mine, and when you're up to it, we can go and get some gear from your place."

Hannah frowned. He wanted her to stay with him. The thought was oddly comforting.

"Well, I'd get your stuff myself, but I'm afraid to set foot in your house."

"Right, thanks."

He took the cup from her hands and put it on the table next to the bed, next to her purse.

"You got my purse." She reached for it and winced as a spark of pain shot across her rib. He handed it to her. Hannah rummaged through it.

It was gone. The photograph of Danny. Had Rex seen it? Had her attacker taken it? *Oh, God, Danny.* She looked up and their eyes locked. He was reading the panic in hers.

"You missing something?"

"Uh, no. I…no, nothing."

His brow creased. "You sure?"

"Yes. I'm just feeling…confused. I need to move, to get up."

Rex walked over to the closet and pulled out a T-shirt, a sweatshirt and a pair of dark-blue track pants. "You're gonna swim in these, but," he flashed her a rakish grin, "it's better than nothing."

She pulled the covers up around her chin. "Thanks."

He lay the clothes in a pile on the end of the bed. "I'll be in the next room. Take your time. I think you may've fractured a rib or two but the best we can do for that is rest. Let me know if you discover any other aches or pains."

"I keep forgetting you're a doctor."

He opened the door connecting to the next room.

"You *are* a doctor, aren't you?" *Or had he lied about that, too?*

"I haven't practiced that kind of medicine for a while but, trust me, I've seen way worse than you out in the field."

Hannah frowned. The movement hurt the cut above her eye. "The field?"

His hand was on the doorknob. He filled the door frame. "I got my med training through the British military. Cut my teeth treating troops out in places like Zambia and the Middle East. That's before I specialized and went into research." He closed the door behind him. The room felt suddenly empty.

Hannah sat forward and squinted into the light coming through the diaphanous white drapes, the bed covers falling to her waist, exposing her breasts. She noticed the indentation in the pillow next to her, the rumpled sheets. He'd lain beside her. She touched the depression in the pillow with her hand. His head had rested there. The thought filled her chest with a spurt of tenderness, but it brought pain, too.

She remembered all the nights she had spent lying in bed, thinking of him, missing him, the pillow beside her empty.

She looked down at her breasts. She had no panties on.

He had lain next to her naked body. She moved the covers aside and gingerly set her feet on the floor, testing, before transferring her full weight onto them. She eased herself into his pants. The T-shirt was not so easy. She had definitely damaged a rib.

Hannah reached for the phone. The number would show up on his hotel bill but she figured that was okay. It was her mother's telephone number and there was nothing that would give her son away.

"Mom, hi, it's me, how's Danny?"

"Hannah, are you all right? You sound strange."

"I'm fine." She attempted a casual laugh. "I—uh—I tripped when I was out running and I knocked my head. Got a bit of a shock, that's all. I'm fine, really."

"Have you seen a doctor? You could have a concussion, you know, and not even be aware of it. Remember that football player in your ninth grade class? He—"

"Mom, I'm okay. I saw a doctor. He's…he's taking good care of me." Rex *was* taking good care of her. He made her feel safe.

"How's Danny, can I speak to him?"

"Oh, he's great. Jim and I are loving his company. I'm so glad you let him come. Jim's taking him fishing again today. I hope to put trout on the menu tonight. Ellie and Frank are coming over for dinner. Frank still keeps asking after you, you know. Oh, here's Danny."

"Hey, Mom." Breath hitched in Hannah's chest at the sound of his clear little voice. She tilted her head back and scrunched her eyes so that tears wouldn't spill out. She was a mess of emotion.

"Hello, my boy." The thought of nearly losing her life, not being there to take care of him was overwhelming. She had to let him know he had a father, someone besides her mom who could be there for him if something happened to her.

But would Rex Logan be there for Danny? Hannah wasn't even sure who Rex Logan really was. She thought she'd known. Now all she knew for sure was that he was a mysterious stranger who lurked in a sinister and secret underworld.

"Mommy, are you there? Did Gran tell you I'm going fishing with Uncle Jim? We've got worms an' everything. Gran's packed us a picnic."

Hannah strained for a sense of normalcy. "Ugh, worms. Why doesn't Jim teach you to fly fish, sweetie, it's much cleaner."

"It doesn't matter *how* you catch 'em as long as you catch 'em and we have to catch some fish 'cause Gran wants to cook them for dinner."

"Well, be careful of those hooks, honey. And, Danny—"

"Yes, Mom."

"If you need to speak to me over the next couple of days, try calling me at the office." Hannah brushed a small tear from under her lashes. "I'm probably not going to be at home much, sweetie. I've got lots of work to do before you get back."

"'Kay, Mom."

"I love you, sweetheart."

"Love you more."

"Not possible. Now, go get Gran for me."

Sheila McGuire took the phone. "You still there, hon?"

"Still here. Are you sure you're okay to drive Danny back?"

"I'm looking forward to it. I haven't been up to White River for a while now. Jim's not coming, though. He's promised to help Frank with the new garage. We'll drive up Friday. If we get the early ferry, we should be there just after lunch."

Four days. Hannah tried to run her hand through her hair. It stuck in the knots, and she winced at the sharp pain the movement delivered to her ribs. She had just four days to sort things out.

When Rex opened the door, she was lying back on the white pillows, claimed once again by the healing hands of sleep. A tumble of knotted gold fell about her shoulders. She looked so pale, so fragile in his bulky sweats. There were bruised purple smudges under her eyes, her lips were dry and cracked.

He felt the rage simmer again as he looked upon her. He clenched his fists. He had a violent urge to avenge this act. He wanted to hurt whoever did this to her. He filled his lungs slowly, taking back control. Allowing emotions like that to fester only clouded judgment. Then you made mistakes.

He walked over to her bedside and pulled a comforter over her. And he bent, brushing her cool forehead with his lips.

Pensive, Rex walked over to the French doors, fingering the book of matches in his pocket. He looked out at the slopes, the sleeping snow guns. He knew that in another month or two, when the temperatures dipped to freezing in the valley, those guns would fire up, suck water from the river and blow a fine haze of sharp white crystals into the sky. They would fall onto the slopes, man-made snow helping nature along in the rush to dress the slopes for winter.

He wondered about Hannah. He knew the intimate corners of her body but he knew so little about her, really. Why had she come here to White River? Why had she quit the job she was so passionate about? Did she ski? What did she look like with a veil of fine white crystals, sitting like little diamonds in the gold of her hair? The image swam into his brain—Hannah, like a snow bride. He crushed it. The mere concept was outrageous. Where in hell had *that* come from? He had to get this job done and get the hell out of this place.

The matches. He pulled the book out and read the hotel name again, Fireside Lodge. Rex had found the book of matches on the loamy soil where Hannah had been pulled from the river. He had checked while she slept. CIA agent Ken Mitchell, under the alias Mark Bamfield, was registered as a guest at the Fireside Lodge.

The woman was still alive. It could end up costing them everything. He gingerly fingered the fresh suture along the top of his cheekbone. The local was starting to wear off, his cheek starting to throb. They were both in the way, Logan and McGuire. That *had* to be rectified before the conference.

He gently massaged his leg, wincing at the pain radiating out from his knee. They had until Friday—only four days. That was when the buyers would start to arrive.

Chapter 7

Hannah was sleeping. Rex wasn't. Couldn't. He'd tried, lying there in the next room with the connecting door open, listening to the soft rhythm of her breathing.

It hadn't worked.

He'd come, instead, to look for Mitchell at the Fireside Lodge after bribing the front desk clerk at the White River Presidential to call him on his cell should anyone come looking for him or a Hannah McGuire.

Rex shifted slightly in the brown leather chair. It was almost midnight and still no sign of Mitchell.

He had intended to surprise the CIA agent in his hotel room while he slept. Picking the lock was a cinch, but the room was empty. Nothing in it to give him away, either. All Rex found was a scrap of paper with Hannah's address scribbled in pencil. Under it was the name Grady Fisher and another White River address. Who was Grady Fisher and how was he connected? That would be the next step. Find Fisher.

The flames in the monstrous circular stone fireplace crackled in spite of the fact it was late August. The nights in these mountains were cool and the flames friendly, especially at this hour. The fireplace dominated the lobby. Rex had chosen his seat for its clear view of the front entrance.

He lifted his newspaper to cover his face when he saw Mitchell come in through the door. The CIA agent crossed the slate-tiled floor, making his way slowly toward the elevator. Rex saw he was limping, favoring his right leg. His face was battered, a puce colored gash under his right eye.

Rex stood up, casually folded his paper as Mitchell punched the button calling for the elevator. He crossed the lobby, still hidden from Mitchell's line of vision. He waited for the CIA agent to get into the elevator and pick his floor. As the doors started to close, Rex slipped in between them.

It was just him and Mitchell now, in the confined space. The elevator started its climb.

Mitchell said nothing. He simply turned to watch the lights flick above the door. But Rex had caught the slight flare of recognition in the man's eyes.

"Haven't seen you since Marumba, Agent Mitchell, or is it Mr. Mark Bamfield?"

Mitchell tensed but remained silent, watching the floor numbers light up as the elevator slowly climbed. The muscle in his neck twitched. Rex leaned casually back and hit the emergency stop.

The car jerked to an abrupt halt.

He stepped forward. Mitchell took a small step back.

"So what happened to your face, Mitchell, and what's with the limp? You take a bullet yesterday?"

"Would've gone to the cops if I had, Logan. Canadians don't take kindly to citizens brandishing firearms."

"You're real funny, you know, Agent Mitchell. What're you doing in White River?"

"Same as you *Agent* Logan. Here for a conference."

Rex lifted his hand to touch the surgical tape covering the neatly stitched slash on Mitchell's face. He pressed slightly. Mitchell winced.

"What happened here, huh? Got a bit of a gash?"

"Fell off my rental bike. Now get out of my face, Logan, before I have security haul your ass out of here."

"Neither of us wants to draw attention to ourselves, now, do we?" Rex turned and released the emergency button. The elevator jerked, sputtered and started to hum. The doors opened on the seventh floor.

Rex held them open as the CIA operative hobbled out. "Oh, just a word of warning, Mitchell, I'm watching you. You stay clear of Hannah McGuire." Rex watched the flicker of interest cross Mitchell's eyes before they shut down. The subtle stiffening in his posture did not go unnoticed, either.

"Yes, she's still alive. I find you within a two-mile radius of her and you get hurt, buddy. Real bad."

"Don't threaten me, Logan." But Mitchell's voice was weary. Rex watched him turn and limp down the passage. The man looked tired, spent.

Hannah felt a little more like herself after having showered and combed the wild tangle of knots from her hair. It was Tuesday morning. She'd lost yet another day, having slept off most of Monday. But she had to admit, it had done her a world of good. Despite the pain in her ribs and a general stiffness, her energy was coming back. Rex had found her a change of clothes, another pair of track pants and a sweatshirt, a white one. It was fleecy inside and soft on her skin, but huge. She really needed to get some of her own clothes, yet she was absurdly comforted by the voluminous warmth of his garments against her skin.

Rex had ordered breakfast and was serving it alfresco. Hannah pulled a chair up to the small round table on the balcony. Rex lifted the silver dome off a golden cheese omelette. There were small rounds of herbed tomato on the side. The steam curled up and was swallowed by the crisp morning air. Hanna pushed her hair back from her face and inhaled the warm, savory scent. "Looks good, Rex. I must admit, I'm starving."

He slipped half the omelette onto her plate and poured two cups of Earl Gray before taking his seat at the little round table opposite her. The French doors behind them were open, and the curtains sighed gently with the wafts of cooler air coming in off the slopes of Powder Mountain.

Hannah drank it in. It had a different smell. She imagined she could smell the ice and snow of the glacier. She was sensing everything so keenly this morning. It was as if her world had been altered, a veil lifted to reveal crisper edges. She cut into her omelette and lifted a forkful to her mouth.

Rex was studying her, his gaze intense. "Hannah, I can get you into a safe house until we have this thing sorted out." He sipped his tea, eyes unwavering over the cup.

She halted, fork midway to her mouth. She set it slowly down. "It's that serious?"

He nodded.

She suddenly didn't feel so hungry anymore. She pushed the food around her plate. "What do mean a 'safe house'?"

"A place out of province where you can lie low until this is over."

"Where?"

"I can't say. But we could get you in there by tonight."

This was bigger than she ever imagined. And she was slap-bang in the middle of it. But there was no way she could go to a safe house. Not without Danny. And she certainly didn't want to tell Rex about her boy now. She wanted to keep him right out of this. He was safe with her mom on the island. She just had to make sure he didn't return before things were back to normal.

Yet, deep down, she had a nagging feeling things would never quite get back to normal.

"Shall I make the arrangements?"

Hannah swallowed against the tightness in her throat. She reached for the sugar bowl and spooned sweetness into her tea. She stirred. Then looked up into his eyes. "How is it, Rex, that a pharmaceutical company can organize a safe house?"

"Hannah, these guys mean business. Someone tried to kill you."

"You're not answering my question."

"Hannah—"

"It's not Bio Can Pharmaceutical, is it? You work for some other agency, don't you? The Bio Can thing, it's just a cover."

He sighed, set his teacup deliberately on the table. "Yes. You're right, but I can't tell you more. I'm sorry."

He looked so damn proper. A British rogue. Hannah blew her breath out in frustration. "Forget the safe house."

"It's for the best—"

"Forget it."

"Whoever killed Amy probably tried to kill you, Hannah."

"Why're you so sure she was killed?"

"I'm not. It just adds up."

"Well, I'm in the middle of this now and I'm going to

see it through.'' She reached for her cup and took a sip of the sweet warm tea.

He leaned forward, dropping his voice. ''Okay. You don't want a safe house, you got it, no safe house. But you stay here, with me. Got that?''

Hannah drew the cool air deep into her lungs, drawing down resolve. ''No. I told you, I'm not leaving my home.'' It was her sanctuary. Where she felt grounded.

''Hannah, you really only have two choices. If you don't stay here, at the hotel with me, I'm going to start making arrangements to get you out of province and into that safe house. And believe me, once I get the ball rolling, you're not going to have any say in the matter.''

He meant it. She could see it in the frightening intensity of his eyes. She hesitated. It was the lesser of two evils, staying with him. At least she could maintain some kind of control over her life. At least she could leave Danny out of things. But the thought of being so close to Rex terrified her.

She cleared her throat. ''If I stay here, will you at least tell me who you think tried to kill me?''

''I don't know who it was.''

''Right.''

''It's the truth, Hannah.'' He leaned forward. ''So what is it, safe house or me?''

She didn't like the way he put it. But she really had little choice. This way she could buy time, keep Danny out of the picture, and maybe find out what happened to Amy.

''All right, Rex. I'll stay here. But only for a while.''

''Good,'' he said. ''Now, tell me what you remember about the attack.''

She nodded, took a slow, steadying sip of tea, and called to mind the traumatic series of events. She told him about the bridge, the way the man had come over it, jerked and swayed it, about the mirrored glasses she had shattered, about the gash under his eye, the thick oozing black blood, the bandanna, the baggy pants and gray hooded sweatshirt.

"Then he just let go of my ankle and let me drop into the river." Just talking about it had her chest tightening up again. She hugged her arms into her waist. "I don't remember anything after that."

"So you wouldn't recognize him if you saw him again?"

"No, not for certain. Anything that might have distinguished him was hidden."

Rex mulled over the facts. The man he'd seen bending over Hannah, the one he'd fired at, could have fitted that description. He must have tossed the hooded shirt, though. He wasn't wearing that, or glasses from what Rex had been able to see in the dim light. As far as he could tell, it had been Mitchell hunched over Hannah on the riverbank. It had been Mitchell he'd shot at. Mitchell with the gash under his eye, the limp. The bastard had probably gone downriver to finish her off.

But Rex had to bide his time, be sure. At the same time, he needed to keep Hannah from further harm.

She looked so fragile, so small and pale in his huge clothes. Yet she was so strong. He'd do anything in this world to keep her from getting hurt. But, Christ, he was hurting inside. He couldn't bear being so near, not being able to take her in his arms, not being able to share the truth of his life with her. This was torture. But he had to bear it. Move forward. "Hannah, do you know a Grady Fisher?"

Surprise lit her eyes. In this light they were luminous pale gold. And he could see those pricks of forest green.

"Grady Fisher, he's the one who signed out those

books you found in Amy's apartment. I haven't had a chance to tell you.''

"Do you know him?

"No, and the librarian wouldn't give me his address. Why?''

"Found his name in Mitchell's room. I think Fisher's address is number 10, 256 Hillside Road.''

"You were in Mitchell's room?''

Rex shrugged. "Technically.''

Hannah looked away. He could see she was struggling. He reached forward to touch the smooth skin on her hand.

She pulled away, turned to him, her eyes bright. "I don't know you at all, do I, Rex Logan?''

A band tightened instantly across his chest. He felt his cold mask slip into place. He didn't want to go there. Couldn't.

"It was all a lie, wasn't it? In Africa?'' The moisture pooling in her wild honey eyes tore at him.

"Hannah—'' He reached out to her.

"Don't.'' She stood. "I have my pride, Dr. Logan. As much as I need to know, I'm not going to prostrate myself, beg for answers. If I was worth it, you'd tell me.''

She'd thrown down the gauntlet. Lanced him to the core. She turned, walked back into the room. But not before he'd seen the emotion in her eyes overflow and tears slide silently down her cheeks.

He got up to follow her. But she was in the bathroom. Door closed. He could hear her soft sobs.

His gut twisted with self-loathing. He lifted his hand to knock, dropped it, stalked across the room. "Christ!'' He stormed out onto the balcony, gripped the railing, turned his face up to the sky. "Lord, help me here.''

By the time she came out, her face was wan, her eyes rimmed with red. But there was a steel resolve in the line of her mouth, her posture. She walked straight up to him.

"Let's go, Rex. We've got work to do. I need to get this over with."

"Go where?"

"The Mad Moose. If anyone knows who Grady Fisher is, it'll be Amy's friend Cindy. She runs a café in the village."

He nodded. Yes, they needed to get this the hell over with. "Fine. We'll go there as soon as we've picked up some clothes from your place. And as soon as you've phoned Al Brashear and told him you need a few days off work."

Rex pulled up in front of Hannah's condo and started to climb out of the SUV.

She turned to face him. "Please, wait out here in the car. I'll be quick."

"What's the deal with your house, anyway?"

Her home, her belongings, Danny's things, they were like her last frontier. "Please, just give me this space."

"Not this time, Hannah."

"You have to. Or you can forget my cooperation. I'll go to the cops."

"Christ, woman." He dragged his hands through his hair in exasperation.

She didn't budge from the car.

"All right. Take the phone and leave the door open. And make it snappy this time. I'll give you fifteen minutes to grab some gear, otherwise I'm coming in after you."

Hannah left Rex in the car and unlocked the door to her condo. It wasn't the same. That familiar warmth she used to feel coming home was not there. The hallway seemed empty, cold. In spite of her earlier spurt of re-newed energy and hard-won bravado, Hannah felt sud-denly lonely and sapped in her own home, her sanctuary. Her world really had changed since Friday.

She climbed the stairs, feeling tired and sore. She walked into her room and looked at the double bed with its pale-green duvet and matching pillows. She hadn't shared that bed with anyone. She had not had a love interest since Rex, not since Danny was conceived.

She pulled open her closet doors and sifted through her belongings, tossing clothes into her bag.

She told herself the emptiness, the loneliness she felt deep in her bones was because Danny was away. When he came back, when Rex finally left town, she could get her life back on an even keel. She'd almost drowned in that river. Maybe she should expect to feel different. But she didn't like it, this new sense of vulnerability.

She shrugged out of Rex's comfy sweats and pulled on an old pair of faded denims and a pale-pink T-shirt. She preferred to wear light, pastel colors when she felt down. Bright colors took too much energy. Black depressed her further. She gathered up a few cosmetics, zipped her bag shut and made for the downstairs hallway.

Hand on the doorknob, Hannah stopped, turned and looked around her condo, at her belongings, at the sunken living room that led off to the left, with its picture-window vista of Alabaster Lake and the mountainous range beyond. And she made a vow. She promised herself that the next time she came back, she would have things under control.

She pulled the door shut behind her.

The Mad Moose was hopping. Reggae music mingled with the scent of coffee and spice and spilled from the doors out onto the small stone patio. Voices fought to be heard over the Jamaican beat.

From the entrance Hannah could see Cindy, blond dreadlocks hanging from a thick ponytail high on her head, busy at the espresso machine. She turned to Rex.

"Why don't you grab the table out there on the patio and I'll see if I can get Cindy to spare us a minute."

Cindy looked up as Hannah approached the Mad Moose counter. Hannah loved her sparkle. She could see why Amy and Cindy had been such close friends. They came from very different backgrounds, but they had a common zest for life in the mountains. When not working at the Mad Moose, Cindy was practicing to be a pro snowboarder.

"Hey, Hannah. How're things?"

"Good. Cindy, I need a minute of your time. I need to talk about Amy, can you take a break in the next few minutes?" She had to raise her voice above the music.

The bright smile, the dimples faded. "Sure, right away. Matt, dude," she called to the dark-haired guy clearing tables. "Can you take over here for me, thanks."

Cindy wiped her hands on her dark-green apron before untying the strings and stepping out from behind the counter. "Can I get you a cuppa Joe or anything?"

"No, thanks." Hannah led her to the table outside. "This here is Rex. He's, ah, an old acquaintance of mine."

Rex smiled, a devilish slash of white against his strong, square jaw. Again she saw the impact he had on women.

"Hey." Cindy held out her hand to Rex.

He stood up, took Cindy's hand and pulled out a chair for her.

She sat. "Thanks. Hey, Hannah, trust you to have a real gentleman friend. I haven't had a White River dude stand up for me since I been here." She ran her eyes over Rex. "And, it's been almost five years now." She smiled, eyes bright, dimples creasing her cheeks. "Maybe it's the hair, huh?" She tossed her dreadlocks. "Whaddya think?"

Rex said nothing. He was leaving this to Hannah.

"Cindy, you know the coroner has ruled Amy's death accidental?"

She nodded.

"But Al and I are still trying to find out why she went up the mountain so unprepared, without telling any-one—"

"Man, don't I know it. Amy used to *love* hiking alone. Knew it wasn't the smartest thing, but she always left me this, like, list of where she would be going and what time she figured she'd be back."

Cindy turned to Rex. "Amy and me, we used to share a place when she first came to White River. I always figured she was kind of obsessive when it came to stuff like that. Girl Scout stuff. You know, she would pack in the bear spray and bug spray and sun spray and the maps and the flashlight and warm gear and everything." She looked down, picking at a loose thread on her shirt. "She used to say to me, 'Cinds, just in case.'"

Hannah placed her hand on Cindy's arm. "I know. That's why we're still trying to figure it out. Cindy, did Amy have a friend called Grady Fisher?"

She looked up. "I don't think so. She never mentioned nothing about him to me."

"You sure? I thought maybe he was a new boyfriend of hers or something."

"Sven Jansen, the mountain dude, he was the last guy she went out with, so far as I know. Amy dumped him not long before she went missing. She never talked about a Grady. But Sven, he was still, like, having trouble tak-ing no for an answer." Cindy leaned forward, dropping her voice in a conspiratorial tone. "You know, Hannah, Sven was always, like, so possessive over Amy he was scary. I always figured he could hurt her. He's such a big powerful dude. When she went missing, I have to admit I thought about him."

Cindy sat up as another group of people entered the Mad Moose. She waved a greeting before turning back to face Rex and Hannah. "People say Sven has been real weird since Amy disappeared. And he just took off into the mountains after her body was found. You know, he was there when they found her. But hey, Hannah, I must go, work calls. Let me know if I can be of any more help. I knock off at six." She nodded at Rex.

"Thanks, Cindy. We'll be in touch."

Cindy pushed her chair back and bent over to whisper in Hannah's ear. "He's got the coolest eyes. They're, like, not human."

Hannah laughed and waved Cindy off.

"What's the secret?" Rex asked.

"Nothing. Just girl talk. What's next?"

"We go find this mountain guide, Sven. Perhaps there's nothing more to this than a love triangle." Rex stood up, offering Hannah his arm. "Can this dude escort you?"

Hannah stood up, hesitated, then took Rex's arm. "The accent doesn't become you, Dr. Logan. I prefer the James Bond sound. Besides, you have to say 'deeuwd,' like you're holding your nose."

"Deeuwd."

Hannah laughed. The movement sent pain sparking through her chest. Reality shot back with the pain. She was getting swept into the moment with Rex, like before.

She dropped his arm. "The best place to start looking for Sven is at the ski patrol cabin up at Base One on Powder. The search-and-rescue guys work out of there in the summer as well as winter. There's a dirt road that leads up to it. We'll have to take your four-by-four."

She strode out a step ahead of Rex, making her way across the village square for the parking lot. If she held her upper body stiff, she could minimize the pain in her ribs. The painkillers Rex had given her were wearing off.

''Whoa, there. Wait up, Hannah, what're you running from?''

You, that's what—away from Rex Logan and his secrets. She slowed her pace as he caught up to her.

He grabbed on to her elbow, turning her around with a chuckle. ''Look.'' He gestured with his eyes. ''Looks like you have company, Hannah.'' She followed his gaze and saw the garish red nose first. It was set against a paste of chalky white. A clown. He had ridiculous striped pants swimming around his legs and he had a polka-dot shirt with enormous lapels. He was mimicking her painfully stiff walk.

An irrational anger started to boil inside Hannah as she watched the stupid clown make fun of her in the village square. A small crowd was starting to gather, laughing at his antics. At her.

Then a Japanese couple walked by, and the clown abruptly shifted his attention to them, imitating their tiny quick steps, stopping every time they looked behind them. The crowd was lapping it up.

At the far end of the square a juggler was spinning skittles and flame. The sights, the sounds of the village square suddenly crowded into Hannah's head, competing for space. Her ears started to buzz. She was losing it. Her life was one big joke, a farce.

She turned and stalked out across the cobbles. She was being oversensitive. She knew it. But she didn't seem to have any control. Hot tears pricked her eyes. She reached the trees and a little strip of lawn on the opposite end of the square.

''Hannah.'' Rex came up behind her, grabbed on to her, forcing her to face him. She looked away, trying to hide her raw emotion.

"Oh, Hannah." He took her face gently in both hands. His voice was soothing, his large hands protective. "Look at me." She opened her eyes into his, clear as the sky behind him.

"You're still in a state of shock. Don't push yourself, don't overdo it. You can't rush the healing process. Give it time."

She wanted to melt into those strong, beautiful, doctor's hands. She wanted to bury her hot tears in his male chest. She wanted to seek cover there, refuge from the madness, breathe in the warm scent of him.

Their eyes locked. The crazy laughter faded around her. She could hear nothing, see nothing but those blue eyes. She was losing herself in them, falling into them.

Rex bent slowly and let his lips touch hers. It was tender, nonthreatening. It was a question.

Her answer was hungry.

She pressed into him, her mouth crushing against his. She could taste him, the warm saltiness.

She invited him in, teasing with the tip of her tongue, and he came. His tongue rough in her mouth, urgent, demanding. Hannah felt herself melt somewhere inside. She felt his hand on her behind, pulling her up toward him. He was hard. She could feel his male need pressed against her pelvis. Her breasts were up against the solidity of his chest. And deep, deep down, she was swollen with warmth and aching for him.

He deepened his kiss, pulling her into him, and pain sparked across her rib, a sharp lightning cracking through her haze. She gasped out in pain.

He pulled back instantly. "Oh, God, Hannah, I am so sorry."

"It's okay." She was disoriented. She held her hand up against her rib, under her breast. She felt suddenly self-conscious. Stupid.

"Rex, I—"

He covered the hand on her ribs with his own. "I'm sorry, Hannah. I never wanted to hurt you. Never." His voice was gentle but it was out of step with a depraved hunger, a wildness still swimming in his eyes. She was both drawn by it and afraid of it. And she was terrified of how her own body was betraying her.

The noise of the crowd was seeping back into her brain. The laughter. The crowd was laughing at the clown who was now passionately smooching an imaginary lover in the middle of the cobblestone square.

Rex grunted. "Well, we sure gave them a show." He placed his hand in the small of her back and gently escorted her from under the shelter of the trees toward the parking lot. "What's with the circus acts, anyway?"

Hannah was still stunned. She'd been sideswiped. Her lips were still swollen from his kiss, the taste of him lingered there. "The circus stuff." She marshaled her thoughts. "There's a festival that comes into town each year, with a circus, for the last weekend of summer before school starts. It gets crazier and busier until after the weekend, when things should get back to normal."

Normal. She wanted normal.

He opened the car door for her. She climbed in. "I hate clowns."

Rex looked at her, brow raised in question.

"They disturb me. They're macabre. Like they've got some hidden grim message."

"Yes, sometimes they cut a little too close to the bone. The mirror they hold up to reality can be a little too stark."

He shut the door and walked around to the driver's side.

Chapter 8

"Sven Jansen? You're in luck. He just got back from a walkabout in the hills. You'll find him in the locker room downstairs, unpacking." The Australian patroller pointed to the stairs. "It's that way."

Hannah and Rex found the mountain guide ministering to an injured dog. Sven Jansen did not look up as they approached, his attention focused solely on the border collie, its paw dwarfed in his large roughened hands. He was applying a strong-smelling antiseptic lotion, small and gentle movements out of sync with his massive Nordic physique. He filled the room with his sullen presence.

A green locker door hung open behind him, contents tumbling onto the tiled floor. There were ropes, carabiners, boots, a sleeping bag and a map covered with plastic.

Hannah sat on the bench beside Sven. Rex leaned against the doorjamb, watching, reading the signs.

"Hey, Sven. The beard's new since I saw you last."

It was bushy, very blond against a face browned dark from the sun. He looked up at her. There was pain in his pale-gray Viking eyes.

He turned his attention back to the dog, reached for a bandage and started wrapping the paw. "Ja. Been in the backcountry for a bit." The sing-song of his Nordic accent was stronger than Hannah remembered. Sven had been spending a lot of time on his own. Too much.

Hannah reached forward to pet the dog. He was one of the best avalanche rescue dogs in the province and one of the only ones to have ever located someone buried alive under snow in Canada. In almost all other cases, given the vastness of the country's terrain, search crews had not made it out in time to save anyone. "What happened to Snooper?"

"Hurt his foot. Had to come in for supplies."

Sven was not one for small talk. Hannah knew that. She figured it would be best to cut straight to the chase. "I was hoping to talk to you about Amy, Sven. This is Rex. We're looking for someone called Grady Fisher, do you know him?"

He stiffened.

"Sven?"

He turned to face her squarely, a storm sparking fierce in his gray eyes. His sudden anger was tangible. It hung solid in the locker room air. He was a young man but an awesome and powerful presence. Hannah found herself drawing back on the bench. Rex remained motionless against the doorjamb but she could sense he was poised to spring.

"That scrawny wuss! I will ring his neck!" Sven hurled the bandage roll at the row of locker doors. Snooper dropped off the bench, crouched low on the floor, eyes never leaving his master.

"We were hoping to talk to Grady." She found the fire she'd unleashed in the young man unnerving.

"I have not sniffed the weasel since Amy disappeared. I have looked at his apartment. He was gone. She left *me* for that *coyote*." He squeezed the tube of antiseptic in his fist as he spat out the words. Ointment oozed onto the bench.

"Amy was going out with Grady?"

"I don't know what she saw in that weak massage therapist for that beauty spa." Sven rose to his full height, well over six feet. He slammed gear back into his locker, muttering in his native tongue.

Then he turned and pointed at Rex, then Hannah. "I don't know what you two are after, but I am not answering your questions. The police, they asked me this question and that question. People, they think because I loved Amy that I hurt her." He smashed his locker door shut. "I loved her, damn it. You can all go to hell!"

The sun had climbed high. The fresh air was welcome after the close atmosphere in the locker room. Rex shielded his eyes and looked up the mountain toward the peak. "That's one lovesick puppy in there. Poor bastard. So, Grady works at the spa."

Hannah followed his gaze, up to where the glacier was cradled in its rocky bed. "You know, Rex, he may be a hothead but I don't think Sven would've hurt Amy."

"I think you're right. Still, you never can tell what people are capable of. Love can drive a man to distraction. Blind him. Like a drug, it twists the senses, fells normal defences."

Shocked by his candor, Hannah looked at him. "You're an expert on love?"

"On the contrary. I have no place for it."

She felt a nauseous twinge in her stomach at the glaring

reality of his words. A part of her, buried deep, so wanted to hear something different.

He turned to her. "Come."

"Where?"

"White River Spa. Let's check out this Grady Fisher."

He'd seen the hurt in her eyes. And yes. He *was* something of an expert on the topic. He knew intimately the black madness that lurked in a man's heart when he could not have his woman.

He'd been its bedfellow for the last six years. But now…now was different. Now the edges were red and raw. Now he could see firsthand the costs. He'd torn at the scars of her pain and laid his own scars open to burn in the air. And into the wounds they'd thrown the salt of a dark smoky passion that still lived and steamed between them. They were killing each other. He had to move fast. The clock was ticking in more ways than one.

"Here, turn here. Then head north on the highway. You'll see the sign."

Rex drove in silence. The turnoff to the spa was only ten minutes away. It seemed an eternity.

"There."

The sign was small, discreet. Very tasteful. Rex took the road that led up into the Moonstone foothills. It cut a sweep through dense, mature forest.

"Quite the place."

"Yeah. Very private. Huge acreage. It's been owned for ages by an East German company, I think."

"It's well established?"

"They started building the actual spa about ten years ago, but it really took off on an international level when Dr. Gunter Schmidt arrived."

"He's the other guy you were lunching with at the Black Diamond?"

"Yes. He's a good friend of Al's. World-famous plastic surgeon. He's the charisma behind the enterprise. You'll meet him."

They rounded a switch-back, and massive wrought-iron entrance gates were suddenly upon them. The gates were flanked by stone pillars and a guard hut. Rex brought the vehicle to a halt. He noticed the security cameras immediately.

"What's this?"

Hannah followed his gaze. "It's to keep the paparazzi types at bay, like me." She opened her car door. "There are some really high-profile clients here, or guests, that's what Gunter calls them. They value their privacy. I'll speak to the guard. I'm sure Gunter will see me."

Rex watched her walk up to the guard hut. She was stiff, walking to minimize the movement around her ribs, but her sway stirred irrational feelings in him still, like that first time he had seen her stride across the bar in Marumba. God, how he would love to take her in his arms, spread that gold hair across his pillow and make her his. The need was so strong. Overpowering. He shifted in his car seat. She had a capacity to do that to him. If he hung around her any longer, he wouldn't be able to stop himself. And it would destroy both of them in the process. She needed more from a relationship. He could see that. Hell, he needed more. But it was not his to give. Not his to take.

"Be strong." He muttered under his breath. "Do your job and then, cheerio, get the hell out of the mountains before you lose your mind."

She opened the car door, climbed back in. "He says go ahead, all clear, Gunter will see us." As she spoke, the iron gates swung sullenly open.

The driveway was paved, a gracious sweep up to the white clinic buildings. Rex could see a carpet of lush green lawn rolling down to a pool where guests were being served by waiters in white with silver trays. He pulled up under the portico and a man, in the same attire as the front-gate guard, stepped forward from the glass doors to open Hannah's door.

They were greeted by the sound of gently splashing water. It burbled from a small fountain in the water feature at the front entrance. They walked into what Rex could only describe as a lobby. Classical music, a piano, tinkling in the background. "They've created a whole different world in here."

Hannah nodded as they approached the reception desk. "Sure have. The White River Spa doesn't have an international reputation for nothing."

The receptionist looked up as they approached, aloof. Rex figured she'd spent some time under Dr. Schmidt's knife herself.

"May I help you?"

"Dr. Schmidt's expecting us." Hannah leaned sideways to whisper to Rex. "It's not like we would've been let in if he wasn't." Her breath was warm and fragrant against the side of his cheek as she spoke. Her tone conspiratorial, smoky, seductive. It snaked through his senses.

The receptionist paged for Dr. Gunter Schmidt and busied herself at her computer.

Rex scanned the entrance area, picking out minute cameras and small flashing red alarm lights. They sure were big on security here.

The door to an office behind the reception desk swung open as a nurse in a white lab coat walked out, a pile of files in her arm. She smiled at the visitors, leaving the door slightly ajar behind her, exposing a figure.

"Oh, look, there's Dr. Gregor Vasilev. He's basically Gunter's right hand when it comes to surgery."

Rex followed Hannah's gaze. The man in the white lab coat was limping across to a desk. "What's with his leg?" Rex whispered the question into her hair. He could smell gardenias, jasmine, the warm evocative scents of Marumba.

"He must've hurt himself. Gregor, hi." Hannah called out to the man and the receptionist frowned at the perceived impertinence.

Gregor looked up, saw Hannah, and froze. His eye was set in a pool of blue-black bruising. Rex could make out surgical tape high on his cheekbone, under the swollen eye.

Gregor waved quickly, indicating he was busy and motioned to his assistant to shut the door.

"Well, he's sure friendly."

"Strange. He usually is." Hannah knitted her brow. "Wonder what happened to his face?"

"Two shiners in two days."

"What?"

"Nothing."

"Hannah, hello my friend." They turned at the sound of the sandpapery voice. Dr. Gunter Schmidt's arms were held wide in welcome as he strode down the corridor. Then he saw Rex.

It was as if a small jolt of electric current shocked through his body.

It broke his stride.

The sudden stiffening of the plastic surgeon's posture was fleeting, a small blip on Rex's mental radar, but it did not go unnoticed. Gunter resumed his stride forward, attention focused solely on Hannah, arms outreached.

"Good to see you, Hannah, my dear. To what do I owe this honor?" Rex noticed he said 'vot'. Dr. Schmidt had trouble with his *w*s.

"Hello, Gunter. This is my friend, Rex."

Rex reached forward to shake Gunter's hand. The grip of the older man was firm, even powerful. He was definitely the man he'd seen lunching with Hannah at the Black Diamond. Even up close, Rex was certain he knew him from somewhere.

"Actually, Gunter, we were hoping to chat with one of your employees." Hannah held her hands up as the plastic surgeon started to protest. "Yes, yes. I know your protocol, no employee talks to anyone even vaguely associated with any media, but I'm not here to do a story." She smiled and tilted her head. "You know me better than that."

Rex watched as she captivated Gunter with the warmth of her smile. She took the surgeon's arm and started to steer him toward the cluster of chairs near a floor-to-ceiling window that overlooked the fountain feature outside.

Hannah certainly knew how to work people. Rex had to suppress a little grin as he watched her sweet-talk the surgeon. Yes, she was smooth. That's what had gotten her to the top of her profession. Beautiful, smooth and brilliant. That's how he remembered her. Yet, there was a difference now. Under it all, she seemed afraid, vulnerable, wounded even. There was a mystery to her. It made him curious. He wanted to ask her about her life since Marumba. But that would mean opening up himself. He couldn't afford to do that.

"We wanted to ask Grady Fisher about his relationship with Amy. I understand he works here as a massage therapist."

Gunter frowned, mouth drawn in a tight line. He sat, motioning for Hannah and Rex to do the same.

"Hannah, this is most unfortunate. Grady Fisher no longer works here." He paused, as if judging her reaction.

"Where did he go?"

"It is a sad story, ja." He sighed. "Grady had a problem, one he hid very well from us all here at the spa. Drink and drugs. It cost him his life."

"What happened?"

Gunter leaned forward, placing his steady surgeon's hand on Hannah's knee. Rex felt himself flex possessively in response.

"Grady killed himself in a motor accident on the highway last year. Most unfortunate, ja."

"Oh." Hannah made more a noise of surprise than a word. The more he watched Gunter, the more certain Rex was that he'd met the man before, perhaps at a conference. But his were not looks that tended to fade into obscurity. Quite distinctive. And Rex had a close to photographic memory for faces.

"There were no other motor cars involved, Hannah. Grady was drunk behind the wheel. He left the road. He went over in the canyon area."

Hannah's brow crinkled. "Yes. I remember now. There was an accident in the canyon late last summer, or was it the fall?"

She turned to Rex. The afternoon light gave her gold eyes the look of a lioness, her skin a luminous quality. "There are so many accidents on that road you forget the names associated with each one."

Rex sat forward. He had a question of his own for the smooth doctor. "Dr. Schmidt?"

Gunter turned abruptly toward him. Rex saw what he interpreted as a fleeting hostility in the older doctor's hazel eyes before they settled into a steady, unreadable gaze. He took in the strong neck, powerful shoulders, the thatch of salt-and-pepper hair. This man was in fine physical shape but none of his distinguishing features, not even the characteristic rasp of his Germanic voice, could find a match in Rex's memory.

"How long did Grady work here? Is he from the White River area?"

"Ach, no. Grady was from the United States. He worked for a high-end spa in California before coming to join us here about two years ago." Gunter cleared his throat. "He was really only with us for about one year in all."

He turned back to look at Hannah, a frown creasing his brow. "Why did you want to speak to him, Hannah?" He said "vye" and "vant".

"We believe Amy may've had a personal relationship, a romantic involvement with Grady. We're still trying to piece together her last movements before she went missing."

"Grady and Amy? A romantic relationship? Nein, I think that is unlikely. He did not seem her type." Gunter took Hannah's hands in his own. "Besides, you should really put this thing to rest. Let it sleep, ja. It is not good for Al that you keep digging this up, Hannah. It makes it difficult for him to say goodbye to his niece."

"Well, we—" Hannah started to explain but Rex coughed and stood up. He stepped forward, holding out his hand to Gunter. "Yes. Well, we had better be going. Thank you for your time, Dr. Schmidt. Interesting place you have here. I feel like we have met somewhere before."

"Thank you." Gunter stood and reached forward to shake Rex's hand. "And, no. I would remember meeting a man such as you. Hannah did not mention your last name."

"Logan."

"I see. Well, nice to have met you. I must get back to my guests now."

"Actually, before we go, Hannah was hoping to say

hello to Dr. Gregor Vasilev…'' Rex turned to meet Hannah's eyes. "Right, Hannah?"

She was quick to pick up on his cue. "Ah, right. Yes. Is he available?"

Gunter was now doing little to hide his increasing agitation. "Hannah, you really must call ahead. Friends are always welcome but at some times we are busier than others. We are extremely busy at the moment. Gregor is prepping for a patient as we speak."

"Oh, I'm sorry. He…he hasn't hurt himself has he, Gunter? I thought I saw he had a black eye."

Gunter laughed. The sound was flat and dry as a desert. He took Hannah by the elbow and started to steer her toward the exit. Rex took the unsubtle hint and fell in step.

"This is precisely why we have this spa secluded and security tight. You see, Hannah, I performed a minor facial surgery on Gregor. He had some skin damage from the sun. What happens with this kind of cosmetic surgery is it can make bad bruises and people like you come asking embarrassing questions." He held the door open for them. "I do not want my guests, or my colleagues, to be faced with uncomfortable questions. They come here to be treated and heal in peace. No questions. And then they go home whole and beautiful."

Hannah smiled. Rex saw it was strained. "Well, Gunter, I'm suitably chastised. Thank you again for your time."

Rex held the passenger door open for Hannah. "I think we touched a nerve somewhere there, partner."

"I just don't get it, Rex. I've never seen Gunter like this. I guess we should've called ahead. And this stuff about Gregor's face, I don't buy it."

Rex fired up the engine of the SUV, waved to the guard

as they drove through the big gates. They swung slowly shut behind them.

"I don't buy it either, but I'm not sure what to make of it yet." He turned to steal a look at her in the seat beside him. She looked tired, wan. She'd been through a lot. He really should get her back to the hotel to rest. Only trouble was he didn't want to leave her anywhere on her own at the moment. "Tell me what you remember about this accident involving Grady Fisher."

"Well, I don't think I was working at the *Gazette* yet, at least not full-time. I remember reading about it." She pushed her hair back from her face. "You know, Rex, I'm not exactly sure when it happened, but we could look at the archives at the newspaper office." She checked her watch. "We could probably head over there now and catch Al before he clocks out for the day."

"I think you've had enough for one day, Hannah, you need to give those aches and pains of yours a rest. A soak in the hot tub would do you good."

"No. Let's do this now. I won't sleep until I find out. Now that I think about it, there was something odd about one of the accidents on the highway last year. I want to take a look at the files."

"Anyone ever tell you you're stubborn?"

"Tenacious." She offered him a grin.

"Okay, tenacious. We'll head over to the *Gazette* now, on one condition."

She looked at him, eyebrows raised. "And what might that be, Dr. Logan?"

"You let me buy you dinner. There's this little place I'd like to try—"

"Rex, don't do me any favors. I just want to get this thing over with."

He turned onto the highway and headed back toward town. "It might do you good to put business aside tonight. Enjoy a nice meal and get some good sleep. We've got a lot of ground to cover tomorrow.''

Rex took the turnoff into White River village. He needed to get hold of Margaret back at the Toronto office and ask her to dig up some information on Dr. Gunter Schmidt and the White River Spa. He'd throw Gregor Vasilev into the mix, too, and see what she could find out about him.

He mulled over the facts as he pulled into a parking space under the windows of the *Gazette* office. Two men with injured faces, Gregor Vasilev and Agent Ken Mitchell. Both with a limp. Had one of them attacked Hannah? If so, why?

Right now his money was on Mitchell. He'd never trusted him as an agent. Rex had found his name in Amy's apartment, in the library book on biological weapons. Mitchell's special interest was biological warfare intelligence. He'd been on the mountain when Amy's body was discovered. Amy must've had dealings on some level with Mitchell. Rex had also seen Grady Fisher's name in Mitchell's hotel room, scribbled on that piece of paper. Grady had also turned up dead.

But the plastic surgeon, Dr. Gunter Schmidt, Rex knew him from somewhere, and the sensation did not sit easy in his gut. The man left a bad taste in his mouth. And his cohort, Dr. Gregor Vasilev, what was he hiding?

He felt Hannah watching him. He turned to meet her gaze. He wanted to hurt the bastard who had attacked her.

''Rex.''

''What is it?'' He placed his hand on her knee, couldn't help himself. She was looking so pale, fragile.

''I need to go into the *Gazette* on my own, by myself.''

''Hannah, you're not safe right now—''

''Look, I know you don't want to let me out of your sight. I appreciate your concern, but you can wait just outside. I'll have Al and the others for protection inside. How's that?''

Those wild-honey eyes were pleading. She really meant what she was saying. She seemed to be having enough trouble explaining his presence to her White River acquaintances as it was. Perhaps she needed a little space, a few minutes alone with Al, her colleagues.

He looked up at the *Gazette* windows from the parking lot. He could see the door from here. He shouldn't be doing this. That's why operatives couldn't afford personal attachment. It clouded judgment. They made mistakes. He hoped he wasn't making one now. ''All right.'' He gave her knee a squeeze. ''You can report back to me over dinner.''

Hannah opened the car door, looking relieved to have won some space.

''Oh, Hannah.''

She ducked her head back into the car. ''What?''

''No more than one hour. Any longer than that and I come looking for you.''

''Margaret, my sweet, you're still at the office.''

''Don't try honey talkin' me, Dr. Logan. Having a good time in White River? Come to think of it, I don't think you're the type to have a good time anywhere. What can I do for you?''

''Before we go any further, can you connect the device?''

Rex engaged the scrambling device on his own phone. He needed to be sure Margaret's end of the conversation stayed secure. He didn't plan on discussing sensitive information, but still, he wanted to be sure what he did say stayed between the two of them. If the feeling in his gut was right, there was something big going down in this little ski town.

"Done."

"Good. Listen, I need you to hunt out some background information on a Dr. Gunter Schmidt. He's a plastic surgeon here at the White River Spa."

"Ah, yes. Heard of him. There was an article on the spa in *Chatelaine* about two months ago."

"Well, I need a check run on his background, anything that relates to his past. Get Scott on it if you need a hand. Also, I want you to see if you can get anything on a Dr. Gregor Vasilev. He also works at the spa."

"Spell that for me."

He did. "And while you're at it, can you run a check on who owns the spa? I'm particularly interested in the names behind what I'm told is an East German company that has held the property for the last decade or so. That's about all for now."

Rex kept his eyes trained on the *Gazette* door as he spoke. He knew there was no back entrance to the office.

"Oh, and, Margaret, get Scott to give me a call on a secure line. There's someone else I need information on."

He flipped his phone shut. He needed Scott to see if he could find out exactly what the CIA was up to in White River. Agent Ken Mitchell in particular.

The *Gazette* door swung open and Rex stiffened. He relaxed when he saw it was Hannah. She was carrying a black bag. There was a fresh bounce in her movement as she came down the steps. Soft color flushed her cheeks. Her eyes sparked with animation as she yanked open the car door.

"Have I got some interesting stuff!" She climbed into the seat, giving a little gasp as she twisted round to reach the seat belt. Her rib was still giving her trouble.

"Well, what is it?"

"Not now, over dinner. I'm starved."

"If I didn't know better, I would say you look positively smug. What's in the bag?"

"Amy's stuff, things they found on her body. The coroner's office sent it up. Al said we could take a look. He wants answers as much as we do, you know."

"What've you told him about us?"

"Nothing. I mean, I told him you were an old friend...lending a hand."

She was avoiding contact with his eyes. She was looking out the window at the mountains washed in the peach and amber tail of the day's sun as it dipped behind the opposite peaks.

"And I told him I took a tumble while jogging over the weekend and that I needed a couple of days off to spend some time with my old friend."

"Thanks."

She turned to face him. "For what?"

"Calling me a friend." He didn't know why it mattered to him, but it did.

The evening chill had crept from shadows and crevices the minute the sun turned a blind eye on the valley. Rex placed the soft fleece over her shoulders and slipped an arm around her waist, escorting her up the cobbled path toward the little stone steps of Ma Maison. She didn't protest and that pleased him immensely. It sent a spurt of warmth through his chest. He felt an urge to protect, to comfort. She fell in step beside him, her body moving in concert with his as they walked. The sensation was intimate, satisfying.

Rex could smell garlic, butter and oregano. The warm scents of country French cuisine called out to them, luring them through the open doors, in from the brisk evening. As they climbed the steps, Rex saw that herbs frothed and spilled out of green window boxes under long narrow windows flanked by shutters.

For a moment everything seemed perfect. He was escorting his woman into a fine little French restaurant for a candlelit dinner.

Only, she wasn't his woman. It was a fragile facade. One that would crack, splinter into delicate shards the moment either one of them started to talk of the future. Or the past. But right now, in this moment, it was perfect. It made Rex want to think about tomorrows.

But a life of love and tomorrows was not for him. His life was the Bellona Channel. Tomorrow a new assignment. Another country. No room for love. Never had been. Well, thought Rex, that was not strictly true. There had been room once, a cavernous hollow he'd felt as a child. It had been a vast ache for the love of his father, the love of a family. But he'd learned early it was not to be. He'd learned early how to slam the door on that aching vault of need.

He looked at the woman beside him. It disturbed him greatly that being with Hannah made him poke about in those painful wounds of his memory. He couldn't afford to dwell there. He needed to stay focused. Needed to keep her safe. And then his job here would be done. They'd both be free.

He watched them go into Ma Maison, arm in arm. This would make things easier. Dr. Logan clearly had feelings for McGuire. The cold Bellona agent *did* have a weakness. He could use her to flush him out. He had to get them both out of the village and into the mountains. Out there he could take care of them. Before the buyers started arriving. By the time their bodies were found, the deal would be wrapped, the players long gone. Everything would be set in motion. There could be no turning back.

And he had a plan.

But it would have to wait until the boy came home.

Chapter 9

"*B*onsoir, Hannah, how lovely for you to come. I have not seen you in Ma Maison for, oh, it seems like years already."

The buxom woman hugged Hannah, squeezing the breath from her. She scrunched her eyes in pain as those large arms crushed her injured rib.

"Isabelle, they're going to have to put you on the wrestling team." Hannah's laugh was breathless. "Got a table for two?"

Isabelle gave Rex the once-over, approval registering in her twinkling eyes. She threw Hannah a knowing grin and obvious wink. "*Mais, oui.* It is good to see you out with a date, Hannah. Come this way. I have a nice secluded spot for your evening." She led the way through the tables to a little alcove set in a bay of windows overlooking the herb-filled courtyard.

Rex guided Hannah through the tables, his hand at the small of her back. He could feel her muscles move along the base of her spine as she walked.

Isabelle gestured to the table. "And how is Daniel?"

Hannah went rigid under his hand.

"Uh…he's well. Everyone is well. Thanks, Isabelle." Her tone brooked no further discussion.

"Well then, I will leave you to enjoy your dinner, *bon appetit.*" Isabelle gave Rex a warm, conspiratorial smile and turned and made her way back to the door to greet an older couple.

Rex pulled out a chair for Hannah. "Who's Daniel?"

She sat, placing the bag of Amy's belongings carefully beside her on the floor. Her eyes were wide gold pools, picking up the flicker of the candle flame on the table. She looked like a wild animal, cornered.

"He's…he's family."

She was hiding something. Not trusting him. But then, who was he to talk about being open. Trusting Hannah, telling her the whole truth, would mean betraying the Bellona Channel and the men and women who upheld its values. He'd shared too much already.

But it ate at him. Was Daniel a lover? He took a seat opposite her, shelving the subject, for now.

"So you've dined here before? I've been eyeing it since I arrived in White River." Rex opened the menu. "What can you recommend?"

Her eyes softened in relief at the change of topic. The mellow candlelight played on the velvet of her skin. Sitting there, across from him, she was just as she had come to him in his dreams.

"I haven't eaten here in ages, but the seafood is still supposed to be excellent."

Who brought you here to Ma Maison last, Hannah? he wanted to ask her. *What are you doing in this ski town in the Coast Mountains? Why did you leave CNA so suddenly? Who is Daniel?* What mysteries was she harboring? Rex figured from what Isabelle had said, Hannah hadn't been on a date for a while. He'd hoped she would've moved on after he left her in Marumba. Found someone, settled, had a family. He wished for her the things he didn't dare to wish for himself. She was a woman who deserved the best, deserved it all. But a secret part of his soul was guiltily satisfied she hadn't. That secret part of him jealously wanted her for himself.

Rex ordered a crisp, dry Riesling and a seafood platter for two.

The sommelier filled their glasses and Rex raised his in a toast. "To solving the mystery." And to moving on.

She lifted her glass. "To finally wrapping things up."

She was right. He'd come full circle, from Marumba to White River, to finally wrap this thing up. It wasn't just Hannah. He had a sense that what started going down in Marumba would play out the notes of its finale here in the Canadian mountains, a full six years later.

The pale-gold liquid swirled against the side of her glass as she lifted it to her lips, taking it in. His stomach did a lurching swirl of its own as he watched her lips, lush against the rim of the wineglass. She set her drink on the table and looked out of the window. He followed her gaze. Darkness was coaxing shadows into the courtyard. Little candles in jars shivered and flickered outside in the evening mountain breeze.

"You don't go out much."

She turned and faced him. "Is that a question or a statement?"

"Both."

She turned away from him, her attention back on the winking lights outside. "I'm busy. I have commitments."

"You're single."

She flashed a warning look at him. "Another statement?"

He reached out, gently took the tips of her fingers in

his hand. "Is there a man in your life, Hannah?" Rex knew better than to tread here. Yet the woman in front of him was a drug. He was the addict slipping deep into the abyss. The more he saw, tasted, the farther he slid, the more remote his control.

She looked down at his fingers touching hers. She was staring at the silver ring. He wondered if she remembered. He'd never taken it off. During that heady time with her in Marumba, she'd intoxicated him beyond sound judgment. He had thought he would get a copy of the ring made for her in platinum. She deserved the finest. God, he had thought to make her his forever. He had never been able to bring himself to take the little silver ring off.

She looked up from the ring, at him, her eyes shimmering in the glow of the flame. Her voice was smoky, thick and heavy with emotion. "I had a man. Once." She bit the bottom corner of her lip. "I loved him."

He felt his muscles react, his jaw set. Her comment pierced to his core.

She turned her hand to face upward under his, running her soft fingers along the underside of his palm. His stomach dipped. The sensation was exquisitely sensual. It roused the serpent of desire that lay coiled in the pit of his belly. Rex sucked in air, slowly. Very slowly.

She held his gaze with those glimmering pools of emotion.

"Rejection is painful, Rex. No matter what form it takes. It breeds a kind of hate."

He knew it well, the hate that cloaked the pain of rejection, had known it most of his life.

He gripped her fingers, hard. She recoiled in surprise. But he held on to her hand, pulling her closer as he leaned in toward her. "God, I'm so sorry, Hannah. I never wanted to hurt you. I...I never knew."

One tear slipped from her left eye. The candlelight

caught its shining trail down her cheek. When she spoke, her voice was soft. So soft. "You never knew what, Rex? How much I once loved you? How I bled when you left?"

He clenched his teeth, fighting at the dam of emotion swelling in his skull. He didn't trust himself to speak.

Her eyes didn't leave his. They bored into his, searching for answers. Answers he couldn't give.

Then she pulled her hand suddenly out from under his. "Look, Rex, I don't want to talk about the past. Or the future. I don't want to talk about me, any more than you want to talk about you. So let's stick to the business at hand, okay?"

"Hannah, I—"

"Do you want to know what I found at the *Gazette?*"

Rex drew air in through his nose, sucking it deep down to his gut as he mentally swept his mess of emotions back into a black corner. "Right. Business. Let's get this over with." He took a swig at his wineglass. "The sooner the better. What did you find?"

She crossed her arms on the little table covered in white damask, her hair a shining fall over her shoulders. Her jaw was set firm. She cleared her throat, but still the pain lingered in her eyes. When she spoke, the smoky thickness of emotion still threaded her voice. "It's pretty astounding, really."

"Well, you going to share?"

She reached down and pulled a Manila folder from the bag at her feet. "I printed out the article and photo that ran in the *Gazette* at the time of Grady Fisher's accident." She opened the folder and pulled out the copy. "Sven was right. Grady doesn't look like he'd be Amy's type. Kind of scrawny intellectual. Amy had a thing for athletic, macho males."

Hannah laid the printout on the table. "The reason I didn't remember more about the canyon accident was because Grady Fisher went off the road the day after Amy disappeared. We were all so engrossed in the search-and-rescue efforts I guess no one really paid a whole lot of attention.''

"So Grady Fisher disappeared the day after Amy Barnes went missing? Now, that *is* interesting.''

He watched her smooth out the paper on the table with those beautiful hands.

"Al had a journalism student helping out as part of a work experience when Grady's accident happened. He put this story together."

She took a sip of her wine. "And there's more." She reached into her bag and pulled out a stapled document. "The RCMP initially suspected drunk driving. That's what the student reported in his story. However, he did send for a copy of the coroner's report. It must have arrived some weeks after he went back to school. It ended up getting filed and forgotten in all the turmoil. No one ever followed up with another article."

Rex looked at the document in her hand. "You got the coroner's report?"

"Yes. And guess what? Toxicology tests showed virtually zero blood alcohol content. Grady Fisher reeked of booze at the scene and apparently there was an open whiskey bottle found in the car, but there was not enough inside him to legally declare him an impaired driver."

Rex whistled softly through his teeth. "This is looking serious, Hannah." It smacked of a setup. He'd seen this kind of thing before. Perhaps Fisher's death was no more accidental than Amy's. "Do you know if anyone got prints from the whiskey bottle?"

"There's no mention anywhere of prints in what I could find at the office. But police did find a vial with traces of something called GHB back in Grady's apartment."

"Gamma hydroxybutyrate? It's an anaesthetic and hypnotic. Like Rohypnol, it's being used more and more frequently as a recreational drug and has been implicated in date-rape cases." Rex took a sip of his wine. "Liquid GHB is common in some club scenes, but when mixed with alcohol, or taken in too high a dose, it can result in breathing difficulties, coma and death. It's got a host of trendy names, one of them Grievous Bodily Harm."

"Well, apparently routine forensic toxicology tests don't look for drugs like that."

"Right. But if Fisher's blood alcohol was so low, they must have tested for other routine drugs."

"They did. But according to the report, there was no trace of the usual suspects—cocaine, morphine, codeine or cannabis. After they discovered the vial, police did ask for a special benzodiazepine analysis but nothing was found."

"Well, those tests might have shown if there was GHB in Grady's system, but only if they were done in time. How long did it take to find his body?"

"A full day after his car apparently left the road. Actual cause of death was head injury and blood loss."

"So it was many hours before they ran those tests. You see, that's the trouble with stuff like Rohypnol and GHB. They have a short half-life and you have to take body fluids within a relatively narrow timeframe to detect them. The way I understand it, inactive metabolites can be detected in blood only for about four to six hours after administration."

"You know your stuff, Doc."

"I head up a pharmaceutical division, I should know my stuff."

"Right." Hannah reached for her wine. Rex was pleased to see a healthy sweep of color brushing those aristocratic cheekbones.

"The coroner did note that Grady's employer indicated he'd been having substance abuse problems and that he hadn't been himself a few weeks prior to the accident. But he said *if* drugs were a factor in the actual accident, there was no forensic evidence to confirm this."

"So the bottom line is Grady Fisher's death was ruled accidental, like Amy's?"

"You got it." Hannah gathered up the report and print-outs as she saw two servers approach bearing the Ma Maison specialty. "Ah, the food. Good, I'm absolutely starved."

One of the waiters set a burner on the table and lit two little tea lights. The other set a platter on top of the burner. Steam spiraled from the lobster, a fiery coral in color. It was set amongst prawns, oysters, mussels and thick fillets of succulent white fish. There was garlic and herb butter, lemon wedges and little finger bowls.

Hannah peered at him through the gently curling steam. A hint of a smile tugged at her lush lips. "Rex, this was a good plan." She shook out her napkin and set it on her lap. "I think I must be drooling."

She reached for a prawn, split the skin and dipped the white meat into the lemon and herb butter. He watched as she savored it, licked the juices from her lips and reached for another. It drove a hunger of his own, one quite unrelated to prawns drenched in garlic and herb butter.

He squeezed lemon onto the oysters. "Looks like I better tuck in before you polish it off without me."

"Mmm." She reached for her glass. "Oh, the other thing the student dug up during an Internet search was an old Orange County newspaper article. Seems Grady Fisher had a bit of a shady past himself. According to the article, Grady was charged in California several years ago for drug possession, but the charge never stuck."

"So the theory that he was abusing drugs fits. Interesting stuff, Hannah. Well done…partner." He raised his glass.

She grinned at him, her lips slick with sauce.

He paused to split open a prawn. "What was found with Amy's body?"

"Not much. It sure looks like she wasn't going on a hike, though. She had a flashlight and a reporter's notebook with her. It has notes in it from the last couple of interviews she did before she went missing. Nothing really stands out as unusual. But, on the inside cover, there is a telephone number for the White River Spa with Grady Fisher's name. Next to his name are the words 'Grizz Hut, 5 p.m., to trail, meeting, BW. Urgent.'"

"Grizz Hut, that's the cabin up near the glacier where she fell?"

"Yes. Grizzly Hut."

Rex lifted the bottle to top up Hannah's glass. She moved her hand over it. "No, no, thank you." Her eyes trapped his. "I've had way more than I need. We missed lunch, you know. Wine's going straight to my head."

"Sorry, that's my fault." He topped up his own drink. "Years of bad habit. I tend to ignore my own hunger until it's too late."

She scooped a delicate mussel from its pearled shell and slipped it between her lips. "If I do that, I get ravenous. Then I eat too much, overindulge and seriously regret it later." She maneuvered another succulent piece of flesh from its blue-back shell and dipped it into the butter sauce.

He felt like that now, ravenous, mad with hunger, a rapacious need as he watched her lips, slick, lush with juices. He'd glimpsed that same dark hunger mirrored in her golden cat's eyes. He sipped his wine, allowing it to linger on his lips, watching her lick the butter from her finger.

If he coaxed her gently, softly over the edge, tipped her into a blind, maddening swirl of need, would she overindulge? Would she suck him in with the same delight, the same fervor with which she was tucking into those firm, butter-drenched prawns? He'd gone way too long with this need. How long could a man turn a blind eye to the hunger that was devouring him?

He speared a piece of fish with his fork. Damn. She was driving him wild. It wouldn't be so bad if he couldn't see she wanted him, too.

She was watching him as she chewed. Their eyes locked, meshed. It was as if she was reading his thoughts, the words hanging unspoken, charged, shimmying with the candlelight between them.

He broke the silence. "So how's your rib, are you up to it?"

She raised her eyebrows, almost choking on her food. "Up to it?"

He grinned, the serpent in his belly writhing. God, he was sure up to it. "Up to a hike tomorrow, to check out this hut on Powder Mountain." Then he leaned forward, dropping his voice to a smoky whisper, words meant only for her. "Unless you had something else in mind."

Her eyes caught the glint of the candle flame. He could see it reflected there, flickering, dancing gold, the dark coffee rims around the lighter amber of her irises feline.

She swallowed, said nothing. Just looked at him, her fingers playing gently along the stem of her glass.

The night air was crisp on her face as the water churned in warm bubbles around her limbs.

He was right.

This felt good. She was glad she'd relented and allowed

Rex to persuade her to pick up a swimsuit at the Presidential's boutique.

Her aches, mental and physical, melted away as she rested her head back on the lip of the tub and looked up at the night sky. A giant's brush had flecked the heavens with twinkling gold. A gibbous moon hung heavy and huge just above Powder Peak. The mica shimmered silver off the top of Moonstone.

She sat up out of the water suddenly. "Oh look, Rex, a falling star."

"A shooting star."

"What's the difference?"

He wasn't watching the sky. His eyes were intently fixed on her. She sank back into the frothing water, conscious of his gaze upon her breasts.

"I have no idea. I would guess a shooting star goes up and a falling one goes down." He laughed, the sound rich, baritone. It rolled over her, through her.

"There's a sense of direction, purpose and future about a shooting star. A falling star, well, it's time has come. It's a has-been. No future."

Like us. She challenged the look in his eyes, the weighted meaning of his words. "Weird thing about the heavens, Rex, is it's *all* about the past. Many of those stars up there, they're long gone. What we're seeing is their history, a beautiful explosion, a glory spent, yet the memories, the light of them still hurtles through space to remind of what once was. What will never be again."

His eyes were suddenly serious. Deadly so. She saw the dangerous edge in them. And the hunger. "Hannah." His voice, low, curled through her blood, raising the small hairs on her nape.

"What?" She could barely manage the word. It came out a throaty whisper. He was undressing her with those Arctic wolf eyes. He was taking off her bikini top, watching as her breasts spilled free of the thin fabric, buoyed by the effervescence of warm bubbles. It sent an electric thrill to her core.

"It's not over, Hannah. You know that."

She swallowed against the tightness in her throat. She could feel the throb of her heart in the warm water. His eyes were undressing her. Mentally, he was stripping her naked. She could read it in the feral set of his features, hear it in the depth of his breath. And it was insanely titillating. The wine must have gone straight to her head because she was powerless to resist the image. All she wanted was to make love to him. Now. Here in this tub. Under this sky, while people watched from darkened balconies of the hotel rooms above.

His eyes held her entranced. And she lost sense of the sky, the hotel, the lambent water of the adjacent swimming pool, the steam rising into the night air. All she knew was him, and her, cocooned in the hot froth of the tub. She was falling deep, mentally, physically, right into the moment, just like six years ago. And like that time, she was just as blinded, just as bewitched by the sheer male sensuality of the man inches from her near-naked body. This alpha wolf. This loner. His arms, thick and muscular, rested on the rim of the tub. The dark hair on his broad chest was wet. He had never had any intention of staying with her six years ago. And he had none now.

He was programmed to roam wild.

Like Mac. Like her father.

And he was right. It wasn't over. Not yet. It lived hot between them.

She narrowed her eyes, pinning him with her gaze. "Let's finish it, then, Logan. Once and for all."

"Do you know, McGuire, that your eyes are the color of an African cat and right now, they're just as wild. Just as dangerous."

She wanted to look away. Couldn't.

"One hell of a challenge to look a cat like that in the eyes."

"What do you mean?"

"A hunter who comes face to face with a lioness, looks into those eyes, he needs nerve."

"For what?" She attempted a laugh. It came out hollow. "To raise the rifle, kill her?"

He raised his hand, reached forward, cupped the side of her face. "Yes. McGuire."

She shifted back slightly. "The cat's no match for the gun, Rex. He's a coward, the hunter."

He dropped his voice to a low, gravelly whisper. "No." He edged closer. She could feel his thigh, all hard muscle, alongside hers, under the water. "A hunter, foolish or arrogant enough to get that close to the lioness, is left with two choices. Shoot, or try to walk away."

"She'd kill him if he turned his back and walked."

"Exactly...but he couldn't shoot."

Something huge and indefinable welled up in her chest. "He walked? She killed him?"

His voice was raw, rough and naked male. "Mortally wounded. The hunter was left half a man." He was closer now, his lids low over the glitter of his glacial eyes.

"Why, Rex, why?"

"Why what, Hannah?" The low timbre of his words, the purling tone, licked over her, sucked her in as he bent closer. She could feel the warmth of his breath in the cold night air.

"Why'd he hunt the lioness?"

"He was hungry, Hannah. A hunger determined only by destiny. He had no choice."

"And...and her?"

"She haunts him, still. Her eyes. In his dreams. Always." His breath was now warm against her ear.

She could hardly speak. Her words came out a hoarse whisper. "Rex...what do you want from me?"

"What I want, Hannah McGuire—" the left side of his mouth dipped in a wicked, lopsided grin "—is to pull this little string here." She felt his hand on the bikini strap at her back. "Pull it and free those beautiful firm breasts of yours." A shiver marched up her spine.

He lifted her hair back from her neck and allowed his lips to whisper against her bare, damp skin. The mountain air was cold, the water warm and she shivered under the touch of his mouth. The contrast of temperatures set her nerves on edge. She was trembling. He teased her lobe with the tip of his tongue while he slipped a hand under the wet fabric of her bikini top and found her nipple erect. He moaned. Deep. The sound so primal. Hannah felt cold reason swallowed by hot lust, by blinding, throbbing need.

"Rex..."

"Shh." His eyes were heavy-lidded, deep and darkened pools now. He brought his mouth down onto hers, stealing words, crushing her lips, invading her with the roughness of his tongue, his taste male, wild. She was drowning, yet exquisitely aware of the churning bubbles tickling her limbs as they floated to the surface to be released into steam as they met the cold night air.

She was without logic, without choice. She met his hunger with her own, tasting him, letting her tongue slip, mate and dance around his, feeling his teeth, the inner seam of his lips. She had a need to wrap him in her legs, take him, suck him in and feed her deep inner yearning.

She splayed her hand wide on his chest and ran it down the fine ridge of dark hair, down into the water, down his hard belly, pressing, urgent. He groaned and deepened his kiss.

A deep splash jolted her out of her haze.

Someone had dived into the pool next to the hot tub. Waves churned the water into an oily dance, black against gold in the night as a lone swimmer cut through the pool in a graceful crawl.

Rex cleared his throat, the lids of his eyes still thick with desire, his voice husky. "I think we are no longer alone."

Hannah quickly pulled the fabric of her bikini top back into place. "I...I think I'm going to call it a night, Rex. I'm not thinking straight. I'm tired. Very tired." Her body, her heart had just won a round with her head. Again. And she just did not have the resolve to fight it. Or even begin to understand it.

She stood up and reached for her towel and the thick white terry robe provided by the hotel.

She half expected, half wanted, him to reach out and yank her back down into the warm foaming water, into the dangerous whitewater of their relationship. She pulled the robe around her and tied the belt, tight. She walked, brisk and erect, into the hotel and made for the elevator without looking back.

He didn't come after her.

Hannah kicked off her slippers. She let her robe slip off her shoulders, and she climbed out of her wet bikini. She hung her bathing suit in the bathroom, took a fresh robe off the hook and walked over the hotel room carpet to the French doors, feeling the soft pile beneath her toes.

She threw open the doors, stepped onto the balcony. The stone was smooth and cold under her feet. She let her robe fall open. The night air kissed her skin with its frigid embrace. She wanted the cold. She wanted to clear her body and head of the hot passionate haze that had engulfed her.

She breathed in the mountain scent, feeling her nipples pucker tight against the night. Goose bumps prickled over her skin. She leaned over the balcony, looked down at the pool, the hot tub. She expected to see him there. He was gone. The swimmer was also gone. The surface of the water gleaming, unbroken. As if it had never been. As if a dream.

Then she gasped at the small sound that came suddenly from behind her.

Hannah's throat closed in fear as hands grabbed her wrists, yanked them roughly behind her back. Before she could scream for Rex, her wrists were caught in the tie of her robe and bound behind her.

Chapter 10

"Don't walk out on me like that!"

Rex spun her around. "Anyone could've been waiting up here for you."

Her eyes were wide with fear. She was naked under her robe. It splayed open, exposing her full, rounded breasts, nipples dusky, hard and tight. The sight stole his breath, his thoughts. His stomach swooped in a roller-coaster lurch, down, in a hot wave to his loins. Her hands were bound behind her back but it was him held prisoner. Her body trapped his eyes, drawing them down the imperceptible swell of her belly, down to the dark gold delta of hair at the apex of her thighs. Lean, long thighs.

He looked up, mouth dry.

Her lips were parted as she breathed, her breasts rose and fell as if from exertion. He'd shocked her. Yet a fine flush of arousal brushed her cheeks and those cat's eyes were alight with an untamed fire. They ignited his need. It burned ferocious, hot and out of control, in the crucible of his belly.

His body screamed to take her at once, roughly, savagely, drink her in, feed on his years of pent-up need. He saw the same kind of need mirrored in the strange dark tempest raging through her gold eyes as she challenged him. He saw the way her eyes flicked down to the towel at his waist. And under her gaze he felt himself swell and pulse where he hung hot and heavy between his thighs.

He reached up, reined in his ferocious fire and gently cupped one breast, scraping the hard nub of her nipple with the pad of his thumb. He spoke against the lust thick in his throat. "God, Hannah, you're beautiful."

Her breath hitched as he pinched her nipple between his thumb and forefinger. He wanted to taste it. Suck it in. He came closer. Her lids flickered, low, her vision swimming. She was delirious, weak with desire. He could see her passion, and it fueled him.

Rex moved his hand up onto her neck. A small sound came from somewhere deep in her throat. He felt as if his knees would buckle under a wave of pleasure that ripped through him. He traced the aristocratic line of her collarbone and let his hand slip down between her breasts, down over her belly to cup the hot mound between her legs. She struggled weakly against the bond at her wrists.

But he didn't free her. He slowly parted her, held her open, slipping his finger up into her heat. She was slick and swollen with need. Another dizzying wave seared through him. He plunged another finger into her core, moving, stroking, coaxing.

Her legs sagged. She moaned and allowed herself to sink deeper onto his fingers.

The world closed in on them.

"You want me, Hannah?"

She said nothing. Just held his gaze, lips parted, and rocked gently on his hand.

He swallowed an oath and swept her off her feet, carried her in from the cold.

He laid her on the bed, freeing her bonds. And his head swam with the vision before him. She was like an angel, like she had come to him in dreams. Her gold hair, damp, splayed out over the virginal white of the pillow, her tawny, dusky nipples, the dark-gold mystery nestled between her legs, was his for the taking.

She reached up and pulled the towel from his waist. He swelled free into her hands. Her soft hands worked with deft movement, stimulating, tantalizing, coaxing.

His brain unraveled with the sensation. It was so much better than he'd dreamed. His mind lurched back six years.

And he stopped.

Grabbed her hands.

''No.''

Her eyes were wide with surprise, her voice a soft throaty whisper. ''Rex?''

He couldn't. What kind of a man would do this to her? Hurt her like this. Again. He couldn't stay. He couldn't do this. There was no future. None.

Rex pushed her hands gently aside. ''Hannah…I'm sorry.''

Anger, pain flashed in her eyes. She gripped his wrists, fingers digging into his flesh. ''Damn you, you bastard.''

''Oh, I want you, Hannah. Like nothing before—''

''You've taken me this far. Take me all the way…or has the great hunter lost his nerve? Is he not up for the kill?'' She ran her hands down his belly as she spoke, reached between his legs, coaxing the hot life that pulsed there.

Hot ribbons burned, twisted through him. His vision blurred. ''I…I can't promise you anything, Hannah.''

Emotion glistened in her eyes but her voice was a low,

throaty growl. "You think I'd be that stupid...twice."
She rubbed, teased. The blood left his head. "I know you
won't stay. I'm not asking for tomorrows. But I need this.
Maybe we both need this. Maybe then we can let it all
go, finish it. Take me, Rex. I know you want me."

She opened her legs to him, her lioness eyes calling,
bewitching.

His restraint snapped in that instant. He edged himself
between her thighs, forcing them wider with his knees,
and she reached up with her hips to him. Straining, urgent,
demanding.

He rocked into her...slowly. At first just the tip, slipping in. Out. Then each movement plunged him deeper.
She was slick, gilded and hot with need. She moved with
him, rhythmically, fervently, the friction driving them
both higher. He could feel the skin of her inner thighs
against him, smooth. Soft. Firm. He drove into her,
ground into her. Faster. She bucked under him. Wild. He
came closer. Higher. He moved until they were slipping
and slick with the heat. Until scarlet waves colored his
mind and his nerves sang. Until he wanted to scream, mad
and primal, like a conqueror of the night.

She seemed to sense he was on the tip. He could feel
she, too, was poised, quivering on the edge. For an instant
he paused. He looked into her eyes. They were open wide,
dark and carnal. Then they swam blind, lids low, her
moans animal. He watched her face as he felt her climax,
wave over rippling muscular wave. He felt her erupt hot
around that part of him buried deep in her. It was too
much. He shuddered and burst into her, spilling himself
in exquisite release.

The waves rolled deliriously over him and over him.
He wanted nothing more than this woman. He wanted to
shelter her, fight for her, love her. He wanted her to bear

his children. The tide of thoughts that surged over him, through him, were not coherent but there as a primal need.

He understood need.

He had lived with it.

It didn't mean it could be fulfilled.

He fell back into her arms. Spent, they lay in silence, the pregnant white drapes billowing softly in the cool night breeze.

When Rex woke, Hannah was nuzzled into the crook of his arm, her breathing soft and rhythmic. He lay there listening to her. His arm went numb, but he didn't move. He didn't want to disturb her. He didn't want to face reality. He'd seen her pain. Things shouldn't have come to this. It was his fault. Yet she'd blinded him.

They were destroying each other.

Hannah woke to the warm scents of bacon and coffee. She opened her eyes to a room filling with the yellow gold of morning sun, vaguely aware of a subtle throb between her legs. It had nothing to do with the slight pain in her rib or the stiffness of her limbs. Sex. It had everything to do with a night of hot glorious sex. He was a perfect lover.

But he wasn't hers.

There was no way she could've halted what had surged between them. She had no regrets over their lovemaking. But he still wasn't hers. At least this time she had no naive expectations. This time she *knew* he'd walk. And she would accept that, with pain. But could she accept that for her son, for their son?

She turned to find Rex watching her, his eyes, Danny's eyes, catching the bright clear light of the morning. He needed a shave, but she liked the look. The dark shadow on his jaw offset the sharp whiteness of his teeth as he smiled at her, eyes creasing with warmth. She didn't think she had noticed it before, that tender warmth in his smile. He was beautiful, in a rough and wild way, like these granite hills. Like the way he'd made love to her.

She couldn't help but return the affection in his smile. "Good morning."

"It is a good morning. Coffee?" He held up the pot.

"What, no tea? What have you done with the Brit in you?"

He paused, coffeepot poised above cup. "My dad was the Brit. An English army colonel. But my mother, she liked coffee. Good Italian coffee."

He poured, steam curling.

He'd never spoken to her about his parents. "Your mother isn't British?"

"Wasn't British."

He stirred in cream and sugar. It pleased her that he remembered how she took her coffee.

"My mother died when I was fifteen. She was Italian, a singer."

He brought the coffee to her in bed. She accepted the cup, warm in her hands. His fingers brushed against hers. "I guess that's where your dark looks come from." *Where Danny's looks come from.*

He frowned, turned to pour a cup for himself. "She was dark, with olive skin. A gypsy at heart. I have my father's eyes." He turned them on her now. "People say he has cold eyes, that he's a cruel man."

She sipped, watching him over the rim of her mug. "Is he? Cruel, I mean?"

He stirred his coffee and dropped the spoon onto the breakfast tray. He walked with his mug to the French doors and looked out at the mountain. "I don't know if *cruel* is really the word. He was a damn fine colonel. One of the best. He wasn't noted for expressing his feelings.

He used to say to me, 'Show your feelings, son, and you give people tools to hurt you.'"

Hannah cradled the mug in her hands. "Did that include showing his feelings to his son?"

He turned to face her. Eyes narrowed, jaw tight. "I never saw much of my father. I bore the Logan name but that was about all. My mother was good enough for a night of hot sex but that was it for the colonel. He already had a wife and four children when I was born. I was the bastard son, the family's dirty little secret."

Hannah's chest felt tight. The words hit home. History was repeating itself in a way. A father, a family, were not part of the deal for Daniel Logan McGuire, either. Danny was her little secret.

Rex turned back to look out the window. "But he did his duty. For the colonel, it was always about duty. Never love. He sent the money regular as clockwork. Visited me from time to time. Never at Christmas or my birthday. I was like a tedious little chore, something that had to be seen to. Then he got mother to agree to send me off to a fine British boarding school. It was supposed to be in preparation for the career in the military he envisaged for me. I saw my mother for holidays. She died after my fifteenth birthday." His tone was bitter, his words clipped. "From school it was expected I enter the military. I did." He turned to Hannah. "There you have it."

Duty.

She did not want Rex to be forced to do duty by his son. She wanted her son to have a dad, to have the genuine love of a father in the home.

Love, not duty. Not some tedious little chore.

Rex had told her he could not promise anything. She accepted that. But did she owe it to Rex to tell him? Did she owe it to Danny? Could she cope with the fallout?

Could she cope with a life like Rex's mother's, like her own mother's?

She didn't think she could, but she had to make a choice. Soon.

Today was Wednesday. Danny was coming home on Friday.

She felt trapped, cornered. Nausea and confusion swept over her.

"Hannah?" He was talking to her. "Hannah, are you okay? You're pale."

She set the half-full coffee cup on the bedside table and pushed the tangle of hair out of her face. "I'm fine." She looked into his eyes. "I'm sorry, Rex."

"For what?"

"For what you went through as a child. I never knew."

His face was suddenly wiped clean of emotion. Hannah suspected it was a trick he had learned early in life.

"It's nothing. Some people are cut out for love and family. Others aren't."

She sat forward. "That's not true." She didn't want it to be true. She yearned to reach out to the vulnerable little boy she knew must lurk deep within him. She wanted to comfort him, hold him, tell him everything would be all right. But the man's eyes were once again as cold as Arctic ice. That little boy must sleep very, very deep within that man, she mused. Frozen in a protective shell. She wondered what it would take to melt it away. Or if anything could.

"Come, have something to eat." He changed the subject, moving over to the breakfast tray and lifting the silver lid. The warm scents of food curled out from under it.

Hannah felt her stomach clench in response. "No, I'm not hungry right now. I just need a shower."

She started to throw back the covers and make for the

bathroom when she realized she was still buck naked. She pulled the covers back up over her chest.

Rex grinned, lines fanning out from eyes that held a mischievous spark. He was finding her morning-after modesty amusing. She could feel herself starting to bristle.

He could see it. He reached for her white terry robe hanging over the chair and brought it to her.

"I'll see you in twenty minutes. Dress for the mountain if you're still up to it." Rex closed the door to the interleading room behind him.

Right. They were going up to Grizzly Hut.

It was around 10 a.m. when they made their way across the village toward the gondola building, the sun already warm. The day would be hot, but up high where the air was thin, over to the north, Hannah could see fine threads of gathering clouds.

Rex followed her gaze. "The weather today should be good, but there's a front moving in. Weatherman said it could arrive early in the weekend, possibly as soon as Friday."

Friday. That was when Danny was due home. Hannah felt a band constrict about her chest. Her time was running out.

They dodged through crowds of tourists gathering in the square, waiting for the clowns to start their acts. The village was getting busier, noisier, people flocking in for the long weekend, for the festival, for the conference.

So, thought Hannah, if the forecast was correct, it would rain on this parade. It would be the first time in years. White River had been unusually blessed with sunshine for at least the past four years over the long weekend that eased August into September, summer into fall. It was traditionally the last holiday fling before schools opened for the year and before locals knuckled down for the busy winter ski season.

Rex had insisted on carrying Hannah's jacket and water in his backpack because of her rib injury. His pack hulked huge on his back.

"What have you got in there, anyway?" she asked as she led the way into the gondola building.

"Stuff." He grinned. He was in a good mood this morning despite the sober talk about his family. He was obviously used to sweeping those emotions under the rug. Like his dad, he didn't give much away when it came to feelings.

And now they'd slept together. Again. Would he sweep that under the rug again, too?

"That's the boon of staying in a five-star hotel. You tell 'em you're going on a hike and they organize the backpack and the picnic. Have it ready and waiting in the morning. So, this is where Amy went up?" Rex approached the little glass ticket booth. The hole cut into the glass was designed for a man of average height. He had to bend down to ask the vendor for two lift tickets.

Hannah stopped him. "I have a pass. It's valid year-round. You only need a ticket for yourself."

He bought one and signed the waiver absolving the mountain of all responsibility for injury. The lift attendant scanned his ticket and Hannah's pass as the gondolas swept continuously round, into the building, knocking against metal as they were mechanically guided into the railings, doors opening like little subway trains pulling into the station, closing again as they swept out and were lifted by creaking lines into the sky.

Rex and Hannah allowed the gondola doors to close on a family of five ahead of them, opting for the next car. The doors swung closed as they were rocked free of the moorings and lifted skyward, swaying from side to side.

"Would Amy have had her pass scanned down there?"

"Yes. There's a computer record kept. Her pass was scanned at 4:30 the afternoon she disappeared. The last gondola ride comes down at 5 p.m. She would've just made it to the top before it was time to come right back down." Hannah watched the town shrink as they climbed. "It takes about twenty-five minutes in total to the top, about fifteen to midstation and then another ten to the peak."

"She may have had no intention of coming down via gondola."

"Perhaps not. But she had no gear for an overnight stay."

"Maybe she was going to hike down."

Hannah watched a colorful group of hikers making their way up the gravel road below. They were oblivious to a bear grazing just beyond the trees to their right. "Perhaps." She looked at Rex. "But I doubt it. She would've known they were calling for crappy weather that afternoon."

He was relaxed, leaning against the little seat that ran around the cabin. His limbs were all tanned muscle. He was wearing khaki shorts, hiking boots. He definitely had presence. He filled a vacuum with masculine power, even in repose.

"The weather up here is notoriously fickle as we head into fall. You can have snow up in the Alpine one minute, a heat wave the next. I checked. The freezing level was forecast to plummet the day she went up. Amy would've checked, too."

Hannah rested her head against the glass. It was cool, but the sun was warming her back. "You know, Rex, I can't help feeling there was a sense of urgency about her movements that day."

He leaned forward, reached out, took a tendril that had

escaped her neat ponytail. He tucked it in behind her ear, the gesture gentle, as if he cared for her deeply.

They were high now, closing in on midstation. The wind at this elevation gently swayed their glass bubble. They were suspended from reality, just the two of them together, a sense of no past, no future, just being.

Hannah felt as if it was possible to just live in the moment up here. Not think, just be.

She closed her eyes, enjoying the sun on her back, drinking in the moment, just being with this man. The man she'd hated and craved all these years. The father of her son.

The crash and bump as the car was rocked and guided into the midstation building jolted her out of her reverie.

The doors of their little cab opened, then as the car moved along its metal moorings, they started to shut again for the second stage of their journey.

Rex sat forward. "How would we know if someone joined Amy here at midstation?"

Hannah hadn't thought of that. "I guess we wouldn't. Not unless the lifty saw something." She pointed to two mountain employees chatting in the sun, just outside of their gondola building posts. "As you can see, not much attention is paid to anything up here, unless it gets really busy or the alarm goes off."

"Hmm." Rex reached down, opened the flap of his pack and fished out the reporter's notebook that had been found on Amy's body. He flipped it open to the inside cover, where Hannah had discovered the notations about Grizzly Hut.

He studied the scrawl again. "Looks like she was going to meet Grady Fisher up at the hut." He pointed to the notation. "See, here it says 5 p.m. If she caught a 4:30 gondola ride up from the village, she would have made it up around five, wouldn't she?"

"Almost. It's about a ten-minute hike from the gondola station on top to Grizz Hut."

"And she would've used the Grizzly traverse, the path above Grizzly glacier where she was found?"

"Yes."

"Someone could've been waiting," mused Rex. They were on the last leg of the gondola ride up Powder Mountain. The trees below were getting shorter and stubbier, gnarled from the colder temperatures and shorter summers at the higher elevation. Soon they would be above the tree line, nearing the peak. The air coming through the small window had a different quality. Crisp. Thin.

"But whoever might have been waiting would've had to know she was coming."

"Right. Or lured her up. A trap."

"Rex, that's bizarre."

"Believe me, I've seen bizarre. This looks pretty straightforward by comparison."

"But why would someone want to hurt Amy?"

"Like I said, she was getting too close to something."

"You think Grady lured her up here?"

"I'm not ruling out anything. Just thinking aloud. He could've asked her to meet him. Someone could've forced him to ask her up here, or someone might have known of their meeting."

Hannah could see the blue roof of the gondola station up ahead, the glass and chrome throwing back the cutting glare of the Alpine sun. She put on her sunglasses. "Georgette said Amy got a call at the office that afternoon, before she left. She was the last person to see her alive, apart from the lifty."

"Any idea where that call came from?"

"Nope. We could check records, I suppose. It's going back a year now." Hannah felt her old anger starting to fester. "If the police had only started looking back then we might not be here now."

Rex caught her chin with his knuckle as their gondola knocked into the station. "I'm kind of glad we are."

She faced him as the doors swung slowly open. "I'm not so sure it's a good thing, Rex." She turned and stepped onto the platform.

He caught his hands around her waist from behind and leaned his chin onto her shoulder. "Sure felt good last night."

She stopped. A little lick of lust started to unfurl in her belly at the breath in her ear. It twisted with anger and resentment, a complex braid of emotion. She didn't turn to him. She looked straight ahead, up at the glare coming off old snow in the crevices of the peak. "But where to now, Rex?"

"Let's take it one step at a time. You lead." He nudged her gently forward.

Damn him. He was content to just fall into the moment, take it as it came, then part ways, like six years ago. She didn't know if she could handle that.

She started up the precarious trail.

Chapter 11

Hannah drew the crisp Alpine air down deep into her lungs as they climbed the rocky trail from the gondola station up to the traverse across the top of the basin.

She was enjoying the burn in her calves, the pull in the muscles of her thighs. Little stones rolled and clacked down the mountain, dislodged by their boots as they made their way to the traverse. She could hear Rex breathing deep behind her as she set the pace.

They were alone. The sky, not above them but around them, was a lucent atmospheric dome of shades ranging from bright white and pale blue to a cerulean that melted into a deep far-off indigo. Hannah imagined the indigo was where the earth's atmosphere met the blackness of space and infinity beyond. All around them were jagged white-capped peaks. They felt as if they were above it all, on top of the world.

To the north, over on the horizon well beyond Moonstone Mountain, sparse wisps of cloud were filling out and beginning to mushroom into monstrous columns of white cotton candy.

She stopped when she reached the point on the traverse above where they'd found Amy and turned back to face Rex. He looked so vital, his powerful chest rising and falling with each deep breath, a dark male silhouette framed by the bright dome of sky. His eyes were the same pellucid blues. It was like looking right through him into the infinity beyond.

Danny's eyes.

It threw her.

She often teased her little boy by saying she could see through him right into the heavens. He would shutter those eyes with his thick dark lashes and say, "No you can't, Mommy, not if I don't want you to."

She turned away from the image and looked down at the unforgiving planes of Grizzly Glacier below. The glacier appeared innocent enough to the uninitiated but below the surface lurked fissures and crevasses, convoluted caves of sheer blue ice. The rope below the trail warned that the glacier was out of bounds.

"This the spot?"

Hannah nodded, still trying to catch her breath. "They found her down there, near that band of rock that forms a lateral moraine."

Rex slipped the pack off his shoulders. It thunked to the ground. He took sunglasses out of his pocket and shielded those eyes. Hannah was glad for her own dark lenses. The glare off the glacier was blinding.

"I recognize it from the television news coverage." He turned and followed the trail with his eyes. "Does that lead up to Grizzly Hut?"

"Yup." She held her hand to her brow, shading her eyes, and looked up the trail. "Grizz Hut is the first in a series of huts along a loop of a trail through the backcountry. The cabins are really quite rustic, basic stuff. They're used by hikers in the summer and skiers in winter. It's not in the ski area boundary.''

"How far to the hut?"

"About a five-minute hike from this point." She sat on a rock outcrop alongside the trail and stared down at the stony gray ledge close to where Amy had been entombed for a winter. She pointed at the rope. "They take that down when there is enough snow and people ski here. Thousands must have gone right over her while she lay sleeping under the ice."

Rex sat beside her. She could feel the warmth emanating from his muscular thigh. The hair on his olive-toned skin was dark. He was looking at the moraine where the glacier dropped sheer and almost vertical below it.

"I saw you on TV."

"What?"

"On the news, when they found Amy's body." He was still assessing the scene. "And I saw Mitchell in his suit, and a man beside you, thick hair, mostly gray. I thought I recognized him but it turns out I don't know him. It was Dr. Gunter Schmidt."

"Oh, right. Gunter was up here that day, going for a hike."

"Is that unusual?"

"Hell, no. He's a fitness freak."

"Tell me about him."

Hannah rubbed her nose. It felt cool despite the warmth of the late-morning sun. After noon they would cook up here, but when the sun dipped, the ground could freeze. "Gunter's a nice enough guy. I don't know him that well. Not married. Very European, as you could see. He's well respected for his work and his research in the field of cosmetic surgery."

"Does he socialize much?"

"With Al, he does, and other top dogs in the community, like the mayor and his wife and the CEO of Powder Mountain, that kind of thing. He helped bring the conference to town, the toxicology conference."

Rex turned his attention from the ice to her. "Really?"

"Well, it's no big deal. A gazillion conferences come to the resort each year, some of them on an annual basis. White River sells itself worldwide on its conference facilities. One week it's a gathering for the funeral industry, the next, a world trade organization and everything in between."

"But Gunter had a specific interest in the International Association of Toxicologists Conference this year?"

"He told the mayor it would be good for the community, that more of these scientific organizations may follow suit. The way I understand it, Gunter was instrumental in getting the resort to put in the bid to host it."

"So, Gunter Schmidt, plastic surgeon extraordinaire, wanted those particular delegates in White River."

Hannah picked up a stone and tossed it down onto the ice, watching it slide and bounce its way down to the moraine. "Is that so curious?"

"Mmm. I've seen that list of delegates. Interesting participants, scientists who were disenfranchised after the end of the cold war. Some are for sale to the highest bidder. And there are countries attending who unofficially thumb their noses at biological weapons control. Gatherings like this are not uncommon, but it is what brought me here, and it looks like that's what brought the CIA, too."

She tossed another pebble, harder, faster, this time. Who did Rex really work for? And who would've thought that White River, the small town where she'd come to hide, to raise her son, was looking to be the center of some sinister international affair. What had Amy stumbled into?

"And Dr. Gregor Vasilev, how well is he known about town?"

"I really don't know Gregor at all. He's been around for dinner once or twice. He's not that forthcoming. I just know that he's Gunter's right hand, literally, when it comes to surgery. I suspect he's being groomed to take over the clinic when Gunter can't hold back the inevitable tide of retirement any longer."

Rex picked up a stone and launched it in a skittering chase after Hannah's pebble. "What about the rest of the staff at the spa? Where do they come from?"

"Many are local. I've heard potential employees get a pretty thorough screening."

Rex stood up, stretched like a bear and hefted the pack onto his back. He held out his hand to Hannah. "How're you feeling. How's that rib?"

She grabbed on to his arm and pulled herself up. "Good, actually. I'm feeling really strong today. Thanks, Doc."

The elevation gain to Grizzly Hut was minimal, but the scenery spectacular. There was freedom out here. Rex sucked it down into his lungs. He would love to see the night sky from this vantage point.

By the time they reached the hut, the sun was high and white in the heavens. The clouds on the northern horizon had bubbled higher and changed shape as Rex watched. The view of Hannah's backside wasn't bad, either. He was enjoying the low level of arousal he experienced as he hiked behind her, watching her muscles flex in those long lean legs, the curve of her behind in her shorts, the fall of her ponytail sashaying across her back.

She stopped suddenly and bent forward to tighten the

lace of her boot, her shorts exposing more of the back of those lean, tanned thighs. Something slipped in his belly. All he had to do was reach forward and grab her around the waist...

She turned around to face him, and he adjusted his sunglasses. Now was not the time. They had work to do.

"The cabin is there."

He saw where she pointed—a rustic, wooden A-frame building set off the ground, presumably because of deep winter snowpack. Beyond the hut was an aquamarine tarn, still as glass, fringed on one side by a tumble of sharp white-gray rock and scree.

He blew out a whistle. "This is breathtaking."

He set down his pack and offered Hannah some water. He drank after her. "I can see the young reporter coming up here to meet her amour for a little romantic rendezvous."

"Yeah, but with some gear, a sleeping bag, candles, maybe a bottle of wine."

"Now, there's an idea."

Rex followed Hannah up the wooden steps. Inside the smell was woodsy, a little damp. There was a large map tacked to the one wall, a couple of bunks, a table and two benches and an old blackened woodstove. From the window he could see the tarn.

Groups of hikers and skiers would've come and gone since Amy was supposed to meet Grady here. If that was even what happened. He pulled the young reporter's notebook out of his pack and flipped it open to the inside of the hard cover.

He read the notations again. "Grady, Grizz Hut, 5 p.m., to trail. Meeting. BW. Urgent."

BW. In his world that stood for biological weapons. In Amy's world it could stand for anything, but judging by the books in her apartment, she could well have understood the significance behind those two little letters.

Rex moved over to study the laminated map tacked to the wall. Little dotted lines in black and red denoted connecting trails. What connection did Amy Barnes have to CIA agent Ken Mitchell, he wondered. His name was in her apartment, in the books. Rex had also found Grady's name in Mitchell's hotel room. The links were there. He just couldn't see where they led.

"To trail." What did those words mean to Amy as she jotted them in her notebook?

"Hannah, can you get down to the spa on a trail from here?"

She came and stood close beside him to examine the map. He could breathe in her smell. Soapy, clean, mixed with the salty warmth of exercise.

She pointed up at the map. Her arm smooth, the muscles lean and defined. "You can. But you have to go down here, to where you can cross White River and get onto the flanks of Moonstone." She traced a thin dotted black line with her finger. "Over here is a cable crossing with a little tram thing hikers use to pull themselves over the water. It joins the trail on the opposite side."

She pushed delinquent tendrils of gold off her face. "The river at that point runs through a really deep, narrow gorge. I don't even know if that tram is still operational. I haven't been that way in years."

"Let's go take a look, shall we? How far is it, do you think?" He ran his eyes over the cabin interior slowly as he spoke. He was trained to notice anomalies.

"About half an hour, at least, I should think."

Something caught his eye, almost beneath the leg of the table. It was trapped between the gap in the floorboards. He bent, tried to fish it out. He couldn't get at it with his fingers. It was wedged tight.

"What did you find?" Hannah was at his side, bending down to see, her hair falling and teasing his face. He could detect the faint scent of vanilla.

"You're blocking my light. Step back a minute." Rex flicked open his pocket knife. "It's probably nothing, but I have a hunch."

"Don't tell me, you always follow your hunches."

"It's kept me alive."

Rex used the blade to lever the glass vial carefully out from between the floorboards. It was still stoppered, the remnants of a clear liquid evident inside.

He reached into the pocket of his pack, emptied two power-bar snacks from a plastic bag and dropped the vial inside, securing the bag.

"What do you think it is?"

"Not sure. It could've been left by anyone, but it was stuck tight in the boards which means it could've been here awhile."

"You mean like from when Amy went missing?"

"We have a lab in Vancouver where we sometimes contract work. I can have it couriered there overnight for analysis. Then we can talk about possibilities."

Hannah drew her brow down, the furrows pinching in above her nose. She was irritated by his guarded release of information. It would irritate any journalist, especially this one. He reached out and smoothed the lines of her brow with his fingers. "It doesn't become you."

She turned from him and stomped toward the cabin door. Rex knew the depths of Hannah's insatiable curiosity. She was being extraordinarily controlled. Either that or her silence was an indication of anger. The cabin door slapped shut behind her.

Rex sighed, ran his hand through his hair. She was in too deep already. He couldn't keep her totally out of the loop. He needed her continued cooperation. Christ, he needed her. Period.

He jerked to his feet, swung open the door. "Hannah!"

She stopped, turned slowly to face him. Her face said it all, her features a painful mix of anger, hurt, betrayal. And he knew it wasn't just about the vial.

"I'm sorry," he called out to her. *In more ways than one.*

She said nothing. Just stared up at him on the cabin steps.

"Okay. I'll stay on the level with you. I want to see if the stuff in the vial is related to the stuff found in Grady Fisher's room after his accident."

She took a step toward him. "You think it might be liquid GHB?"

"Who knows? A test will rule it out if it's not. If it is, we *may* be placing Grady Fisher in the hut. Or we may be placing someone else here. Someone who drugged Grady with GHB. But really, that's all it might prove."

"You think someone used GHB on Amy?"

"One step at a time, Hannah."

The climb down into the White River watershed was steep. Hannah could feel a slight tremble in her knees by the time they reached the cable over the river. Far down in the rocky cleft between the two mountains, a steam of spray rose above the white noise of the river. She shivered, holding on to her elbows, hugging herself, the memory of her fall into this same river etched fresh in her brain.

Rex placed a large hand on each of her shoulders. "It's okay, Hannah. If the thing is not secure, we turn back." His presence as a protector, big and strong, was comforting. It was a childish notion. She knew that. Yet she felt she could trust him. With her body, anyway. Not with her psyche. He'd done enough damage to her spirit.

"You wait here. I'll take a look at that thing."

"It's a thing all right." The two cables looked solid and taut enough. Hannah saw they were joined on each end to a steel A-frame structure fixed into rock on either side of the gorge. A metal car, a box really, rested at their end.

The idea was to climb into the box that hung from a pulley on the top cable. Hikers then pulled themselves across the crevasse by hand, using the lower cable.

She watched as Rex tugged on the cables. She loved his hands, the thickness and power of his forearms. He stepped into the box, bouncing his weight against the resistance of the strands of metal.

"Looks good." He started to pull himself across, setting out as their guinea pig.

The cable bowed under his weight, dipping to a definite sag at the middle. Hannah held her breath. Rex stopped and jounced the car, high above the steaming water. It held. She relaxed as she saw him pulling, hand over hand on the cord of metal, back to her side.

"Works just fine." He stepped out, hefted his pack onto his back and held out a hand for Hannah. "All aboard."

She tried not to look down at the hungry, steaming maw below. Fine droplets of spray reached up from their depths to taunt the two of them as they hung high above. They moved slowly, jerking across, drawn by the power of Rex's arms.

Once safely on the far end of the gorge, Hannah rubbed at the indentation in her hands. She'd been gripping the edge of the metal box way too tightly. This whole business was getting to her.

They started the last leg of the climb down to the vast

spa property that sprawled out over the Moonstone foothills.

They were deep in the cool shadow of Moonstone peak
when they came abruptly up against a fence. "Stop!" Rex
pulled her back, pointed to the bright orange symbols of
a man being zapped by lightning.

"It's electrified?"

He nodded. "Must run for miles." The charged fence,
about eight feet high, snaked into the distance through
trees and brambles of berry bushes. Rex pointed to a security camera. There were others like it placed at intervals
along the property line. "These guys mean business," he
whispered.

A crude road, two depressions of tires molded into the
ground, ran alongside the fence. Rex and Hannah followed the road for what seemed like a mile, keeping to
the trees in an attempt to stay out of the camera scopes.
Hannah felt furtive, as if she were some criminal sneaking
up along the spa property line like this.

Rex pointed. "Gate. Careful. Don't touch the wire."

Hannah could see that whatever vehicle traveled this
rude path used this back entrance to the spa property. At
the moment the gate was locked shut. She leaned forward
trying to get a better view of the dull gray concrete buildings inside the enclosure. They were tucked in beyond a
stand of conifers. She didn't know there were additional
buildings on the spa land.

Rex pulled her back suddenly into the tress, quietly
pointing up to a camera mounted on a rod. It swiveled in
their direction. She could hear dogs barking in the distance, closing in.

"More cameras," he whispered. "Guard dogs."

He pulled her briskly back along the path. "Let's go
before the hounds arrive. I really don't feel like explain-

ing to Dr. Gunter Schmidt why we tried to come in the back way."

Hannah scrambled behind Rex as he led the way along the crude road and back up the trail toward the cable crossing. The rough vehicle track veered off down to the left as their trail took a fork up to the right. "See that?" He pointed to the track. "It must run from the property here down into White River Park, where you go jogging. You can probably access this through the back of the park and get down to the highway."

Hannah's lungs were raw by the time they reached the dreaded metal box. Pain nagged at her injured rib as she panted. Her thighs burned.

The sound of barking dogs faded into the distance.

"Whew. What was that about?" Rex swiped the back of his hand across his forehead.

Hannah didn't have the energy to answer. She struggled to regain her breath against the pain of her injury.

Rex let the heavy pack slide from his shoulders with a thunk to the ground. He dug out the water bottle, offered it to Hannah. His back was damp where the pack had rested.

Pain seared across her ribs as she downed the liquid. She'd have to take it easy the rest of the way.

"Looks like Dr. Schmidt and the spa gang are real serious about security."

"I guess paparazzi can be quite persistent." Her words came in breathy bursts.

"Paparazzi? You've got to be kidding? I can't see it, not back here."

"Hey, if they rent helicopters to spy on a hot movie star they could easily climb out this way to nab a picture and make a quick buck."

"True enough. But I sure didn't see any movie star types back there. And dogs, cameras, electric fences?

Seems extreme." He helped her into the cable car and started hauling them across the gorge. "I'm guessing Gunter uses that back gate when he goes hiking. Maybe his 'guests' use it, too. Access to the wilderness backyard, one of the spa perks." His words came like gusts, with each powerful heft of his hands as he hauled them over the gorge.

"Yeah, well one of those spa perks is absolute confidentiality. Perhaps the heavy security guarantees that."

He grunted. "Perhaps."

The path back up to Grizzly Hut seemed steeper on the return. Hannah was relieved to reach a sunny clearing fringed by fireweed at the halfway mark. She flopped onto the ground.

Rex looked down at her, raised an eyebrow. "Time for a lunch break?"

"Don't look at me like that! It's way beyond lunch. And did you hear me complaining?"

A grin tugged at the corner of his lips. He checked his watch. "Like I said, I've got bad habits."

"You're telling me," she muttered.

"What's that, you said?"

"Nothing. What's in that picnic they packed for you?" She nodded toward his pack—then froze.

She heard a sound.

A huff.

The sound was a mixture of forced wind and a bark. She knew instantly what it was. It curled the fine hairs on the back of her neck and shot adrenaline through her system.

They were downwind from the sound. Good.

She stood up quietly and placed her hand on Rex's forearm in firm, silent warning.

Rex stilled at the urgency in her touch.

She had her finger on her lips, eyes wide. Then she

moved her hand from her mouth to slowly part the dying fireweed. Her gentle gesture sent a silent flurry of soft white fluff into the air. Seeds like snow in summer. Some settled on her hair, a nimbus of gold covered in white fluffs of confetti. She looked like a beautiful mountain bride. The sight of her like that threw Rex. It was a punch to the gut, just the thought of it.

She whispered. "There. Over there."

He turned to follow her hand.

"They don't know we're here. We're downwind."

Yards from where they crouched behind the curtain of fireweed, a hulk of a black beast lumbered toward a smaller honey-colored bear. The big beast's stance was aggressive. Rex figured he must weigh at least five-hundred pounds.

A small black cub moved confusedly, bleating at the golden-brown sow's feet.

"Black bear." She kept her voice low.

"But that one's blond."

"Yes," she whispered. "Black bears come in a range of colors."

Another whoof came in a rush of air from the sow's chest. She stomped her feet, legs stiff and she chomped her jaws making popping sounds, warning off the male. Then she made another little sound, a pleading noise. It sent her cub scampering up a conifer.

The tiny bear made plaintive little noises, crying out to its mother as she fended off the massive male predator below. Rex figured the baby bear's sounds were something between a little goat and a lamb.

The mother bear held her ground as the male paced, irritably, back and forth.

"He's looking to mate with her." Hannah whispered

in his ear. "She won't accept him as long as she has a young cub with her."

The smaller honey-brown bear charged at the massive male, her thick golden-brown fur rippling over her body.

It was a mock charge, but there was nothing deceptive about her intentions. Rex figured she would probably die fighting to protect her little one hanging in the tree. She'd kill to get this male out of her space.

The large bear moved to the left and then the right, evaluating, swaying his heavy head side to side, before slowly retreating.

The sow had beaten him off.

Hannah's hand was still tight on his forearm. He could feel adrenaline humming through his blood.

"Typical."

He looked at her. "What?"

She was still whispering. "The male impregnates the sow and then leaves her alone to fend for the offspring while he goes off, wandering to find another mate." Her eyes were flashing gold sparks of anger. "If that little cub is a male, the big bear will kill it in a few years if it doesn't move on out of his way and find its own territory."

He was surprised at her sudden vehemence. "It's the way of the wild, Hannah. You can't personify."

She paused, looking into his eyes, searching. "It's about propagating the species. Sex. Not that much more to it than that. Is there?"

And she wasn't talking about bears. She wasn't far off. At least that was his experience.

But what he felt for Hannah, that was different.

Sure it was about lust and sex. Exquisite sex. But he wanted more. He wanted to grow old with this woman. To share her spirit for life. To keep her safe. He cared for her.

But he'd known from a young age you didn't get something just because you wanted it. And keeping her safe meant keeping his life and what he did for a living separate from her.

It was best for both of them.

Yet after last night, the world looked a little different. Something deep inside him had shifted. He wasn't sure what. He felt a sudden sick little slide in his stomach at the thought of what they were doing to each other.

He looked back through the fireweed at the mother bear. She was calling her cub down from the tree. Gentle, encouraging little sounds.

He studied Hannah's face as she watched the little cub scamper and slide backward down the tree. Her eyes shimmered with emotion. This vignette was tugging at her heart strings.

He touched her gently on the arm. ''Perhaps we should take our own picnic elsewhere.''

''Right. We should move on. I'm not really hungry anymore, anyway.'' Her tone was melancholy as she started slowly up the trail, her shoulders slightly slumped. She was tired. They should rest at the cabin.

He hefted his pack onto his back and followed in her steps, pondering her sudden switch in mood.

It was close to five o'clock when they reached Grizzly Hut, almost time for the last gondola ride down.

Rex set his pack down on the wooden stairs leading up to the hut, noting the pile of chopped wood tucked under them.

Hannah sat on a rock nearby. She looked so alone, so tired against the vast backdrop of sky. He went to her. ''We have choices, Hannah.''

''I know.''

''We can catch the last gondola down. We can hike

down once we've rested a little. Or, we could camp out here. I came prepared.''

She looked up at him. "Prepared?"

"I have a sleeping bag. Just in case. It's big enough for two."

A flicker of humor lit her eyes, chasing away the shadows he'd seen lurking there. "You're something else, Rex. You're a regular Boy Scout, aren't you?"

"Military training."

"Right." She sighed and looked out over the amphitheater of peaks. "I don't have the energy for a hike down." She took a deep careful breath, as if her rib was troubling her again. "And I really don't feel like going back down to join reality right now." She smiled, gentle, soft, a little sad, up at him. "Let's camp."

"My thoughts exactly. You need to rest. And it doesn't look as if anyone has the cabin booked for tonight. There's wood, and I have sustenance."

"And that, I need."

"Why don't you unpack the food? It's in the pack. I'll get a fire going out here."

He looked out over the jagged horizon. Those mushrooming white clouds he'd seen earlier were now clustering, dense and black, in the distance. "It looks like the weather will hold for some time yet. We can move into the hut later."

"What about getting that vial you found to the lab?"

"It can wait." It had to wait. He needed time with Hannah. He had a sense it was running out. And he wasn't ready to let go yet. "I can get it down to Vancouver tomorrow morning and have a same-day result."

Hannah yanked open the top of the backpack still wallowing in thoughts that had flooded her brain as she watched the sow fend for her cub. She believed there was more to life, more than propagating the species and fending for your young. There was friendship, love. It wasn't just the way of the wild, dammit. Humans were more evolved. Weren't they?

She must be more tired than she thought. Rex was right. She was personifying. She shouldn't confuse that battle between the sow and the black beast with her own life. Yet she couldn't ignore the symbolism. It butted against her brain.

She looked up at Rex gathering wood, building a fire, his muscles defined through the woven fabric of his shirt. There was a wildness about him, a dangerous feral quality.

How could she expect, or even dream, of love from a man who didn't know love. His family, his father had rejected him. Like that male bear, the colonel had left Rex's mum to feed and shelter him until he was barely old enough to go his own way and carve out his own territory. Alone.

Hannah sensed that the concept of real love, family, was absolutely foreign to Rex. The only real family he'd known was the military. He did his duty. He did what he believed was just and for the greater good of man. He did it out of an honorable sense of duty. But not out of love.

And that wasn't good enough for Danny. Or was she just being selfish? Maybe she owed Rex a chance to be the father the colonel never was. Would he even want that chance?

Oh God, in one day Danny would come home. She had choices to make. She scrunched her eyes shut, squeezing back the emotion that pricked there, and dug into the backpack.

She touched glass, cool and smooth.

The devil.

He had planned this.

Hannah pulled out a bottle of red wine. There was also a blanket, her fleece, a tin of smoked oysters, crackers, cheese, French bread, a container of wild blackberries. A sleeping bag. So this is what he'd been hefting about all day.

"Rex."

He looked up at the sound of her voice.

"You're wicked."

He grinned, a devilish slash of teeth white against the shadow of his sculpted jaw, eyes dancing as bright as the flames licking the wood to life.

Chapter 12

Hannah laid the blanket out near the fire and took two plastic wineglasses from Rex's backpack. "Look at all this. There's got to be a romantic buried deep in that hard heart somewhere."

He just winked at her as he uncorked the bottle. Wine burbled rich and red into the glasses, the fire cracked and shot sparks of bright orange high into the thin Alpine air.

The far-off indigo in the dome of sky was deepening as the blackness of space crept in for the night.

Hannah leaned back on the roll of sleeping bag propped against a rock and sipped her wine. There was no other sound. Just the pop and crack and whisper of flames. The air was tinged with wood smoke and the scent of old snow and ice. She could see the first star of the evening.

They ate in intimate silence, as if afraid to speak into words the turmoil of emotions each housed in their bodies. Hannah's feelings were beyond the shape of simple words. They were too complex. Too big. What they both needed was time. Time to be with each other. Time to understand.

Time she didn't have.

Time he would never have.

To speak now, at this perfect moment, would bring reality crashing in. She just wanted to savor it. Drink it in. While it lasted.

She lay back, her face turned up to the heavens pricked with pins of light. The moon was rising, an enormous, pale, luminous shape. It was monstrous, so close. She could make out the pocks and craters. It bathed the far-off glacial peaks in an eerie glow. Hannah felt like a speck in space and time. Insignificant.

She started as Rex leaned over and brushed a plump blackberry against her lips. She opened her mouth, took it in, crushing the wild ripe flavor between her teeth. His eyes spoke to her as he took a berry between his own lips, watching her as he crushed it in his mouth.

Then he leaned down above her. Pressed those berry-stained lips against hers. The taste of wine and wild ripe fruit, the scent of smoke, it made her senses swim. Her blood coursed warm through her veins.

His kiss was gentle, lingering, searching, questioning. It brought tears to her eyes. Sweet pain.

"Hannah?"

"Shh, Rex." She raised two fingers to his lips. "Not now."

He nodded, reached out, wiped the wetness from her cheeks and lay back beside her. Together they watched the heavens, fingers laced, fire spitting.

By the time they moved into the cabin, an Alpine wind was whistling softly through the flue of the woodstove and roiling black clouds had blocked the rising moon.

Rex stoked the fire and turned to face Hannah. Her

hands were raised, untying her hair. She let it fall, soft and gold, down onto her shoulders.

She was an angel, teaching him to feel. To want. She made him yearn for things he'd never dreamed possible. Not for him.

She was wearing the large T-shirt he'd brought for her. The swell of her breasts pressed against the soft white fabric. She was kneeling on the sleeping bag he'd laid out on the floor in front of the woodstove, her legs sunbrowned and bare beneath her.

Rex knelt down behind her. The glow of flames flickered and wavered against the cabin walls, making shadows dance. The wind moaned gently through the flue.

From behind he slid his hands up under the T-shirt. He stopped just under the swell of her breasts. He leaned forward, whispered into the fall of her hair. "How's your rib, Hannah? You doing okay?"

She just nodded, leaned slightly into him.

"You were pretty tired coming back up the mountain."

"I feel more rested now. It's just so much has happened—"

He nuzzled against the smooth warmth of her neck. "I know."

"Rex, there's something I have to tell you. I—"

He slipped his hands, one over each breast feeling the soft, heavy weight of them. Her nipples reacted immediately to his touch, spitting hot fire to his groin.

He held her, whispered into her ear. "What did you want to tell me?"

She gave a small shiver. "Nothing. It can wait." Her voice was thick, throaty. Aroused. It fueled the need growing tight against his clothing. His chest felt tight. Oh, how he needed this woman.

She reached, hands behind her back and found the buttons of his shorts. Her fumbling there took the blood from

his head. All his heat settled into an almost painful throbbing desire between his thighs.

She found her way through the buttons, slipped her
hand into his shorts. He tried to speak. It came out a low
groan. He stood to free himself of his clothing and then
he bent to lift the T-shirt from her body.

The sight of her stole his breath.

She knelt, in front of the flickering warmth of the
flames, in white panties, breasts bare, dusky nipples
pointed. She looked up at him, her lids heavy with need
over those leonine eyes.

He knelt slowly down behind her and ran his fingers
from her neck firmly down the ridges of muscle that cradled her straight spine. She shivered under his hands,
arching her back. He coaxed her to kneel forward on
hands and knees. She took his lead, holding her chin high,
hair splaying down her back. He slowly removed her
panties, ran his hands over her, kneading, squeezing her
full, soft, firm buttocks.

She moaned, arched farther, exposing the mound of
rough gold curls between her legs.

The sight of her like that swallowed him in primal
need.

He slid his hand over that mound protruding out from
between her thighs and felt her heat. She moved against
his hand, parted her knees wider, dipped her back farther,
opening herself wider to him.

He stroked those engorged, swollen lips until she glistened with desire, until his fingers were slick with her
need. Then he thrust his fingers deep into her. She pushed
back, onto his hand. Her moan was feral. His need wild.

He took her like that. Mounted her. Rocked into her as
she braced with her hands against the force of his thrusts,
breasts bouncing in the flicking light.

The heat sang in his core as he plunged repeatedly into

her. She threw her head back, arching her back, her hair a wild mane. And he heard her noise. Animal, as wave upon blinding wave crashed over them. The sound was deafening in his ears.

Sated, they lay together, in silence, as the flames in the woodstove slowly died to glimmering coals and the depth of night closed in. The wind was more plaintive now, a low wail. A loose board clacked intermittently against the Alpine hut. Through the little window, ripples skittered across the surface of the tarn.

Rex had a sense time had run out. Something between them had crested. He didn't know what lay on the other side. He rolled onto his side and looked at her.

She smiled up at him. But he could see a sadness in her eyes.

He brushed her cheek with his hand. And he knew then that he wanted to come back here, to the White River Mountains, in the winter. He wanted to ski wild down the slopes with her, cut through fine powder as deep as his knees, to hear her laugh at the spray of fine crystals against her cheeks. He wanted to spend nights in deep snowbound backcountry huts. To make infinite love.

But there was the Bellona Channel. There was her safety.

Choices.

Scott had made a choice. He'd taken a wife and they'd borne a child, but Scott's job had cost them their lives. He couldn't take that road. Not after having seen what happened to Scott. Not after that letter he got threatening Hannah's life in Marumba. He couldn't have both, Bellona and Hannah.

Choices.

He lay on his back and looked up at the rafters of the wooden hut. For the first time ever, he thought about the possibility of leaving Bellona. A life-style change. He couldn't do fieldwork forever. He'd have to face that sometime. Old injuries were acting up. And there were young guns bucking for a crack at his position.

This golden angel resting at his side had opened a door. Just a crack, but through it he glimpsed something. Something he had never dreamed possible. A life, a future with love.

But he needed time. To work it all out. Perhaps he could come back and spend time with her in the winter. They needed to bridge the pain of old wounds.

"Rex." She sat suddenly up, sleeping bag pulled around her, voice still deliciously thick from passion.

"We need to talk, Rex."

He lifted himself up onto one elbow and studied her face. Her lips were still stained from berries, swollen from his kisses.

"Yes. We need to talk."

"This job you do. I have to ask, what can you tell me about it? What can I know?"

He knew this would come.

"I can't talk about it, Hannah. I need you to understand that."

Her eyes bored into his. "I don't."

He hesitated. "I work for a covert agency. You were right. The Bio Can thing is a cover, but I can't go into specifics."

She looked away.

"Hannah, it's not just about me. Others depend on the secrecy, the loyalty of this organization I work for."

"And you can't even tell me what 'this organization' is called, after all we've been through, after the fate Amy suffered?"

Rex felt sick. This woman had worked the world as a foreign correspondent. She was no babe in the international woods. He couldn't lie to her. If he wanted to be with her, he'd have to trust her. Implicitly. But even then, he could be putting her life in danger, like Scott's wife. Like Scott's kid.

"You don't trust me, is that it?"

"I trust you. God, woman, I care for you more than anything in the damned world."

"Then why can't you be open with me?"

"Because I can't dammit! Because you've scrambled my radar. You're taking me places I am unfamiliar with right now. I don't know the boundaries. I need time."

She reached out, grabbed the voluminous T-shirt, pulled it over her head. She wrapped her arms tight over her knees and stared into the dying embers. When she spoke, her voice was low, with an edge he hadn't heard before. "Why'd you leave me that night, Rex?"

He reached forward to touch her. She shrugged him off. "Why?"

"I had to."

"Your job?"

"Yes."

"I see." She faced him square, chin set in defiance, her eyes narrowed. "It's been good, Rex. The sex."

"Hannah. I want to be with you. Always." The words came out of his mouth before his head had formed them. They came from his gut. But they were true. More true than anything he'd said in a long, long time.

Her eyes widened. "What?"

"You heard me. Be with me."

She blew out a breath in frustration. "All these years, Rex, and you walk back into my life and tell me this."

"I just need some time. To work things out."

She was studying him, her eyes probing. "What about kids, Rex? What if we ever wanted children? Would you just get up and leave in the night because the job called? Would your children not see you for years?"

Rex Logan, Bellona agent, felt suddenly lost. Hollow. Afraid even. She was pushing his boundaries back into black uncharted territory. He'd seen it coming. Yet he felt himself instinctively closing up in defense.

"You see," she said, moisture welling up in her gold eyes. "It can't work. Ever. This job you do, it *is* your life, your family. There's no room for more. Please don't try and take any more from me." Her lashes were wet with tears but her voice was determined.

She'd pushed him into a corner. He didn't like that. It made him want to lash out. He was angry. With himself for getting them to this point. With her for having this power over him. She'd had that power the moment he'd first seen her in Marumba.

Now as he looked at her, amber in the fading firelight, he felt as if he was on the edge of losing her forever. She was slipping from his grasp.

Her eyes held his, glinting, waiting for him to speak.

He felt a tightening in his chest. Panic? It was something he never let in, yet here it was. He was afraid to lose her. Couldn't lose her. Emotions he'd long learned to keep in check were seeping, simmering, bubbling to the surface. Like the molten core of a volcano finding its way to light.

"Hannah, I want more. You've shown me there is more. I'm prepared to make changes. But give me time to try and wrap things up, sort them out. I need to think about this. I need to see if I can make it work that we can be together."

"Don't do me any favors, Rex."

"Christ, Hannah, I'm trying here. I want to be with you. Forever. I love you, damn it!"

She sat back, as shocked as he was at the words that had come from his lips. A fat tear slid down her cheek. She stared at him.

He reached and wiped it gently from her face. "I want to make it work," he whispered. "Like I've wanted nothing before, Hannah. Help me make it work."

She took his hands. "You mean it, don't you?"

"I mean it."

"Then you will tell me why you walked that night."

"I had to."

She sighed. Looked away. "And children?"

God, when she moved, she sure moved. She was covering years of ground here. He was thinking of just one step. One little step at a damn time.

Kids. He thought of Scott's child, dead. He thought of himself as a boy. He had vowed he would never visit the same kind of lonely pain on a child. Yet the thought of her bearing his children was intoxicating. He hesitated before speaking. "Kids were never part of my plan."

Something shuttered in her eyes.

"Hannah, I don't know how to be a father."

Something shifted in her features. She was closing him out, slipping from his fingers as he watched. He reached out. She gently pushed his hand away and lay back, silent, closing her eyes. Tears slid out from under her lids.

He didn't know what to say. Hell, he didn't know what he felt. He had no idea what had just happened. He lay back beside her, unspoken words hanging thick and heavy in the dark air. The loose slat of wood banged louder against the hut, insistent. The whine of the wind in the flue rose, plaintive, as the storm moved in.

She didn't know how long she had lain awake, the black cold of night creeping in around her as the embers died a slow death. She had listened to his rhythmic breathing for what seemed like hours, wondering at his capacity to sleep. She must have fallen asleep herself, sometime close to dawn.

Now in the harsh dull gray light of morning, she knew she couldn't tell him. She couldn't bring herself to tell him about her son. His son.

He didn't want kids. There was no room in his life for her, let alone a ready-made family. She did not want her little boy to face the kind of rejection Rex himself had. And she did not want to live the life of her mother, waiting for a man she craved with every pore in her body, while he toyed around the world carrying secrets he'd never share.

She had to amputate herself from him. Now, while she still could. Before the cancer of this relationship consumed her. Then she had to work at rehabilitating herself—again. Except, this time she would never let him back in. This time she would be the one who walked away. For good.

He wasn't there beside her when she woke, her eyes thick with dried tears. She lay now, stiff as the floorboards under her, the wind an insistent wail, the storm front closing in.

They would have to hurry and try to get the gondola back to the village before high winds shut it down.

She fumbled for her clothes, fingers cold, clumsy.

She stepped over the sleeping bag, reaching for the cabin door. The wind whipped it from her hand as she opened it, slicing splinters into her skin. It crashed back against the side of the hut.

He stood there in the bleak dawn, out on the edge of the cliff. His arms were fisted at his sides, feet astride. He faced the storm as it loomed, out on the horizon. He faced clouds broiling black, purple, puce. He stood, unflinching, as lightning cut sharp, jagged streaks through the sky. The thunder rumbled, echoed and reverberated through the peaks around them like the artillery of warring armies. His sleeves billowed against his strong arms in the wind, his hair a dark and disheveled mass.

The sight stopped Hannah dead.

He looked as if he were the god that had summoned the storm. Wild. Crazed.

He turned as she approached. His Arctic eyes cold, framed by dark lashes, as angry as the weather.

"Come." He stepped down off the rocks and strode past her, making for the hut. He gathered their gear and stuffed it into his pack. "Hurry. Lifts will shut down any minute now."

She pulled her fleece up against her neck as she followed him, trying to keep pace, stumbling over the small rocks in the path. The wind dropped as they rounded the peak and saw the gondola building below. There was some protection there. The lift was still running. For now.

The gondola doors closed on them, encapsulating their silence as the cab lurched from its moorings and began its descent down Powder Mountain. The storm was closing in fast now. Wind buffeted their glass cocoon. Thick drops of rain started to spit and flick sporadically against the windows.

"Rex."

He looked at her, those Siberian husky eyes detached. He'd already closed her out. Just like that. Like before, in Marumba.

"I'll go into the office today. Pack my bags."

"You're not going anywhere."

The gondola lurched, and she grasped at the railing for balance. Far-off black clouds glimmered as they were backlit by a burst of sheet lightning. A purple and orange tinge lit the dawn, an ominous hue preceding the storm.

"I must go." She had to escape his charged presence.

"Not until I can be sure there'll be no more attempts on your life. Then you can go."

She had known he'd say that. Still it burned, the fact that he was prepared to let her go once his job was done. "All the staff will be at the office. I'll be safe there. You can speak to Al if you like. He can call you on your cell if there's something to worry about."

Hannah had no intention of returning to the hotel once she packed her bags. Not ever. Danny would be home tomorrow. If she didn't feel safe, the two of them could pack their car and head north until everything had blown over.

She would go back to the hotel now. She'd shower, pack her things and take everything to the office with her. She had to sever her ties. Now.

He was mulling over her proposal, deep furrows in his tanned brow. It made him, his anger, all the more awesome.

"Fine. I'll take you to the office. You're not to leave there. I'll call you and let you know when I'm coming to pick you up. I'll speak to Al."

She'd be long gone before he could come and pick her up.

"Fine."

Drops of rain the size of small marbles bombed into the earth and erupted into minute clouds of dust as they pulled into the village gondola station. The scent of rain clashing with soil was earthy, musky. It was still only the front end of what was yet to come. The sky was heavy, laden with its dark burden, waiting to burst and spill its sorrow.

White noise rushed in Hannah's head as she pushed through the crowds in the village. There were people everywhere; they scampered for cover from the heavy drops. The weather was crashing in on their parade. Clowns and jugglers were packing up their bright red and yellow and orange sacks. Some acts continued under eves. Bongo drums beat. Her heart echoed the primal sound in her ribs as she hurried toward the hotel.

The large lobby was crowded with delegates coming in for the international conference. Suits, saris, turbans, a gaggle of tongues. She pushed wildly through them, knowing that Rex was struggling to keep up with her. She jabbed the elevator button, closing the doors before he could reach her.

She wasn't sure what she was trying to achieve. She was running on blind instinct. From him. But she was held up at the hotel room door as she had to wait for him and his key card.

She averted her eyes from him as he opened the door and checked out the room before permitting her to enter.

She marched into her side of the suite, closed the door and made for the bathroom to turn on the shower.

She could hear his cell phone start to ring just as water spurted into the tub. Then all other sound was drowned out. She closed the door, finding comfort in the fog of steam that reached up and enveloped her.

"Logan, hey buddy."

At the sound of Scott's voice, Rex punched in the code to activate the scrambler installed in his cell phone. The red LED indicator showed voice encryption had been initiated. It was a sophisticated point-to-point system. Scott had a similar device on his end. Their communication was secure from eavesdroppers.

"Hey, Scott, any info for me?"

Scott knew Rex better than most people. When the agent's wife and daughter were killed, he'd turned to Rex. They'd become close friends.

The two of them had worked on the Marumba mission. When Ken Mitchell had botched the raid and the lab had burned, the Plague Doctor had slipped back underground.

A week later Scott and Rex each got hand-delivered letters from paid messengers with similar wording: "You will pay for crossing me. Your loved ones will die a most horrible, painful death."

Rex had been in Ralundi, camping with Hannah when his message came in the dark of night. Their safari guide had accepted the letter from a Marumba local paid to deliver it. The local had slipped back into the night, and Rex had read the letter by the light of the campfire while Hannah slept in the tent. He had no doubt it had come from the Plague Doctor. And he did not underestimate the danger.

He'd made an immediate decision. Packed and left before dawn broke. No one would use Hannah to threaten him. If they thought she was his reject, she'd be useless to them. She'd be safe.

Scott had also received his letter in Marumba, the night before he was due to ship out. He had believed his wife and daughter were safe back in Toronto. But he was never to see them again. A few days later they died in an horrific car accident. Their vehicle went up in a ball of flames. No one was sure of the cause.

Scott had not been able to save his family. Rex had saved Hannah, but at a cost, to both of them.

He was only beginning to see the extent of that cost now.

"We're still working on your requests, Rex. Should have a full report for you later in the day, but I wanted to get word to you immediately on Ken Mitchell."

"What you got?"

"If the CIA is in White River for this conference, it's not via Mitchell."

"What?"

"He hasn't worked for the CIA for about a year now.

My sources say old Kenny Mitchell went whacko after the Marumba lab fire.''

"Go on.''

"Well, it appears that after the fire, he took it real personal that he'd been responsible for sending the Plague Doctor into the underground to continue with his work. He became obsessed with finding him to the point of irrationality. They had to take Mitchell off that beat, but he still spent his days and nights trying to hunt the Plague Doctor down. Last year he was dismissed from the agency. Mental instability.''

"You buy this?''

"You mean do I think it was just the ploy of a double agent to get out from under the CIA? I don't think so.''

"So what has Mitchell been up to in this past year, then.''

"That's why I don't think he was scamming. Mitchell was institutionalized late last fall. He was becoming a bit of a public hazard in his zeal. I think CIA brass was worried he might be a loose cannon with serious secrets to spill.''

Scott cleared his throat and continued. "According to my sources, Mitchell was raving to one of the shrinks at the institution about a young reporter up in Canada. He maintained this reporter and her friend had stumbled onto something at a spa in White River. Her friend worked at the spa and reportedly found a secret lab where a surgeon was working on some superpowerful biological agent.''

Now Scott had his attention. Rex paused, listened to make sure he could hear the shower in the next room before continuing. "If Mitchell was locked up in a nut house, how come he's here in White River now?''

"Got out last month. They haven't seen him since. Lost track of him.''

Rex blew air through his teeth. "I'm going to have to

have a little talk with Mitchell and see if I can get into the White River Spa and take a look around myself.''

''Rex, Mitchell…he's unstable. Could be dangerous.''

''Got it. But somehow I don't think he was that loopy when he was talking about a reporter and her friend. Turns out a young reporter here, Amy Barnes, died early last fall. So did her friend, who worked at the local spa. He died only a day later. Somehow they're connected. I'm really going to need that background information on the top two doctors at the spa, Gunter Schmidt and Gregor Vasilev. Looks like we're in deep crap here.''

''I'm on it.''

The shower was still going. ''Oh, and, Scott, I'll be expecting some lab results from Vancouver sometime to-day. I'm going to courier a sample down there as soon as I hang up with you. The lab will phone the results in to Toronto.''

''Good enough.''

''Okay, thanks, buddy.'' The shower was being turned off. ''Speak to you later in the day.''

''Right. Say, have you seen the McGuire woman since you been there?''

Rex had told Scott Hannah was in White River. Scott knew how much it had cost Rex to walk out on her in Marumba.

''Been kinda tough to avoid her. She's gotten herself right into the thick of this.''

''How so?''

''She was suspicious of the reporter's death. She works at the same newspaper. She's been digging around too much and it seems to have landed her in hot water…or should I say some very cold water.''

''So?''

''So what?''

''You know what I mean. I've seen nothing in this

world that can mess with your brain like that hotshot foreign correspondent.''

Rex looked over at the closed door of Hannah's room. ''She's not a foreign correspondent anymore. She quit.''

''Why?''

''Damned if I know. Nothing you need to worry your head over. I'm going to wrap this up and then I'm outta here.''

''You know, Rex, if I had to choose, if I had to do it over again, I'd choose my wife and child over anything. Hell, I'd work as a clerk in a gas station just to have them back.''

Rex was silent, taken aback by his colleague's sudden candor.

''You there?''

''Yeah, still here. Sorry, Scott. I know what you're saying. It's just not for me.''

''You know, Killian is thinking of stepping down as Bellona board chair. There's going to be an extra seat there. If you got on the board, you could call the shots instead of dodging bullets out in the field.''

Rex appreciated what Scott was trying to do. ''I'm better in the field, buddy.'' His head was starting to hurt. He rubbed the pain in his temple. ''Never been one for a family, anyway.''

''Word is they're naming you as candidate for the board, Rex. It's an ace opportunity. You get to keep your Bio Can job and you get a shot at a normal life.''

''Normal life. It's a farce.''

''That's the cynic in you speaking. Hey, it worked for me. Until…''

''I'm sorry, buddy.''

Silence.

''Yeah, well, you take care of that McGuire woman. I'll check in later today.''

Rex flipped his phone shut and slipped it into his pocket. His head felt thick. He walked over to the connecting door, turned the knob, pushed it open.

Hannah was gone.

Chapter 13

"Yes, she's here but she's on another call."

Never mind tenacious, that woman was stubborn, infuriating. Rex felt the small muscle in his jaw begin to pulse. "Georgette, put me through to Al Brashear then, please."

"My pleasure."

Al's voice was as rough as Georgette's was pleasant. "Yes, Hannah's here."

"I'm Rex, a friend of Hannah's and I—"

"I know who you are. She'll be fine."

"Look, Al, I'm not sure what Hannah has told you, but she needs to stay inside the office until I come and collect her this afternoon. No going out for lunch, nothing. And I need your help."

"Yeah?"

"Call me at this number if anything strange happens. Anything."

Rex gave Al his cell number. Hannah should be okay

as long as she stayed with her colleagues inside the newspaper office. It would give him time to pay Mitchell a
visit and to see if he could wangle his way into the spa.

Hannah, receiver cradled between ear and shoulder, listened to her mother's voice.

"So, we thought we'd come up a day early, dear.
Danny said he didn't want to miss the circus in the village."

Hannah's mind reeled. Rex. Danny. Home today.
Early. She felt dizzy. Words failed her.

"Hannah, are you there?"

"Uh…yes, Mom. That's great. So, uh, what time do
you think you'll be arriving?"

"Don't fuss or anything. We should be in White River
around four or five this afternoon. I've still got the key
to your house. We'll be there when you get home from
work, sweetheart. I'll fix dinner. We're bringing up some
groceries."

"Thanks, Mom."

Hannah placed the receiver back into the cradle, numb.
She felt as if she was in another time zone. This afternoon. Danny would be home this afternoon.

"You okay, Hannah?"

Al was watching her, blue eyes peering over his thick
half-moon reading glasses.

"Yeah. Thanks, Al. Been a crazy few days." She
rubbed her temples.

"That Rex guy?"

"It's that obvious?"

Al pulled up a chair. "Hannah, this 'friend' of yours,
where'd you meet him?"

She tried to shrug off his question. "Long time ago.
Another place. Another life. So, you ready to edit this
piece or what?"

Al didn't take the bait. He leaned forward. "He's the one who followed you from the Black Diamond the other day, isn't he?"

She looked into his eyes. "Yeah. He's the one."

"Hannah, if you're in trouble—"

"Al, I'm fine."

He nodded. "So how come he's helping us with Amy?"

She swallowed against the tension in her throat. "Al, I really don't want to have secrets from you. I just can't talk about it right now. Can you understand?"

He reached out and patted her arm. "Sure, hon. But tell me, what's this guy's last name?"

She paused. Trapped. "Logan."

"I see." Al pushed his chair back, stood, looked down at her. "Want some tea?"

"Sorry, sir." The clerk smiled up at him. "Mr. Bamfield checked out early this morning."

Damn. Mitchell had left the Fireside Lodge. What was he up to?

Rex walked out of the lodge into a sheet of drenching cold rain. The storm had settled in. He pulled his jacket up over his head and made for the hotel. The wind had died but thunder still reverberated in the peaks.

He would need to break in to the spa tonight, take a look around. But first he'd need backup, someone to watch over Hannah.

He had missed lunch. Once in his hotel room he ordered a late-afternoon snack, coffee and a chicken salad sandwich, and punched in Scott's cell number.

"Hey, any news?"

"Good timing."

"What've you got?"

"First off, Dr. Gunter Schmidt checks out. So does his

partner Dr. Gregor Vasilev. Schmidt's records show he
grew up and trained in Switzerland and worked most recently at an exclusive surgical clinic in Berlin. Vasilev
did his training in Russia, where he apparently developed
some ground-breaking cosmetic surgery techniques at a
spa in Odessa where he worked on top Soviet brass,
among others.''

"Russia, huh? What brought the two of them to White
River?"

"That's where it gets interesting. The White River Spa
has been held for at least a decade by a shell company.
The assets of that shell company are in turn controlled by
a Russian and East German-based consortium, Die Waffenbruder. Loosely translated that means brothers or com-
rades-in-arms. It's never been proven, but Die Waffenbruder is suspected to have links to the Russian mafia and,
more ominously, to money laundering and the financial
backing of some key terrorist organizations.''

Rex whistled through his teeth.

"It appears Die Waffenbruder brought Schmidt and
Vasilev out to head up the spa about five years ago.''

"Sweet Jesus. I'm going to need backup here.''

"One step ahead of you. I'm heading up from Vancouver as we speak.''

Rex laughed. He could always trust Scott. "I'm at the
White River Presidential, room 641. Looking forward to
seeing you. Any luck with the lab reports?"

"Yeah, they gave it top priority. The stuff in the vial
was liquid GHB, gamma hydroxybutyrate. Where'd you
find it?"

"Up in a cabin on Powder Mountain. I suspect it was
used in the death of both the reporter, Amy Barnes, and
her friend Grady Fisher.''

"You been able to link them?"

"Only circumstantially. Mitchell is a common denominator but I haven't been able to find him. I need to get into that spa tonight. If there's something there, they could have it all cleaned out in no time if they get wind we're on to them.''

''Gotcha. I should be up there some time this evening.''

Rex hung up and punched in the *Gazette* phone number. Hannah would probably be knocking off work by now. He could leave her in Scott's care while he checked out the spa under the cover of the storm.

''*Gazette,* how may I help you?''

''Georgette, Rex here.''

''Sorry, Rex, Hannah's not taking calls right now.''

So she was playing games. He felt anger start to prickle. Things were coming to a head and he didn't have time to waste.

''I need to know when I can pick her up.''

''She says she'll be working late this evening.''

''Get her to call me.''

''I will.''

Damn Hannah. He'd give her an hour and then he'd march over there and drag her back himself. He kicked off his shoes and flopped back onto the hotel bed. He lay there, mentally sifting through Scott's findings, trying to join the dots.

Hannah was about to wrap up for the day when she saw Georgette standing wide-eyed at the door of the newsroom. The receptionist was speechless; her jaw hung slack.

Hannah jumped up from her desk. ''Georgie?''

Georgette swayed and reached out for the doorjamb, as if to steady herself. ''It's, it's…oh, God, Hannah…it's…it's your mom—''

Hannah stormed forward, grabbed Georgette by the shoulders. ''What? What's happened, Georgie?''

Hannah could feel Al's hand on her shoulder, restraining her.

"She's...she's on the phone. Line one."

Hannah dived for the receiver. "Mom!"

"Oh, God, Hannah, I'm so sorry. Hannah, I'm so *so* sorry."

Fear dug talons in around Hannah's throat. She couldn't breathe. Danny. She knew. As if by sixth sense, she just knew.

"Where's Danny?" She could hear the hysterical shrill of her own voice. "My God, Mom, where's Danny?" Her hand strangled the receiver. "Tell me!"

"They got him, Hannah. He took him."

"Who?" She screamed down the line now. "Who took him?" Her body was trembling. She could feel Al's hand on her shoulder.

"The man. He was waiting at your house. He—" Her mother broke down into racking sobs.

The sound of her mother crying tempered Hannah. "Where are you, Mom, is someone with you?"

"I'm at the health care center. The police are here. They've just shut down the highway. No one can get in or out of White River. They *will* find him, Hannah."

Her legs buckled under her. She crumpled into her office chair. "Are you okay, Mom, have you been hurt?"

"No, no. Oh my God, I'm so sorry—"

"Mom, put one of the cops on the line."

The officer took the phone immediately. "Corporal Van Kleef here. Miss McGuire, I am sorry you had to find out this way. We do have an officer on his way over to your office."

"What in hell happened? Where's my son?"

"Your mother and son were confronted at your home by a male suspect. Your mother was knocked to the ground and your son was kidnapped. Your mother says she did not recognize the perpetrator.''

She had no time for laborious cop-speak. ''For God's sake, just tell me what he looked like!''

The corporal cleared his throat. ''Big, tall. He wore a gray hooded sweatshirt, baggy pants, a bandanna over his face. He had dark glasses on.''

''Oh my God.'' Hannah covered her mouth with her hand. He fit the description of the man who had tried to kill her. What did he want? Her tongue felt thick, too big for her dry mouth.

''Miss McGuire, we've closed the highway. He won't get out of White River with your son.''

Al took the phone from Hannah, and Georgette rushed to fill a glass of water.

''Rex…I…I have to call Rex.'' Her words came hoarse from her throat. Dazed, she moved to pick up the receiver just as a bright shock of orange hair in the doorway snagged her attention.

A clown.

The ridiculous creature stood where Georgette had stood seconds ago. Mocking. Surreal.

''Hannah McGuire?'' He didn't sound like a clown, but then she didn't suppose she knew what a clown should sound like. Hannah felt like she'd slipped through the looking glass into a bizarre landscape, the numbness of shock laying claim to her body. ''I'm Hannah,'' she told the clown.

He took a clumsy step forward with his long red polka dotted shoe, held out an envelope. ''This is for you.''

Hannah stood, reached forward with her trembling hand and took the envelope. She didn't want to know what was inside.

''Where'd you get this?''

''Someone slipped me a wad of cash to drop it off.''

"No!" She grabbed him as he turned to go. "Who paid you?"

"Some dude in a big gray sweatshirt. I didn't ask questions. Hey, it's raining cats and dogs out there. I wasn't going to make any other cash on the streets today. Gotta go. Got another delivery."

Hannah hardly noticed the clown leave as she fumbled at the envelope, dropping it in her haste. Al bent forward, picked it up off the floor, opened it for her. He held out a piece of plain white paper. She took it from him, read the black block-printed letters: "Come up to Grizzly Hut at once. Talk to no one or your kid dies a most horrible painful death."

Hannah crumpled the paper into a ball in her fist and made mechanically for the door. Like a zombie she reached for her rain jacket, a peaked cap and her ski pass.

"Hannah, where are you going?"

She ignored Al, pushed past Georgette and walked on wooden legs from the newsroom, out of the *Gazette* door, down the steps and into the solid shining sheet of gray-black rain.

Rex turned the facts over and over in his brain. He *knew* Dr. Gunter Schmidt from somewhere, but he still couldn't place him. His cell phone rang, jolting him.

"Rex, here."

"Rex…Hannah, she's gone. Her son has been kidnapped."

"Al?"

"She's left the office."

"What son?"

"Hurry." Panic laced the publisher's voice.

"I'm on my way."

Rex tied his boots, lunged for his jacket and pulled open the door. What did he mean "Hannah's son"?

A clown with a bright shock of orange hair stood, hand raised to knock. He stumbled back in surprise as Rex burst out of the room.

"Uh, are you Rex Logan?"

"What you want?"

The clown handed him an envelope and turned to run in clumsy strides down the hallway. Rex tore open the white envelope, read the black block-printed letters on the plain white sheet of paper. As he absorbed the words he flashed back six years to the plain piece of white paper with black block lettering he'd received in Marumba.

The writing was identical.

He'd never forget it.

It was etched into his brain. The words were almost identical: "We have her. Grizzly Hut. Come or your loved one will die a most horrible painful death."

Your loved one will die a most horrible painful death. The exact same words. He was here in White River. He had to be. The Plague Doctor was here.

Rex shoved the note into his pocket and raced down the corridor to where the clown waited nervously for the elevator. Rex grabbed him by his big bow tie. "Where'd you get that letter?"

Perspiration shone through his white pancake makeup, his red nose askew. "Hey, man. Chill out. A guy paid me, like I told the woman. He gave me cash. He told me the times I must make the deliveries. He said the first letter was to go to the woman at 5 p.m. at the *Gazette* office. Then I was to bring this one here, to you."

The elevator doors opened. Rex grabbed the oversize lapels and shoved the clown up against the wall. "Don't go anywhere, Bozo. The cops will be wanting to talk to you."

The elevator wasn't fast enough. His usual methods of staying calm were not working. Rage clouded his vision.

Rex found Al and Georgette huddled in the newsroom with an RCMP officer. He motioned to Al from the door, behind the officer's back. He didn't need to attract attention to himself just yet. He had to see what he could do before the cops started poking about.

Al excused himself and joined Rex in the reception area.

"What happened?"

"Hannah's son was kidnapped. She got a note from a clown and ran off."

Al's words hit Rex sideways, like a mallet to the head. "Hannah has a son?"

Al sighed, took off his glasses and rubbed the bridge of his nose. "I guess she didn't tell you."

Rex grabbed the front of Al's shirt. "Tell me what?"

"She has a boy. Daniel." Al reached up to remove Rex's hand from where he'd balled his shirt fabric into a fist. "Do you *mind*."

Rex dropped his hand. He was losing it. For Hannah's sake he had to stay in control. "How old is Daniel?"

"Five, going on six. He'll be six in October."

"His father?"

Al positioned his glasses back on his nose. Rex could see he was struggling with the information.

"Where in hell is the boy's father?"

Al looked Rex directly in the eye. "The boy's name is Logan...Daniel Logan McGuire."

Rex felt his stomach slide, as if he had swallowed a heavy, cold stone. His words came out a harsh whisper. "Logan? His middle name is Logan?"

"As in Rex Logan."

"*My* son?"

"He looks like you. I'm sorry it had to come out this way."

Chapter 14

Her rain jacket kept her torso dry and the cap helped with her hair, but her pants were drenched and sticking to her legs by the time she reached the gondola station. Thank God the lift was running. The wind had died, and the lightning had stopped, but rain still poured, relentless.

She held her pass out to the lifty, who looked her up and down as he scanned it. "You know it's snowing heavily in the Alpine at the moment, ma'am?"

"I'm just going up to the restaurant." The restaurant was at midstation. She didn't need to tell anyone she was going right to the top, to Grizzly Hut.

"Well, you're in luck. Only reason we're running the gondola tonight is because of the party up there." He smiled. "The big buffet kicks off the long weekend. Make sure you're down by eleven. That's when we shut down."

"Uh...did you see anyone else go up. A man with a little boy?"

"No kid, ma'am. Just two other guys within the last

hour or two. One and then the other a few minutes after him. Weird thing was they both had cuts on their faces. In the same place, just under the one eye."

Hannah wrapped her arms tightly across her chest as the gondola doors swung shut. She was shivering. From cold. From fear. She was nauseous with worry for Danny.

The cab lurched out into the dark rain and started its climb up into black clouds.

She felt exposed, vulnerable in the glass bubble as it swayed and lurched into the dank mist. She did not get out at midstation, and there was no one to see her continue the last leg of her ride up to the peak.

She willed the car to go faster. As it rose higher, the driving rain turned to thick wet flakes of snow that plastered one side of the gondola. The weather was freakish at this elevation, at this time of year. By the time the sun came out tomorrow the snow would probably all have melted. No sign of it. But where would she be when the sun came out? Would she be holding her boy? Would the mountain claim them, like it had Amy, leaving no sign of the tragedy that was unraveling around her?

Hannah shivered in her wet clothes as she shouted out the window. "Oh, Danny. Where've they taken you? What do they want?"

Nothing in this world could have prepared Rex for the twisted tangle of emotions that assailed him.

Outside the *Gazette* office he had to stop to collect himself. He gripped the cold metal of the staircase banister. *Why hadn't she told him?*

A son.

A prickle of exhilaration burgeoning in his gut slammed head-on into anger. She'd kept the secret for six bloody years. He would've dropped everything had she told him. Now he might never see his son. The Plague

Doctor had him. If he didn't hurry, they'd have Hannah, too. They would use his woman and his boy to get to him.

Rex sucked in the damp air, trying to find control. Six years ago he'd walked out on Hannah so that this would not happen.

Now it had.

They had all come full circle to see this thing finally play out.

He had to get to them, to Hannah. He would not let six years of agony come to naught.

Driven by a force alien to him, Rex flew down the stairs, two and three at a time. He would let nothing come between him and his son.

He checked that his .38 was tucked into his hip holster and ducked into the rain. It would be dark soon. It was probably snowing in the Alpine. He needed gear. Fast.

He vaulted up the stairs of Expedition, a rental and retail store off the village square. It was quiet, no other customers. Rex ordered his gear, making clear it was urgent. The clerk raised her eyebrows but said nothing as she gathered up two head lamps, gloves, hats, a backpack, emergency space blanket, a water bottle and first-aid kit. Rex flashed his credit card and quickly stuffed the gear into his new pack.

The village was nearly empty as he ran through the cobblestone streets to the gondola station. The clerk at the store had told Rex it would still be operational because of a party up at the midstation restaurant.

He saw the lifty chatting with another young guy as the gondola booths swung through the berth, opening and closing empty before starting back up the mountain.

Rex considered running past the lifty and hijacking the cab with the doors just closing. But he figured if he didn't go over to the booth and buy a ticket they'd shut the lift down and have security waiting for him up top. He couldn't risk it.

He pushed his cash through to the ticket seller. "One. Anyone else gone up recently?"

She looked up at him through the hole in her glass booth.

"Been real quiet today with the weather and all. We had a woman a short while ago and two guys before her. Should get busier closer to seven though, when the party up at the restaurant gets going." She pushed the ticket and the waiver form out to Rex. "Sign here."

He spoke as he scribbled on the form. "Who bought the last ticket up?"

"Can't give out that information. Sorry."

Rex slipped a fifty-dollar note under the window of the ticket booth. The young woman looked up at him, surprised, unsure.

"Can it hurt?"

"I, uh...I guess not." She flipped to the last waiver form that had been signed. "Here it is. Mark Bamfield."

"Did he have a little boy with him, about six years old?" *My son.*

"No, sir. Haven't been any kids going up since this morning."

"And the woman and the other bloke? Who were they?"

"They used passes. I don't have their names on waiver forms."

"Your lifties scan the bar codes on the passes, don't you? Their names show up on your computers."

The woman hesitated. Rex slipped another fifty-dollar bill under the glass. Her dark brown eyes opened wide.

"Everyone has their price, sweetie." If money didn't work, there were other ways.

She turned to her computer monitor, opened a window

and scrolled down a page. She looked at the times of the scans. "The woman was Hannah McGuire. The man—" she scrolled farther down the computer page "—I'm sorry, there's no particular name registered against that bar code. The pass he used was a corporate pass that belongs to the White River Spa. Their staff use it and they also give it out to guests. It could've been anyone."

Rex left the booth, handed his ticket to the lift attendant and climbed into a gondola car.

There was no way to go any faster. Mitchell, the loose cannon, was up there with Hannah. Who else? And where was Daniel Logan McGuire? The Plague Doctor was behind this. Rex was certain of it. After all these years everything had converged in this quiet mountain town. Had the Plague Doctor been hiding up here, in plain sight, while he continued his diabolical work?

Rex flipped open his cell phone and punched in Scott's number.

"Scott here."

"Where are you?"

"Down here in the lobby of the Presidential. I got into White River earlier than I expected. Where are you calling from?"

"I'm in a gondola heading up Powder Mountain. I need your help."

"Shoot."

"I'm gonna keep it brief. McGuire has a son. He's been kidnapped. I suspect they're using the boy to flush her and myself out. They—and I think the Plague Doctor is involved in this—are luring us to the Grizzly Hut up on Powder Peak. I don't know where the boy is…or even if he's still alive. I need you to get to the White River Spa and check it out. See if the boy is there. Mountain staff haven't seen a kid go up in this lift since this morning. He was kidnapped around four o'clock this afternoon, but there's a back entrance to the spa. You can get to it through the back of White River Park.''

''What's the boy's name?''

Rex felt his voice catch. ''Daniel...Daniel Logan McGuire. He's almost six. See what you can find. I'm going to see if they've got Hannah up at the hut.''

''Logan McGuire?''

''Yeah.''

Scott was silent for a minute. Processing the information.

''Take it easy, Rex.''

''You, too, buddy.''

He watched from the shadows of the mountain-top gondola station as she emerged from the building and stumbled up the rocky path into the swirling gray. After six years, it was all finally going to come to an end. Like a festering boil, it had taken until now. Here, in White River, all the links were coming together. He felt a sense of relief. Finally he could purge himself.

He watched as she slipped. Then he stepped out from the shadows to follow her up to the cabin. He knew the man was waiting for her there. He had followed the man.

Hannah slipped in wet snow that was starting to compact on the trail up to Grizzly Hut. Without the aid of a flashlight she groped her way into the snowy bleakness. She had to concentrate. Accidents happened when you lost concentration, when you panicked. But she could feel the panic licking in her stomach. She willed herself to push it down. Danny was counting on her.

Her legs and toes were numb, her wet pants now icy and abrasive against her skin. She stumbled again and stopped.

"Danny!" She screamed into the swirling snow. Her words were sucked into a flat absorbent void.

She was at the traverse now, where the trail crossed above Grizzly Glacier, where Amy had gone down. She hugged the side of the mountain, her fingers red and raw from cold. Darkness swallowed the trail ahead. She rounded the ridge, feeling her way. Then she saw it. The light above. It flickered, wavered. Dim in the distance. It was light from the hut.

"Danny!"

The wind sucked the yell from her mouth. This side of the ridge was unprotected, and the flakes of snow became small, driving ice pellets. They stung into her face like a million needles.

Hannah groped her way to the cabin, bent double against the stinging snow. She stumbled up the cabin stairs and crashed into the door. It swung open under her weight and she tumbled into the room.

He sat there, beside a flickering candle. There was no fire. The cabin was cold, dank. He watched her, one side of his mouth pulled down in a derisive grin. Mocking. The fresh scar under his eye was puce.

This was not the Dr. Gregor Vasilev she knew. This was the man who had tried to kill her, tried to drown her in White River.

The cabin door crashed shut in the wind behind her. Trapped. Just her and Vasilev, in the dull flickering light.

"What have you done with my son?"

She forgot the cold. She forgot the numbness in her legs and feet, her raw hands. She took a step toward him. "Where is my boy, you bastard?" Clumps of snow dropped from the peak of her cap.

He didn't get up. He hardly moved. Vasilev just waved his hand indicating the bench opposite him. There was a glass of amber liquid in front of him. It was catching the light of the weak flame. An empty glass vial rested beside it.

Hannah looked back at Vasilev. It was then she noticed the glint of the gun in his other hand, resting in his lap.

She moved woodenly across the floor, toward the table. She didn't sit. "I want to know where Danny is."

"Take a seat, Hannah, my friend," he laughed, the sound flat and sharp. It grated like metal in her head.

"Take a seat, have a drink. A bit of brandy to warm you up while we wait for your lover to come."

Hannah eyed the glass, the empty vial.

"Go on, take it. It's a sundowner." He cackled again. "Except the sun has already gone down for you all. Drink it while we wait for the famous Rex Logan."

It flashed through her mind. Amy. Grady. The GHB drug in alcohol. The brandy. The empty vial on the table. She had to buy time.

"What makes you think Rex will come after me? He doesn't know I'm here. I told no one, like the note said."

"Good girl. But Logan got his own note. I had it delivered after yours so that we could have a little time together before he arrived."

So, Vasilev wanted to drug her before Rex arrived. Danny had been used to lure her. She saw it all now. This monster probably had no intention of keeping her alive. Her purpose as a lure had been served. She felt sick. Her stomach felt as if it had turned to water. She prayed that her son was okay.

"Why are you doing this?"

"You're in the way."

"Is this how you did it with Amy?" Hannah pointed to the drink on the table.

"She was easy, the nosy little carbuncle. She thought she could play with the big time." He snorted. "She took the drink with no problem. I told her Fisher had asked me to come and meet her in his place. I told her that we had urgent, vital information for her, that she had to come at once and we would go down to the spa.'' He laughed. He was enjoying this, finding sadistic pleasure.

Hannah tried to keep him talking.

''What then?''

''She was helpless from the drug by the time I sent her down the glacier. She managed to scream before her system shut down completely. Nature did the rest.''

''What about Grady Fisher?''

''His big mistake was using the phone at the spa. We have them all monitored. We knew what he and Amy had discovered. We heard them plan the meeting at the hut. He was going to show her the lab, our research and come down the back way to the spa. We dosed him up. After the nosy reporter was out of the way, I put him in his car and sent it over into the canyon.'' He motioned to the vial. ''It doesn't leave much trace.''

He leaned forward, eyes boring into hers, menacing, the fresh scar on his cheekbone bunching. ''Sit. Drink.''

Hannah stood her ground. ''I'm not doing a damn thing for you until you show me Daniel.''

In one fluid movement Vasilev was up, forcing the glass up to Hannah's mouth. She could smell the brandy fumes.

''You'll never get away with this.''

''Watch me.'' He held the back of her head and pushed the glass of lethal liquid up against her lips.

She'd be damned if she would acquiesce and allow him to pass off her death as some accident. If she was going to die, she would go down fighting. She would make sure he left telltale marks all over her body.

Hannah shoved his hand away from her mouth. The force of her movement sent the liquid splashing up into his eyes. The glass crashed to the floor. He winced and lashed out at her with the back of his meaty hand, sending her flailing to the ground.

She lifted herself up off the floor with one arm as Vasilev grabbed the heavy iron fire poker from beside the woodstove. He raised it above his head. Hannah raised her arm in a weak effort to fend off the blow as he started to bring it down on her head.

A sharp crack splintered the air.

Hannah watched in astonishment.

In slow motion, Gregor Vasilev's knees buckled under him. The poker crashed to the floorboards and he started to slump forward. His body caught the edge of the table as he came down. He groped for the gun that lay there. He aimed, squeezed the trigger as he sagged down onto the floor.

Hannah screwed her eyes shut, waiting for the thud of impact in her body.

Nothing came. Just the sharp crack of gunfire.

Then silence.

She slowly opened her eyes. Vasilev had fallen faceup over her legs. His eyes stared out at nothing. She stared in horror at the small black hole in the middle of his forehead. It was oozing thick blood. Spittle seeped and bubbled from the corner of his open mouth.

Her heart stampeded against her rib cage. She turned slowly to face the cabin door.

He stood there, leaning against the jamb, a hand clutched to his chest just under his left shoulder. There was blood seeping out between his fingers.

"Mark?"

He cleared his throat, stepping forward into the cabin, hand still pressed into his chest. "You can call me Ken, Ken Mitchell. I think you know by now who I am."

He tucked his gun back into his pants and moved over to Vasilev, slumped over her legs. He felt for his pulse.

"Good and dead."

Revulsion leaped suddenly into her throat. She struggled to pull her legs out from under the bleeding body. Ken lifted Vasilev, helping Hannah free her legs.

Ken coughed. He pulled a handkerchief out of his back pocket and pushed it under his jacket and shirt, up against his chest wound.

"You all right, Hannah?"

"I...I'm okay." Her words came out in a dry croak. "You've been shot."

"I'll be fine." He coughed again. "Surface wound. Can you make it down to the spa? They have your son there."

"Danny? He's all right?"

"I followed Vasilev after he kidnapped your boy. I was watching him as he staked out your house. He's been watching your house for days. I saw him attack the older woman and take the boy. I followed them back to the spa. I couldn't get in through the gates so I waited. Vasilev," he nodded toward the corpse, "came back out a few minutes later without the boy and headed for the village. I followed him up in the gondola. I knew he would've sent for you, and for Rex Logan. He wanted to get you both away from the village where he could deal with you."

"You're sure Danny's at the spa? He's okay?" A spring of hope erupted in her chest.

Ken reached for Vasilev's backpack resting on the bench. He pulled out a head lamp, grunting in approval. "I don't know if he's okay. We must hurry."

"How're you involved in all this, what's going on?"

"U.S. Central Intelligence. We're after a doctor who escaped capture in Marumba. We believe he's here, in White River."

Ken positioned the flashlight on his head. He took Vasilev's gloves and hat and gave them to Hannah. "Here, you'll need these. We're going to hike down."

The dead man's gloves. His hat. She recoiled.

"Go on."

She took her own sodden cap off her head. The ends of her hair were still encrusted with clumps of melting snow. It dripped down her shoulders into pools on the cabin floor. She racked her brain, trying to pull into focus what Rex had told her about Ken Mitchell, that he might be a double agent. She pulled the dead man's hat low over her ears. She would follow Ken since he could lead her to Danny. She'd play the cards as they were dealt her. But she'd trust no one.

"Logan is after the same doctor." Ken Mitchell opened the door into a night that was saved from blackness only by the whiteness of the blowing snow. "All the players are onstage now. All the same ones from Marumba, even you." He clutched tightly at his chest, coughing, as he ushered her out into the cold.

"Even me? What do you mean, 'even me'?"

"I followed Logan in Marumba, after the lab fire. It was part of my assignment to keep an eye on him. He'd managed to get real close to the doctor and we thought that if the doctor was still alive, if he'd survived the fire, he'd probably go after Logan, thinking he'd been responsible for things. I watched him in that bar in the capital, in Penaka, when he first saw you."

Hannah stumbled out into the night. "I never met Rex in a bar in the capital."

"No. But Logan saw *you*. Next thing he was taking an unscheduled vacation in Ralundi." Ken coughed. "It was most out of character, very contrary to his CIA personality profile. You sure have some hold over the famous Bellona Channel agent."

Bellona Channel agent? Hannah felt the bitter taste of

bile rise in the back of her throat. Nothing was as she knew it. Nothing was as it had seemed. She felt violated. In her line of investigative work she'd heard mention of the Bellona Channel. It was a top-secret civilian agency, and few knew more about it except that it was a funnel for information on biological terrorism and warfare. It contracted to governments and helped head up and co-ordinate research projects. She didn't know it had field agents. So Rex was a Bellona agent. Now she knew. He'd followed her to Ralundi. Now she knew.

The beam from the flashlight on Mitchell's head probed a narrow tunnel into the void. Around it swirled a madness of snow.

"Stick close. Hold on to the end of my jacket if you want. Watch your footing. It'll get slippery down by the gorge, but hopefully the snow will turn to rain down there."

She looked at the marks in the snow made by Mitchell. He was not only leaving footprints but drops of blood, black against the snow.

"Why don't we take the gondola?"

"We need to get into the spa the back way." He had to yell against the wind whipping at his words, tossing them out to the peaks. "Don't want to risk the gondola. Cops will be everywhere. It could screw this up."

Hannah considered making a bolt for the gondola station. But Ken had the flashlight. He had a gun. She didn't know what game he was playing. "Screw what up?" She slipped in the slush and regained her balance grabbing on to his jacket.

"I think I know where he's holding your son. If police decide to descend on the spa, they'll need a warrant. There'll be too much warning. Everything will be gone. We'll lose him again, the doctor. And we could lose your son."

He wasn't making much sense to her. She had to grasp on to the notion he might be telling the truth, that he might know where Danny was.

"Who has Danny? Who is this 'him'?" She screamed the words into the wind as she followed in his trail. He was still dripping blood. He was badly injured.

"The Plague Doctor."

Hannah felt her head swim. Things were getting more and more bizarre. "Keep focused, Hannah. Do it for Danny." She whispered the mantra to herself, over and over, as they descended the trail to the cable crossing. Beyond it lay the spa. And Danny.

Rex cursed aloud. He was trapped in the glass bubble as it rocked in the dark against the blinding rain. Water ran in shimmering black rivulets over the glass.

He checked his watch. He'd been stuck like this for twenty minutes now. He hadn't even reached midstation.

He swore again.

He knew this happened on ski hills. He'd skied often enough to know that lifts occasionally stopped for some reason—a mechanical hitch, someone having trouble getting on or off. There was nothing for it but to wait. If the gondola was broken, ultimately rescue would come.

But he felt impotent, suspended in time and air. The drama was unfolding up there on the mountain, and he was halfway between here and there, bobbing in the storm. It could cost lives. He tried his cell but he wasn't getting reception.

Then he felt it jerk. It stopped. Then it jerked forward again, the cabin lurching forward as the cables swayed and sagged. Then the humming was regular. The lifts were running again. Thank God.

He fixed the head lamp onto his head before his gondola cab docked at the peak. He pulled on gloves, secured his backpack at his waist, made sure his gun was still accessible. Rex made quick work up the trail to Grizzly Hut. He could see two sets of tracks in the snow but they were obscured by the thick white blanket that kept falling.

With his tunnel of light, he could make out the warning rope above Grizzly Glacier where Amy had gone down. He could no longer see the path, but he kept parallel and well above the rope, hugging the far edge of the trail.

The window of Grizzly Hut was illuminated by weak flickering light. He could see it as he approached. He could feel the bite of the wind here, around the edge of the ridge.

Rex kept low, working his way around to the window. He killed the light from his lamp and carefully raised himself to look inside.

He could see nothing apart from the faint flicker of a candle flame starting to sputter and drown in its own wax.

He moved around to the front of the hut, the snow muffling the sound of his tread. He crept up the small stairs, felt for his gun. He waited. Listened. Then he crashed through the door, firearm leading.

Dr. Gregor Vasilev lay on the floor. A pool of thick gelatinous blood congealed around his head, his glazed eyes wide, oblivious. The stare of death. The sick sweet smell of death. A gun lay at his side.

Rex moved cautiously forward. He slipped his own weapon back into its holster, removed his glove and felt for a pulse where he knew there'd be none.

Vasilev was dead all right. Bullet wound to the head.

Rex clicked over to autopilot as he searched for signs. He saw the empty vial on the table, the same kind of vial he'd found in this very cabin and sent off for testing. He checked Vasilev's gun. It had been recently fired.

He saw the shattered glass. He lifted the broken base

of the glass to his nose and sniffed. Brandy. The fire poker lay near the table. There had been a scuffle.

He moved over to the door. More blood there. Life sputtered suddenly from the candle. Rex clicked on his lamp, the only light in the cabin now coming from the flashlight on his forehead.

He stepped outside into the swirling snow. The flakes were bigger, softer now, the wind dying. Then he saw it, the scuff marks and prints. They were being covered quickly but the indentations still remained.

He dropped down into a crouch, examining the trail. Blood. Someone else had been injured. God, he hoped it wasn't Hannah. If Vasilev was dead, Ken Mitchell must have her. He was a wild card. Unstable. There was no point in trying to second-guess his moves. He would be behaving irrationally, and Hannah's life, his son's life, were at stake.

Rex could make out two sets of prints, leading away from the hut into the dark mountain night. The spa. Mitchell and Hannah must be making for the spa.

Rex crouched low, following the trail. He'd lost valuable time.

Chapter 15

Hannah slipped in slush as they negotiated the descent to the cable crossing over White River. She slid into Ken Mitchell's legs, causing him to collapse on her.

She scrambled back up as Ken struggled to right himself. Hannah saw a puddle of blood where he'd fallen. She had some of his blood on her glove and on her sleeve. He was weakening.

"Why don't you give me the light, Ken, let me lead the way?"

He brushed her aside. "I'm fine. Just a flesh wound."

"That's no flesh wound. You need a doctor."

He pushed forward. "Yeah, well, we're going where I hope to find one. A special one. One I've been hunting for years."

They reached the point where precipitation hovered between slushy snow and thick rain. A little lower, as they neared the cable crossing, the ground was muddy, slick, and the slush turned fully to rain. It was not as relentless as it had been earlier. Hannah figured the storm must be moving through. Yet without the snow, it was blacker.

White River roared somewhere down in the dark as Hannah picked her way blindly along the edge of the gorge. Fear lay heavy and liquid in the pit of her stomach as she climbed with Ken into the metal box.

Ken was too weak to move the primitive car along the cable himself. He used only his left arm. Hannah helped him pull, hand over hand. She was thankful for the dead man's gloves as she gripped the cold metal, hauling the car forward in slow, jerky movements over the unseen maw below. She could hear the whitewater raging, gurgling, hungry beneath them.

It was easier going down to the spa enclosure. They hugged the electrified fence line, as closely as possible, moving slowly along the rough road toward the gate. Hannah knew the cameras Rex had pointed out earlier would be capturing their movements. She was glad. Ken Mitchell frightened her. He didn't seem rational. Someone would see them and come and find them. Soon.

She was surprised to see the back gates to the spa property hanging open. Lights mounted on poles burned harsh and white several yards inside the enclosure, throwing the concrete buildings she'd seen on her earlier hike with Rex into stark relief. It looked institutional.

"They're open. Strange." Ken muttered before he was besieged by another coughing fit. Hannah didn't like the sound of it. There was a moist burble in his lungs. He hunched over, racked by the coughs.

She stared at the open gates.

Should she make a run for it? She could call the police from that building. They must have a phone.

As if in answer, Dr. Gunter Schmidt stepped out from under the shadows of a large, heavy fir. Hannah ran forward. "Gunter! Am I glad to see you. I—" She saw the gun held level with her belly. It was trained on her. She stopped dead.

"His name is not Gunter, Hannah." Mitchell coughed. "He is Dr. Ivan Rostov, the Plague Doctor."

"Mitchell. Drop your weapon or I kill the woman. Now!" Gunter's familiar rasp had taken a menacing tone. It shot frost up Hannah's spine. Her head spun. She realized she was shaking, her teeth chattering, from the wet cold, from sheer fear and exhaustion.

Ken Mitchell raised his head to look at Gunter, but he was still hunched over, drained. He threw his gun to the ground.

Gunter shot a look at Hannah. "So, Vasilev failed. Again. Come. This way." Gunter stepped forward, prodded her sharply in the waist with the barrel of his weapon. He marched the two of them toward the bright building. "Vasilev is brilliant with the surgery but useless for this other business."

Hannah stopped and tried to turn to face him. "My son—"

"Keep moving."

The building seemed empty. Clinical. He marched them into a wide tiled corridor. It was like a hospital. It smelled of disinfectant. The sound of their wet feet played loud through the passage. Gunter walked behind them. He forced them into an elevator.

"Don't try to be heroes. The boy will die."

Hannah whirled around. The sight of Gunter's face in the harsh light winded her.

It was Gunter—but it wasn't. He'd taken off his cap. Gone was the thick thatch of salt-and-pepper hair. He was close to bald with a rim of brush-cut gray spikes running around the back of his skull. His eyes—they were not the warm hazel she knew, but a stone-cold green.

She looked from those unfamiliar eyes to the glint of

the weapon in his hand. "Who the hell are you? Where is Danny?" Her words were whispered, her voice low and threatening. She was in the middle of something she did not understand, but she knew one thing. She would do anything to get her boy.

"Move." The steel elevator door opened. She didn't know how far down into the earth they had gone.

She saw three doors leading off the underground corridor. Cut into each door was a small, thick glass window. Under the windows were Biosafety Level 4 signs along with the interlocking rings of the universal biohazard image. Black on red.

The implications of what she was seeing swept over her in a nauseating wave. She felt as if she was drowning under it. How long had this evil secret been buried under the White River earth? Was this what Amy had discovered? Is this what Rex was after?

Gunter used a card to open a door without the biohazard logo. It was dark as pitch inside. "Get in."

He pushed Ken Mitchell, who stumbled coughing into the dark. Hannah turned to face him. "You won't get away with this."

Gunter laughed in her face, gun at her belly. She recoiled at the warm rankness of his breath. "I've gotten away with it for years. The only real thorn in my side has been agent Logan and his Bellona group. And that idiot Mitchell in there." He gestured at the dark room with his head. "The agent will come for you. You are his big weakness. His *only* weakness. How does it feel, my dear, to know you will be responsible for the death of the man you love?"

"You're a psychopath!" Hannah lunged at the monster. He'd deceived her, Al, the whole community for all these years. He had professed friendship to Al while orchestrating the murder of his niece.

Gunter intercepted her movement, bringing her up short, the muzzle of his gun up hard under her neck. She couldn't swallow with the metal pressed into her throat. She started to choke.

"There is nothing you can do, Hannah McGuire. Go say your prayers. When I kill Logan, I will move my research, my treasures, out. Everything is packed and ready. The rest, what I haven't already destroyed, will be ravaged by fire. You will be burned to a crisp. The place has been wired to go, just like Marumba. It will all look most unfortunate. But I will be long gone. My work here complete. What I have created will shift the balance of power in the world as we know it."

He slammed the thick, reinforced door shut in her face. Darkness swallowed her. She heard Ken coughing. She groped her way toward the sound. "Where's your flashlight, Ken, give it to me."

She almost fell over Ken slumped on the floor. She reached down and felt the headlamp on his head. She worked it free and fumbled to find the switch. Light flooded the small room.

Her eyes adjusted, focused, fell on a small gray bundle. "Oh my God!"

She flung herself into the corner where Danny lay curled in a dark-gray blanket. "Please, please be all right." She shook his small body. "Danny! Danny, it's Mommy. Wake up, Danny! Oh, God, wake up!"

His eyes fluttered open and then closed. Slowly he tried to open them again. The sharp blue of his eyes was darkened by enlarged pupils. He was woozy. His little voice thick.

"Mommy?"

"Oh, my sweetheart." Hot tears spilled in relief. "Are you all right? Do you hurt?"

"No…just…tired." He closed his eyes again.

Hannah realized Ken was at her side. He was devoid of color, pallid as death. He wiped his sleeve across his mouth and it came away stained red with blood. He leaned forward and felt Daniel's pulse.

"He's okay, Hannah. Good, strong and steady pulse. He'll sleep it off, I'm sure, whatever they gave him." He coughed and wiped the pink spittle from his mouth. "Just watch his breathing." Ken slumped with his back to the wall, legs stretched out in front of him. "If his breathing goes irregular, try CPR."

Hannah sat against the wall and pulled her son up to rest with his head in her lap. She stroked his sleek dark hair. It was just like his daddy's.

She bent low and whispered as he slept. "I found your daddy, Danny."

She felt Ken's hand on her arm. He was losing strength as she watched by the light of the headlamp. "I'm sorry, Hannah…so sorry."

"You tried to save us, Ken."

"More than once." He coughed. "I pulled you from the river. Rex shot me for it. Just nicked my leg, though."

"I don't understand."

He coughed. "I don't think I have much time…but I want you to know. Gunter Schmidt is the one who we call the Plague Doctor. I have been after him since his escape in Marumba. I think Logan holds me responsible for that. He's right to do so. I moved in too early. After the fire I wanted more than anything to make it right. It consumed me."

He spluttered. The blood from his mouth a darker red now. His chest was wet, black with it from where it oozed from his wound.

"The CIA got wind the Plague Doctor had survived the fire when a Bellona Agent, Scott Armstrong, received a threat against his family. It was believed to have come from the Plague Doctor. Rex Logan also received a threat…in Ralundi one night…against your life. He dumped you. At least, he wanted it to appear that way. It saved you. Scott wasn't so lucky. Lost his family. No one could prove the connection.''

''They were killed?''

''Made to look like an accident. Like Grady, in a car. Vasilev was in Toronto when it happened.''

Ken's breathing was irregular now. She could hear the air bubbling up through the liquid deep in his lungs. Hannah reached for his hand. It was cold, damp.

''Rex left you for your own good, Hannah. He's a fine man. Must've been hard on both of you.''

Ken closed his eyes. She was losing him.

''I am so sorry…I tried to track him down…Plague Doctor…set it all right. For years I followed false leads. When the young reporter…Amy Barnes…she kept calling the CIA offices last year. They eventually put me on to her. They thought she was another one of my crazy schemes. But I believed her…she told me her friend worked at the White River Spa…overheard a conversation between two doctors. Her friend, Grady Fisher, believed they were cooking up biological weapons. He followed them. Found this lab. He didn't go to the police. He has a bad record…afraid he'd be deported from Canada. He told the reporter…she went after it. She wanted the story.'' He coughed up a glob of blood. He didn't have the strength to wipe it away.

''But I couldn't get to White River. To help. They had me hospitalized. Figured I was nuts. Then I heard she was missing. Came as soon as I was released, just when they found her body. I didn't make it in time…almost a year late…''

Ken's head lolled forward over his chest. ''He will…get away…again.''

Hannah stroked her son's hair and held on to Ken's clammy hand. She sat with them in the airless, empty room. So Rex had always loved her.

"I've been no help... Sorry...I'm so sorry."

He was slipping away. She smoothed the wet hair from his cold forehead.

"You've been more help than you'll ever know, Ken," she whispered.

He closed his eyes and lay still.

"Thank you." Tears swam in her eyes as she cradled her son. They had to get through this. *Rex had always loved her.* She understood now. She wanted Danny to meet his father, no matter the cost.

Rex stood at the open gates at the back of the spa property. He lifted his face up to the cold rain. He closed his eyes, feeling its wetness against his cheeks, and he made a vow. "Get us through this and I will do whatever it takes to be with my family." He spoke out softly into the darkness. Then he said the words again, "My family." He hadn't dreamed it possible.

He had to make it possible. He'd left unfinished business in Marumba. He would finish it here, in White River.

He slunk through the shadows of the trees, eyes trained on the door of the building.

He saw him come out.

He was moving quickly down the path. Rex saw it now, in the movement. He had recognized the stance of the Plague Doctor in Gunter Schmidt's powerful movements, but his appearance had been so altered that Rex had been easily deceived. Damn, he should've seen it. Cosmetic surgery. Different hair. Different voice. Contacts for the eyes.

Rex followed, silent as a wolf closing in on his prey, eyes trained on his quarry.

Gunter headed for a truck parked in the trees. Rex watched. He had to get to him before he managed to get into the truck. He crouched low, running softly over the pine needles.

"Halt!"

Rex froze still as a statue. The Plague Doctor aimed his gun at the source of the sound—at Scott. Scott had his own weapon trained on the doctor, the man responsible for the death of his wife and child. Finally, Scott and Rex had both come face-to-face with their nemesis.

"Drop the gun, Doctor," Scott ordered.

Gun still in his right hand, still trained on Scott, Gunter slowly raised his left hand. He had something in it. "See this? I press this button and it all goes up in smoke. It's wired, just like Marumba. You lose Rex Logan's woman, her son and the CIA agent, if he isn't dead already."

His voice. It was certainly not the voice Rex remembered from Marumba. The characteristic rasp must've been a surgical addition.

Rex, still undetected, raised his gun slowly, aimed for the doctor's head. He let Scott speak.

"The cops are all over the place, Doctor. They should have their warrant by now. The highway is closed."

From his vantage point, Rex could see that Scott had spotted him. He dipped his head slightly in silent acknowledgment.

"If I send this place up in flames, it's not only my lab that goes. It's the whole spa. Patients will die. Innocent people, Agent Armstrong, like your wife and child."

Scott held his ground. "There's nowhere for you to go, Doctor."

The movement came suddenly. Gunter lifted his gun and fired. Scott dove as he saw the doctor start to move. Rex shot and the bullet hit Gunter in the torso. Rex wanted him alive but disabled. He shot again at his knees.

The doctor buckled to the ground. As he went down he hit the button on the detonator in his hand.

Rex heard a muffled explosion. He saw Scott scramble up and head for the doctor.

Rex turned and sprinted for the gray concrete building, making for the door he'd seen the Plague Doctor come out of.

Thin fingers of smoke seeped and curled under the door into their windowless prison. Hannah could smell fire. Mitchell no longer had any pulse. Her son was still sleeping.

She covered Danny's head with the blanket, rushed over to the door and pulled. She kicked at it. It was solid, unyielding. She screamed. She banged with both hands. She was banging them into a pulp. She knew they would soon be overcome with smoke. This airless room would be their coffin.

He ran low through the smoke-filled corridors. He could hear her screaming, muffled by walls. He saw the biohazard signs. So this was where the Plague Doctor was doing his work. Small but efficient. He heard the banging.

"Hannah!"

"Over here! In here! Help!"

"Hannah, can you hear me?"

"Rex! Yes. Oh, God, Rex. Yes, I can hear you."

"Stand well back from the door, all of you. I'm going to fire at the lock. Got it?"

"Yes. Got it."

"I'm going to count to five, then fire…one, two, three, four, five…"

The bullet hit the lock square. He had to fire twice more before he could crash the door open.

He burst into the room.

She crouched there, huddled over her son. His son. Mitchell lay lifeless on the floor.

The smoke was growing dense. He had to hurry. He felt Mitchell's pulse.

"He's dead, Rex. Shot. Vasilev did it."

He shifted his attention to the bundle in the gray blanket. "Hannah, I'm going to take Daniel. You follow me. Stay close. Real low. Hold on to me. We're going up the stairs."

He scooped the small boy in the blanket up into his arms. He was light. Limp. The sensation overwhelmed him. He cradled his son to his chest. Hunkering over him, he ran, Hannah at his heels.

They burst coughing and choking into the cold damp night air. It was still spitting rain. Sirens. Alarms. Fire crews from the village were responding. The clinic building situated at the low end of the property was being evacuated. He saw Scott with a RCMP officer. The wounded doctor was in handcuffs.

Rex ran toward Scott, his bundle still limp in his arms. "I need to get him to a hospital. Now."

"Take my truck. Here're the keys."

Hannah held Daniel in the passenger seat as they bumped over the rough track to the low end of the property where dirt gave way to paved road and wild brush and trees gave way to the manicured grounds of the spa. They drove out through the spa gates against a wave of incoming emergency personnel responding to the fire. Red and blue police lights pulsed against the night sky.

Chapter 16

He could see why she hadn't wanted him inside her home. There were photographs of her and Daniel everywhere. Next to her bed, where she lay now, sleeping with their son, was a picture of Hannah and Danny in the snow with a snowman twice Danny's size.

The little boy was laughing out at the photographer, baby white teeth against olive skin, his eyes a crystal blue, thrown into stark relief against dark hair and thick dark lashes.

Rex picked up the gold frame. He had seen another boy like that once, in photographs his mother had left him. Except, that little boy had not laughed at the photographer like this one did. He traced the lines of him with his finger. "You've done a fine job, Hannah," he whispered to the woman sleeping next to his boy. "You have raised our son so that he finds joy and love in the world."

He looked down at her where she lay. Her hair was

spun gold, fanned out on the pillow, her face in repose, beautiful, pale. She still had dark smudges under her eyes. She'd been sleeping since early that morning.

"And you've touched me so that I, too, can see the joy, the love." He gently replaced the frame on the bedside table and bent to brush his lips over hers. "I'm not going to let you go this time. Whatever it takes. We *will* work through it. All three of us."

Daniel stirred in the bed beside her. There had been minimal traces of GHB in his system, but otherwise he was fine. The doctors at the White River Health Care Center had given Hannah a sedative to help her sleep. She was in a state of exhaustion and shock. Rex had brought them here, back to her house, in the early hours of the dark morning to make room for casualties coming into the small health care center from the spa fire.

He stroked Daniel's head. He couldn't get over the wonder of it. This child. His.

Rex could hear Hannah's mother knocking about in the kitchen downstairs. He'd told her to relax, but she said she needed to keep busy. The poor woman felt responsible for Daniel's kidnapping.

Rex tucked Danny's yellow teddy bear under the covers with him and kissed his son on the forehead. Then he went downstairs to see if he could help Hannah's mom.

"Smells good. What is it?"

Startled, Sheila McGuire turned to face Rex standing in the kitchen doorway. She nervously rubbed her hands on the white bib apron she had found in one of the drawers. "It's pot roast. That other agent, Scott Armstrong, called to say he'd be stopping by. I thought he might want to stay for dinner. I've asked Al, too. But, oh, dear, I think I've overdone things again. Maybe Hannah wants some quiet. Maybe I shouldn't have invited anyone."

Rex stepped forward, took her hands in his. They were

warm and soft. "Pot roast. My favorite. I haven't had a good pot roast since before I went to boarding school. My mom used to make a killer roast."

The smell of the food on the stove, the potatoes, the steaming pots, assailed him. He wished he could go back in time and hug his own mother. She had worked on her own to raise him. He wished he could go back and say thank you.

He lifted Sheila McGuire's hand to his lips. "Thank you."

She looked up into his eyes. "He looks so much like you, Rex."

"Danny?"

"Yes."

"You know? Hannah told you?"

"She didn't have to. He looks just like you. Welcome home, Rex. I hope you're going to stay."

Hannah found them like that. Rex and her mother in the kitchen, surrounded by the scents of hearth and home.

"Rex…Mom?"

They turned to face her. He towered over her small mother. She was flushed pink from cooking.

"How are you feeling, Hannah?" He stepped toward her.

"Rex, I need to talk to you, to tell you about Daniel. I—"

"I know. I know about Daniel."

She was knocked off balance. She had summoned all her courage to come downstairs and tell him immediately, afraid of how he might react.

"You know?" She turned to her mother. "Mom?" She hadn't even told her mother who Daniel's father was. For all these years she'd kept it locked deep in her heart. Her mother stood there now, in the middle of the kitchen, in her dear old apron, tears streaming down her cheeks.

"Mommy." The little voice came from behind her. She whirled around. "Danny. You shouldn't be up. How are you feeling, my boy?" She scooped him into her arms, squeezing tight. "Why don't we all go into the living room and sit down. There's someone I want you to meet, Danny." Looking at Rex, she said, "We need to have a group talk."

Rex saw the wariness as the sharp little blue eyes homed in on him. The likeness between himself and Danny was uncanny. It would take time for Daniel to adjust to the concept of having a father, Rex knew. But he ached to hold him, squeeze him to bits. He wanted to take him fishing, teach him to ski, teach him to fly one of those kites he'd seen...all those things he himself had wanted to do with the colonel. Something melted inside him, and a river of possibility flowed out before him as he watched the small boy, sitting on the sofa beside his mother at the other end of the room.

But he knew he needed to give that little boy space and time. He would overwhelm him otherwise. Daniel was silent, small hand tight in Hannah's, eyes fixed on Rex.

Then he stood up and faced Rex, unclasping Hannah's hand. In his clear little voice, with a strength Rex recognized as his own, he spoke.

"So, you're my dad?" His words were solemn.

"Yes, Daniel. I am."

"I always knew you'd come." He turned to look at his mother. "See, Mommy? He did come. I just knew he would."

Rex did something he didn't know was still possible— he cried. Tears crept out of the corners of his eyes. He

hadn't felt that salty wetness, that kind of cathartic release, since before he'd joined the army as a young man.
He held out his arms wide, welcoming his son.

Daniel walked slowly over the carpet. He stopped and
stood, facing Rex, assessing him. Then he leaped, with
force, into the arms of his father. Rex could feel the little
arms and hands around his neck. There was no stopping
his tears now. Daniel's breath was warm in his neck. He
heard the whisper. "You *are* going to stay, aren't you?"

"Yes, son," he whispered in return, drinking in the
scent of his hair. "I'll stay. If your mother will let me."

He looked over Daniel's head at Hannah, who came to
their side. "I know about the death threat in Ralundi, Rex.
Ken Mitchell told me. He knew about it."

"Hannah—"

"Shh." She put two fingers to his lips. "I understand.
I know why you left me. I just don't know what happens
now."

"I've always loved you, Hannah. More than you'll ever
know. I need you. You, and now Danny, make me whole.
I didn't believe this could be possible in my life. You've
shown me it is."

He could see her eyes glisten.

"What about Bellona?"

"I don't need it anymore—I have you." He reached
out and took a handful of her hair, playing it softly
through his fingers.

He'd done a lot of thinking as he'd watched them sleep
upstairs. He believed in the Bellona Channel but he
needed to be with his family now. That was more important than anything. If he gave it up, if he quit, he would
probably have to forfeit his position with Bio Can Pharmaceutical. But that was all right. He was a doctor, he
could find something else. He was prepared to give it all
up to hold on to what he had never dreamed possible,

what he had never had in his life. Love. A real family of his own.

He closed his eyes, savoring the presence of them both around him, Daniel snuggled against his chest, Hannah at his side. God, it would have been tragic if history had gone ahead and repeated itself. He'd come so close. Like his dad, Colonel Logan, Rex would have sired a child who'd grown up lonely and rejected by his father. Oh, the irony.

He understood it all now—why Hannah had left her job and come to White River. She'd wanted to give time to her son, to raise him in these timeless mountains. She had sacrificed her career for Danny. He loved her and he respected her for what she had done.

He opened his eyes and turned to face her. "Why didn't you tell me, Hannah? Why didn't you give me a chance to be there for you˝and Daniel?"

"You rejected me, Rex." She looked down at her hands. "Perhaps I was wrong to make the choices I made. But you wounded me. I didn't want the possibility of Danny facing that same hurt. I didn't want you bound to us by some notion of duty. I saw what that did to Mac, to my mom, to me."

"Mac?"

"My father. He died on assignment in the Congo, a man torn by a sense of duty to his family and his need for freedom."

"So we're starting from scratch, huh? You and me both. No shining examples of fatherhood. We'll just have to forge our own way." He reached out and took her hand in his. "Marry me, Hannah McGuire."

Her breath hitched, catching in her throat as she spoke. "What are you going to do about Bellona?" Her eyes were wide pools of liquid gold.

"There are more important things in my life now.

Things I treasure. I'll give it up if you'll have me. I can move out West."

"You're sure?"

"Never been more sure of anything in my life."

"Yes, Rex." She whispered the words. "Yes, I'll marry you."

Danny jerked upright. "Does that mean you'll stay?" He had been quiet against his chest. Listening, waiting in anticipation.

Rex threw back his head and laughed a great loud laugh. It burbled out from his belly, reverberated up through his chest and into the air. He had never felt so good. So fine.

The sound of his laughter sparked Daniel into a little chuckle. With relief, Hannah laughed and wept, too.

"What's with all this merriment?" Scott stood at the top of the stairs leading down into the sunken living room.

"Ah, Scott, you're just in time to agree to be my best man."

He started down the steps. "Hey, I *am* your best man."

"No, no, I mean for our wedding."

Scott stopped in his tracks, a large smile slowly spread across his face, setting his green eyes twinkling. He stepped forward to take Rex's hand. "Congratulations, buddy. It's about time you saw the light."

He took Hannah's hand, kissed it. "Congratulations, Mrs. Logan-to-be. And you, young man—"

"I'm already a Logan."

"So I hear." Scott took a seat on the sofa. "So I hear."

Hannah helped her mother serve the roast, and Rex poured the cabernet.

"Grape juice for you, my man." He set a glass in front of Danny.

"Thanks, sir."

"If you want, when you're really good and ready, you can call me dad."

"I'm ready…Dad."

Everyone laughed. Scott raised his glass in a toast. "To the Logans." Hannah had never felt so complete as she raised hers in response.

Al lifted his glass. "To the Logans. And…to my Amy."

They raised glasses in a soft chorus of solemn murmurs. "To Amy."

Scott set his glass down and started to tuck into his potatoes. "You know, Al, if it hadn't been for Amy and what she set in motion, the world could have looked like a different place today."

"That's quite a statement."

"No," answered Rex. "Scott's right. This weekend would have seen evil biological weapons technology pass into the hands of countries who oppose all that the Western world stands for. Amy stopped that. She set in motion a chain of events that ultimately stopped the Plague Doctor from delivering the goods to renegade scientists attending the toxicology conference."

Al shook his head. "I can't believe Gunter turned out to be one of the world's most wanted men. I thought he was my friend, Hannah's friend. He deceived us all here in White River."

"He was hiding in plain sight, working on his research. Thanks to Amy, he was finally flushed out. And Amy brought me together with my family."

He was right, thought Hannah. If it hadn't been for Amy, she wouldn't have been forced into Rex's company. They wouldn't be here now, together, enjoying a family dinner.

Al nodded his head slowly. Contemplative. "So what was the Plague Doctor actually working on?"

Rex caught Scott's eye. Scott nodded. Rex continued.

"Well, the Plague Doctor was trying to complete something he first started in his Marumba lab. It's what we refer to as ethnic bullets. These bullets are biological agents, lethal bugs, that can be genetically engineered to target only certain types of people with common genetic makeup."

Sheila joined the discussion. "You mean a virus or bacteria can be genetically altered so that it only attacks a certain ethnic group?"

"Exactly. The mapping of human genes has made this technology possible. It's the frightening future of biological weapons."

Hannah could hardly believe what she was hearing. The Plague Doctor was doing *that* in White River. "This is crazy, Rex. It sounds like science fiction, like potential genocide."

"It is. What was science fiction is now fact."

Rex forked up a couple of baby carrots, popping them into his mouth. "Good carrots. You tried these, Danny?"

"Uh, not yet…Dad." He was relishing the word playing it over his tongue.

Rex sneaked a carrot off Danny's plate and continued. "After the Plague Doctor escaped the Marumba fire, he was taken by the consortium, Die Waffenbruder, to Odessa, where Vasilev apparently worked his plastic surgery magic on him. He then took on the identity of Dr. Gunter Schmidt. The real Dr. Schmidt rather coincidentally disappeared in Switzerland. It appears his identity was stolen, which is why Gunter's records checked out."

"Yeah." Scott picked up the conversation. "And, Rex, I haven't told you yet, it turns out Vasilev was doing all the surgery at the White River Spa himself. The Plague Doctor is brilliant in his evil genius but apparently he is

not a plastic surgeon. They needed to bring Vasilev in to
help him.''

''What happens to the doctor now?'' It was an uncomfortable juxtaposition, thought Hannah, a doctor, trained
to heal yet working to deliver death. But then, everything
as she knew it had been turned on its head in the last few
days.

''He will eventually end up being tried at the Hague
by an international tribunal.'' Rex sneaked the last carrot
off Danny's plate. The boy smiled in gleeful conspiracy
as his mother threw them a dark look.

''And his work, these ethnic bullets?''

''We have it all now. We have the samples and we
have the technology. We can use it now to work on a
plan for developing antibodies and treatments. Bio Can
Pharmaceutical will do that, under government contract.''

Hannah sighed. ''I still feel for Ken Mitchell. He may
have screwed up in Marumba but he devoted every minute of his life trying to put this evil behind bars. It drove
him crazy.'' She took a sip of her red wine. ''He saved
me, you know, twice.'' She looked at Rex. ''He pulled
me from the river after Vasilev pushed me in.''

''So that explains it. He must have tackled Vasilev and
earned that gash on his face.''

''And a bullet in the leg from you.''

''You have a gun?'' Danny's eyes were wide.

''Policemen have guns, Danny. Your dad was doing a
job like a policeman, chasing the bad guys who tried to
hurt me.''

''Like the bad guy who took me.''

She leaned over and kissed his head. ''Yes. Now eat
up, we need to get you into bed.'' Hannah made a mental
note to call a counselor tomorrow. Danny would surely
need someone to talk to after all he'd been through.

"Who was this Plague Doctor going to sell these magic bullets to?" asked Al.

"Someone at the conference, we think. It could have been a representative from any number of the countries attending. They would have done it on the side. That's how these information exchanges often happen, through conferences like these that serve as meeting grounds. If the doctor doesn't confess and tell us, we may never know. That is why organizations like the Bellona Channel must remain ever vigilant."

Scott cleared his throat, commanding attention. He clinked his knife against his glass. "Speaking of Bellona, Rex, I've been asked to tell you that Killian has named you to the board."

Hannah flinched at Scott's words. She held her breath waiting for Rex to respond.

He turned to look at his colleague. "I'm flattered, Scott, but I have other plans."

Hannah breathed out a sigh of relief.

Scott took a sip of his wine. "I understand, Rex, but hear me out. Killian says he wants to keep you running your division of Bio Can, except he wants it relocated out West here in B.C. And, as a Bellona board member, you call the shots, decide on policy. There is no fieldwork. You get a crack at a normal life."

Rex set his glass carefully down on the table. Hannah could see him weighing the options. She knew what his work meant to him. She could see it in his eyes when he spoke. Until now it had been his life. Could it be possible that they could have the best of both worlds?

"Scott, why would Killian want the indigenous medicine division out West?"

"He doesn't want to lose you." Scott tilted his head, catching Hannah's eye. "None of us do."

Danny piped up. "That's for sure." His interjection raised a chorus of laughter.

Rex looked at Hannah, one brow raised in question.

"It sounds too good to be true, Rex."

"Think about it, buddy. You and Hannah talk it over. The way I see it, old Killian is not too much longer for this world and he's looking ahead."

"You can't be serious?"

"He needs to groom a replacement for board chair."

Danny's eyes were drooping. Hannah stood up. "Come, Daniel, I think you need to call it a night. Let's say goodnight to everyone."

Danny turned to look up at his father. "Will you still be here in the morning?"

Rex reached out and placed his large hand over the little one. "Yes, Danny. I'll still be here. I'm not going anywhere. Ever."

"Will you come tuck me in?"

Hannah could see Rex struggling with his emotions. When he spoke, his voice was hoarse and gentle. "Of course."

He looked up at Hannah. She could see the sparkle, the shimmer in his light eyes. It was as if a swimmer had broken the surface of those cold blue pools, refracting light in a million directions. It was time, she thought, that a swimmer played in those cool depths.

"I'll take him up, Rex. I need to talk to him. We'll call you when he's ready to be tucked in."

She helped Danny brush his teeth and put on his Winnie the Pooh jammies, relishing the beauty of this simple routine. She tucked him and his yellow teddy bear into his bed and bent to hold him. She held him like that for a long time, smelling the mintiness of his warm toothpaste breath, the clean soapy smell of his skin.

"Danny?"

"Yes, Mom?"

"You've been through a lot. I'm going to get someone who is trained in dealing with these things to come and talk to us. To make sure we are all really feeling okay. It's not good to bury things, you know. We need to talk."

She knew it well enough. She had been burying things deep for the past six years. The relief she felt now was beyond description.

"I'm okay, Mom. My wish came true."

She sat up and looked into those eyes, his father's eyes.

"What wish?"

"My wish for a dad."

"Why didn't you tell me about that wish, Danny?"

"'Cause I know it made you sad when I asked about my dad."

His words ripped at her heart. She hugged him tight. "You have him now. *We* have him. Sometimes we have to wait for the good things."

"I know. We have to fight and pass all the tests before we get to the treasure." His clear little voice was imbued with a wise and knowing tone. "It can take many years."

"Where did you learn that?"

"TV."

"I see. So it does teach you something." She leaned forward and kissed him. "You sure you want to sleep in your own bed tonight?"

"You'll be in your bed?"

"Yes."

"And Granny, she'll be in the spare room?"

"Yes."

"And Dad, he will be in your bed?"

Hannah smiled. "I think so. You okay with that?"

Danny grinned over the top of his duvet. "I'm okay with that. Can you call Dad now, to tuck me in?"

Rex climbed the stairs to say good-night to his son, his large frame silhouetted against the light in the stairwell. As Hannah watched him, he turned and blew her a kiss. She smiled. She felt a spurt of warmth in her chest that radiated out through her body, like ripples from a pebble cast into a pond. If Daniel's wish had come true, so had hers. She had her own little family, and they were going to build on pillars of love. It had taken six years to get here, but it was worth every minute of it.

She turned into the kitchen to put the coffee on. Al touched her arm. "I'm happy for you, Hannah."

"Thank you, Al. You were always there for me. You helped me cope during the dark times. If it wasn't for Amy, we might never have come this far."

"That's what I wanted to talk to you about. I feel like I can finally put her soul to rest. Her work has been done." Al paused for a moment. "Will you come up to the glacier with me tomorrow? I want to scatter her ashes. I haven't been able to do it until now. I thought I'd have a little ceremony. She would want it that way, for the wind to carry her ashes over the distant peaks. It's where her spirit will always be."

Hannah felt tears prick at the back of her eyes. "Of course I will, Al. I would be honored to."

"And I'd like Danny and Rex, your family, to come, too."

"Thank you." She kissed Al's crinkled cheek. "We'll all say goodbye. We will set her free."

Al helped Hannah carry the tray of coffee into her sunken living room. Through the large picture windows, the town of White River was a sparkling jewel nestled between the two mountains on the opposite shores of Alabaster Lake. She smiled inside as she handed Scott his coffee. She had vowed to have things under control by the time she returned to her home, her sanctuary. And she did. But not in her wildest dreams had she thought things would turn out the way they had. She'd laid solid foundations for herself and her son in White River. And now they were going to build on them, together, as a family.

"Where's Rex?" Scott asked over the rim of his mug.

"He's still with Danny. I'll go get him."

Hannah climbed the stairs, softly pushed open the door to Danny's room. And her heart cracked. The man she loved was bending over their son, kissing him on the forehead.

"Night, my boy."

"Goodnight, Daddy."

She felt tears slip down her cheeks as Rex tucked the duvet tight around Danny's little frame.

"I'll always be here for you, you know that now, don't you?"

Danny nodded his dark head and snuggled against his teddy bear.

Rex stood, flipped off the light and moved to join Hannah in the doorway. He lifted his hand and gently wiped the moisture from her cheeks.

"No more tears," he said.

"They're happy tears."

He nodded, bent to kiss her mouth. Before his lips touched hers, she felt the warm whisper of his breath. "We've got a lot of catching up to do, Mrs. Logan."

"Yes." She whispered against his mouth. "But we've got a lifetime to do it in."

* * * * *

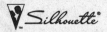

INTIMATE MOMENTS™

STRATEGIC ENGAGEMENT

(Silhouette Intimate Moments # 1257)

by

Catherine Mann

A brand-new book in her bestselling series

WINGMEN WARRIORS

For teacher Mary Elise McRae, returning to the United States could mean her own death. Yet in order to save two innocent children, she had to do just that. Being under the protection of Captain Daniel Baker, however, soon had her fearing for more than her well-being—she could very well lose her heart!

Available November 2003 at your favorite retail outlet.

If you enjoyed what you just read,
then we've got an offer you can't resist!

Take 2 bestselling
love stories FREE!
Plus get a FREE surprise gift!

✂ **Your opinion is important to us!** Please take a few moments to share your thoughts with us about your experiences with Harlequin and Silhouette books. Your comments will be very useful in ensuring that we deliver books you love to read. *Please take a few minutes to complete the questionnaire, then send it to us at the address below.*

Send your completed questionnaires to:
Harlequin/Silhouette Reader Survey, P.O. Box 9046, Buffalo, NY 14269-9046

1. As you may know, there are many different lines under the Harlequin and Silhouette brands. Each of the lines is listed below. Please check the box that most represents your reading habit for each line.

Line	Currently read this line	Do not read this line	Not sure if I read this line
Harlequin American Romance	❑	❑	❑
Harlequin Duets	❑	❑	❑
Harlequin Romance	❑	❑	❑
Harlequin Historicals	❑	❑	❑
Harlequin Superromance	❑	❑	❑
Harlequin Intrigue	❑	❑	❑
Harlequin Presents	❑	❑	❑
Harlequin Temptation	❑	❑	❑
Harlequin Blaze	❑	❑	❑
Silhouette Special Edition	❑	❑	❑
Silhouette Romance	❑	❑	❑
Silhouette Intimate Moments	❑	❑	❑
Silhouette Desire	❑	❑	❑

2. Which of the following best describes why you bought *this book?* One answer only, please.

the picture on the cover	❑	the title	❑
the author	❑	the line is one I read often	❑
part of a miniseries	❑	saw an ad in another book	❑
saw an ad in a magazine/newsletter	❑	a friend told me about it	❑
I borrowed/was given this book	❑	other: _____	❑

3. Where did you buy *this book?* One answer only, please.

at Barnes & Noble	❑	at a grocery store	❑
at Waldenbooks	❑	at a drugstore	❑
at Borders	❑	on eHarlequin.com Web site	❑
at another bookstore	❑	from another Web site	❑
at Wal-Mart	❑	Harlequin/Silhouette Reader	❑
at Target	❑	Service/through the mail	
at Kmart	❑	used books from anywhere	❑
at another department store or mass merchandiser	❑	I borrowed/was given this book	❑

4. On average, how many Harlequin and Silhouette books do you buy at one time?

I buy _____ books at one time	❑
I rarely buy a book	❑

MRQ403SIM-1A

5. How many times per month do you shop for any *Harlequin and/or Silhouette* books?
One answer only, please.

1 or more times a week	❑	a few times per year	❑
1 to 3 times per month	❑	less often than once a year	❑
1 to 2 times every 3 months	❑	never	❑

6. When you think of your ideal heroine, which *one* statement describes her the best?
One answer only, please.

She's a woman who is strong-willed	❑	She's a desirable woman	❑
She's a woman who is needed by others	❑	She's a powerful woman	❑
She's a woman who is taken care of	❑	She's a passionate woman	❑
She's an adventurous woman	❑	She's a sensitive woman	❑

7. The following statements describe types or genres of books that you may be
interested in reading. Pick *up to 2 types* of books that you are most interested in.

I like to read about truly romantic relationships	❑
I like to read stories that are sexy romances	❑
I like to read romantic comedies	❑
I like to read a romantic mystery/suspense	❑
I like to read about romantic adventures	❑
I like to read romance stories that involve family	❑
I like to read about a romance in times or places that I have never seen	❑
Other: _____	❑

*The following questions help us to group your answers with those readers who are
similar to you. Your answers will remain confidential.*

8. Please record your year of birth below.
19 _____

9. What is your marital status?

single	❑	married	❑	common-law	❑	widowed	❑
divorced/separated	❑						

10. Do you have children 18 years of age or younger currently living at home?
yes ❑   no ❑

11. Which of the following best describes your employment status?

employed full-time or part-time	❑	homemaker	❑	student	❑
retired	❑	unemployed	❑		

12. Do you have access to the Internet from either home or work?
yes ❑   no ❑

13. Have you ever visited eHarlequin.com?
yes ❑   no ❑

14. What state do you live in?
_____

15. Are you a member of Harlequin/Silhouette Reader Service?
yes ❑   Account # _____   no ❑   MRQ403SIM-1B